A CAGE OF BONES

JEFFREY ROUND

A CAGE OF BONES

THE GAY MEN'S PRESS

First published 1997 by GMP Publishers Ltd,
P O Box 247, Swaffham, Norfolk PE37 8PA, England

A CIP catalogue record for this book is available
from the British Library

ISBN 0 85449 252 6

Distributed in Europe by Central Books,
99 Wallis Rd, London E9 5LN

Distributed in North America by InBook/LPC Group,
1436 West Randolph, Chicago, IL 60607

Distributed in Australia by Bulldog Books,
P O Box 300, Beaconsfield, NSW 2014

Printed and bound in the EU by The Cromwell Press,
Melksham, Wilts, England

Thankyous and acknowledgments:

People who read the manuscript in its various incarnations and offered their invaluable input: John Davison, who encouraged me to go on casting my net when the waters seemed empty, Shyam Selvadurai for the extra push, Douglas LePan, Dawn Rae Downton, Peter Hawkins, Tara Cates, Linda Spalding, and my generous and insightful editor, David Fernbach, all for their very astute comments.

People who otherwise helped: my parents, Len and Loretta Round, for allowing me to pursue the geography of my own destiny, Irene Dakos who saw it all so long ago, Joanne Ashdown, Jennifer Barclay, Joy Brooks, Andrew Burn, Jim Fenton, Rod Heimpel, James C. Johnstone, Judy Levita, Michael Ridler, Brian Scott, Tony Spinapolice, Barb York, all for various favours, Mark Gannage for the legal counsel, Sarah Martyn who said 'Let geography be your destiny' and opened my mind to life, Duncan Roy for his entertaining hospitality in Whitstable, Reza Mahammad and the Star of India for the physical and spiritual nourishment in London, Dion Fortune for the wisdom, International Top Models Toronto, My Models Milan, Joni Mitchell and Chrissie Hynde for the late-night company, GianCarlo Cardellicchio and his motorbike Andreo, Francesco di Nepi for his insightful comments on Italy and for introducing me to the Riviera, and the numerous other people whose lives and experiences enriched this story when our paths crossed briefly.

* * *

* * *

In memory Gianni Versace 1946–1997

For John James Davison, who showed
me that love is a gift, on his 33rd birthday

* * *

Here is my secret. It is very simple: only
with the heart can you see well. That which
is essential is invisible to the eye.

The Little Prince — Saint-Exupéry

Part I:
The Geography of Destiny

1

From the windows of the plane the coast of Europe spread out below like a patchwork quilt. This region here, that mountain range over there. Blue mists and silver waters covering the earth.

Warden checked his watch. Seven hours out of Toronto. The mid-Atlantic at dawn had been a lonely place. Now, craning his neck, he could make out hilltops and towns cradled in valley basins newly crowned by daylight. It was all fitting together piece by piece.

Up and down the aisles passengers stretched tentative limbs as though unsure of the bodies they had just awakened to. A bevy of blue-capped stewardesses dispensed steaming trays for anyone alert enough to think of breakfast. It was remarkable to consider he was now on the other side of the Atlantic. He'd never left home before and suddenly found himself halfway across the world. It occurred to him briefly that life as he had lived it — quiet, ordered, safe — no longer existed.

It was to be a brand new beginning, Warden knew. Just as he also knew from within a mysterious repository of post-adolescent wisdom, that each beginning contains its own ending. Every journey without is a journey within, a mask concealing a face beneath it which can in turn hide something else.

The previous summer he'd been snagged from a beach full of rowdy volleyball players on Hanlan's Point to portray the all-Canadian boy in a jeans commercial. At the time he'd had vague moral qualms concerning the superficiality of the pursuit and a remembered lecture on the demons of objectification gleaned from a course on Noam Chomsky. Still, he went ahead, scoffing at the idea anything would come of it.

When the advertisement aired, he was amazed how his screen image took on an identity of its own, a secret, alien twin peering back at him through the gates of another dimension. Along with a rise in requests for dates Warden received offers from several established modelling agencies. One agency, Toronto Male, arranged a photography session for him. School had started by then and he did not pursue it beyond that.

A few weeks later someone phoned to say his photographs were being sent to an affiliate group in Italy. Then the Italian agency contacted them to ask about his availability. He wrote to the head of the Italian group, a Sr. Calvino, thanking him for his interest. Warden explained he had just started his second year at university and was not available.

There was no reply. At Christmas, Sr. Calvino phoned him personally, urging him to come to Italy to work with his agency, called Maura's Models. Warden snickered at the name, thinking it someone's awkward attempt at North American-casual. He refused, thanking Calvino again for the offer.

"But darling — I want to make you rich and famous," the voice oozed out of the phone.

Warden laughed again. The man's accent was strange.

"Why do you laugh when I say that? Don't you want to be rich and famous?" the voice asked petulantly.

"Right now, Sr. Calvino, I have to think about school."

"But darling, you have your whole life to read and study. Come to Italy. You would do so well here. Your face is very European."

Warden wasn't sure what he meant.

"You could have the entire continent at your feet."

"I'm not sure I'd have room for it," he quipped.

The voice on the other end did not catch the humour.

"I might have time in the summer but I'll probably be working to make my tuition for next year."

The voice exploded. "But darling — work here! That's what I'm telling you! You could be so rich. Why are you playing these games?"

"I'm not playing games, Sr. Calvino."

"Well, come by February at the very latest so we can work you in. In the summer it's no good here — everyone goes to the seaside. Lazy, lazy," he chided.

"I'll be writing my mid-terms in February," Warden replied.

The voice sounded as though it had been stung. "Darling, you're making things very difficult for me. Call me when you are ready to talk. I'll be waiting." Italy clicked off at the other end.

Warden went to the hallway and stood in front of the mirror.

He turned his face this way and that. Looking at his features as though they belonged to someone else. Sandy hair, high cheekbones, deep-set almond eyes. He could see nothing that would make anyone want him to travel to Italy. Or anywhere else for that matter.

At supper he mentioned the call to his parents. His mother, who had come downstairs to join them that evening, was hesitant and looked to her husband to offer practical advice. Warden's father thought it frivolous and said so. His sister, Lisa, however, declared it "most excellent" that someone so far away should actually phone and ask him to join an agency.

"That's so cool!" she said, her adolescent eyes flashing in defiance of her parents' lack of imagination. "Let geography be your destiny, Ward. Or you'll always wish you'd done it when you had the chance."

* * *

January passed with no further mention of the offer. At reading week Warden returned home with a bewildering pile of books. Another set of exams and two more months of school lay ahead of him. Then two more years starting in the fall. He'd spent the last year trying to convince himself the career path he'd chosen under his father's tutelage had been a good one. He was no longer sure.

He tried studying at the dining-room table but found it impossible to concentrate. Meaningless words danced on the page in front of his face. He gave up, closed his book, and went for a walk. It was a typical February day, the ubiquitous greyness stretching on forever. Land and sky hovered between winter and spring, a dry rattling time of great opposition wearing through the winter-weary heart like tire tracks across snow. People hurried by, clutching coats and hats to keep out the slicing cold. A bus tottered along carrying a cargo of pale, discontented faces returning from the workaday world like conscripts in battle.

Warden cut across the park. Dead leaves hopped about in the wind like mischievous, drunken birds where the snow had lain recently. He felt a twinge of loss. A chance forsaken. With the money left over from his commercial he could probably go to Italy for a few weeks in summer, he mused. He might just be able to afford it.

In a week he would be returning to school, going back to his tiny, cramped dormitory room and the over-crowded lecture halls. He pictured the uneventful days that stretched ahead while a chill wind blew him across the field. A leaf fluttered in the air.

Warden looked over his shoulder. The sky lay in tattered rags along a dark horizon. Clouds were mounting over the lake, closing in with the night. Here and there, daylight leaked through at the seams. Flashes of light at the edge of the sky like phantom gunfire.

Something moved inside him, looking for a face, a name. What was it he yearned for? he wondered, even as he felt its force. Whatever it was, he longed to have it and wrestle it to earth, much more than school or family or staying safe and secure within the comforts and confines of this, his home and native land.

He felt a shifting of forces, the tectonic plates of his interior coming into play. Something had been calling him and now, at last, he understood. It was life itself. A faceless, nameless desire to live in the moment at hand, urging him not to wait in hope or anticipation of a tomorrow that lay forever out of reach. He looked up and laughed. He would go to Italy. He'd have been a fool to miss it.

He ran home, tearing into the house like a schoolboy, bounding up to the room at the top of the stairs. It had once been his room, a secret place where space invaders left powdery streaks on his pillow at night as evidence of their earthly visits. A room that had sustained hours of fantasy. When he left home and moved into his dormitory, his mother began spending more and more time upstairs until they came to think of it as her room. He knew she would be there.

Like the date one first begins to age, Beatrice wasn't sure precisely when she began to feel the pangs of fear and doubt that led her to withdraw from the world. They crept up on her gradually.

At first, it was only a strong desire to remain at home when the others went out. She liked the silence that invaded the house when she was alone. It was soon replaced by a jumble of sounds from outside when the others returned from the skating rinks and movies and the million other worlds people belonged to momentarily when they left their homes and went out of doors.

Sometimes, to prolong it when they returned, she retreated to the attic room under the eaves. Eventually, the space between each succeeding journey to the outside — for that is what they had become, no longer did Beatrice make simple trips to the post office or variety store — became wider and wider. Sometimes the family did not see her for days at a time, knowing she was behind the door at the top of the stairs.

Warden knocked and went in. A canopied bed occupied most

of the space along with a desk, a bookshelf and a bearskin rug spread across the floor. His mother stood by the window overlooking the city's skyline. What had she been watching? he wondered. The lights scattered across the valley? The lines of cars snaking over the bridge in the darkness below? Or simply her own reflection pressed like a cloud upon all these things?

"I've come to tell you I'm leaving, Mom."

"You're going back to school tonight?"

Neat hair framed an oval face. A beautiful woman, her youthfulness had long since vanished, revealing a face whose features became more distinguished and isolated with time.

"I'm going to Italy." He said it quietly.

She stood very still for a moment as though inwardly folding and unfolding a fan.

"But, dear... when did you decide this?"

"Today — I mean, I've known it all along, but I made up my mind just now."

Her look was not one of disapproval or objection, but simply motherly concern that her child — anyone's child — might make a rash decision without thinking and so live to regret it.

"Don't you think you might take more time to decide, if you really want to go?"

That was not what she meant to say. Of all children, this one knew his mind before he spoke it. And once spoken it was made up.

"What about school? Have you given it proper consideration? I know you're not happy with..."

"I have thought about it, Mom. It's what I have to do."

"And how long will you be gone? A week? A month?"

He shrugged.

"I don't know."

"Will you be back in time for school next fall? Maybe if you take a break now you'll be ready to settle down and study when you come back."

"Maybe."

She shook her head at the unknown chasms opening before him. Bewildering thoughts; mothers' worries. But she was already beyond the surprise. Her practicality was coming through.

"I knew you'd go one day," she said. "I always knew it."

Her emotions turned quickly. She stepped outside her anxiety for him. Somehow she'd gotten beyond those minor peaks, like new snow blanketing old emotions, covering them with a fresh layer of hope for this son with the flush of excitement spreading across his face. She smiled and tears formed like stars in her eyes.

"Does your father know?"

"Not yet."

"He'll be upset when he finds out you want to leave school. It was his highest hope for you. You really didn't like it very much, did you?"

Didn't. It was already of the past.

"There's still plenty of time to be an engineer, Mom. Or anything else I choose." He hugged her.

Downstairs in the den Warden's father sat in a chair next to the gas fire. Suspended from the ceiling in the alcove behind his desk was a set of model airplanes he and Warden had carefully constructed when Warden was much younger. They spoke of hours of cautious, deliberate labour, Walter guiding his son each crucial step of the way. He put down a book as Warden entered, folding his hands over his belly. A cat padded around the room looking for a place to sleep, settling in a corner away from anyone else.

"Hello, Ward. How's school?" the deep voice asked.

"Fine, thanks, Dad. Do you have a minute?"

"Come in and close the door."

His father indicated a decanter on the sideboard near the shelves of books extending along one wall.

"Would you like some sherry?"

"No, thanks."

"This looks like it's going to be a father-son talk. Well, have a seat. What have I done?"

Warden stayed standing before his father, silver-haired and handsome despite the deep furrows in his cheeks. The older man regarded his son, waiting for him to speak.

"Dad — I've come to ask your permission to leave school and go to Italy."

Walter studied his son's face.

"I don't really know what to tell you," he said at last. The voice was brusque, but not off-putting. "You want permission to leave school — since you paid for it out of your own wages I can't tell you not to do so."

He paused, balancing his thoughts with what he might have hoped to hear in such a situation.

"Do you think you'll find things easier or better in another country? Or are you simply going in search of excitement? I think on the contrary you'll find it more treacherous in a land other than your own."

Warden explained how he felt about school, how the offer from Sr. Calvino made him aware of opportunities he might be passing up.

"I feel there's something out there for me and I've got to find out what that is."

He was aware how pitifully naïve that would sound to his father.

"For you to leave school and go off somewhere is the last thing I'd wish for you. My own father, who you never met, was a drunkard and a petty criminal. I spent every ounce of energy I could to educate myself so I would lead a decent life and not turn out like him."

He paused for a moment, as though a vague memory had unsettled his thoughts.

"Education is the one thing that will lead you up in this life, Ward. It's the thing that will bring you what you want."

They remained, the father sitting, the son standing, like Phoebus and Phaëthon, the boy asking for the one thing he must have, the older man wishing he would ask for anything but the freedom to choose that one thing.

"What if my happiness depends on it, Dad? If I stay through another two-and-a-half years of school and become an engineer I still might not be happy."

"Happiness is not everything you think it is right now. You won't find that out till later, unfortunately. I just hope it's not too late."

Walter looked at his son. What did he know of this boy, barely a man, standing before him now asking for his freedom? No more than his own father had once known of him, thinking that to beat a boy into submission would obscure the corners of the unknown from his personality, driving its shadows from the face of fact.

"Don't think I don't have your happiness at heart, Ward. The proof is in my fear for you. Look around you. Whatever is most precious is to be found right here, at home. You have everything you could possibly need in front of you."

Warden envisioned the expensive Palladian design on the hallway walls, smooth walnut stripes on the bookshelves extending floor to ceiling, thick oak bannisters on the stairwell lending an air of peace and security to the family home.

"I won't say no to you," he heard his father say, "but I ask you to choose wisely. The years go fast enough of their own accord. The trick is to hold them in."

Walter thought the conversation was over. He hoped his son would go away and think about what he had said and, if he were truly wise, change his mind. Warden remained standing before his father, whose life was solid and secure. It belonged there, in the home he had created for himself. His own course was just begun.

"I want your permission, Dad."

He looked at the boy before him. It seemed years since he had really seen him. The bough had broken.

"Even when you were a boy," he said, "you always did exactly what you wanted, no matter what you were told... and sometimes it turned out to be the right thing. Alright, I'll leave you to your choice and hope your plans work out for you."

Warden sprang to the door, pouring out thanks and delight to his reluctant parent, flying off. Walter looked after him for a moment, then reached for his book and settled back into the chair by the fire.

* * *

Despite Warden's seeming maturity his parents' concerns were not altogether unfounded. Both Walter and Beatrice were aware their children had been raised in a gilded cage, albeit one of modest proportions. Warden's social expertise was average for a boy just turned twenty raised on *MuchMusic, Letterman, Beverly Hills 90210* and the generic wisdom of Macintosh computers. His sexual score card, though, even self-admittedly, was somewhat less impressive.

In high school he had been the first love of a dozen adoring schoolgirls. At university he was popular with his classmates and within a week everyone knew him by name in the dormitory where he lived. Other boys sought his advice on love matters as much as the tedium of schoolwork, even if they seemed to Warden more capable than him. Girls flirted with him openly during class lectures, hinting they were willing to be intimate with him, though he never took up their transparent offers.

Except for the odd bit of inquisitive kissing in junior high school, he'd never sought physical intimacy with anyone. The only time he experienced anything like it was with another boy in his chemistry course. From the first, there was an undeclared attraction between them, though neither ever spoke to the other.

Warden and John, as the other boy was called, always sat in close proximity to one another during class. To anyone watching, the pairing would have seemed as accidental as the casual attraction of sympathetic elements. Occasionally, Warden would glance up at the blonde-haired boy seated languidly at his desk. John would turn, catching his eye as though bored with the lecture. Lingering an instant before looking elsewhere.

One night Warden dreamed he'd stayed late after class and he and John were the only ones there. They talked and laughed aloud as they had never done in real life. When it came time to leave, they walked up the street arm-in-arm until they reached a tall, dark building. John stopped and looked about.

"Where are we?" Warden asked.

John smiled. "African Studies," he replied, as if that told all.

Warden looked up at the building, uncertain.

"We can go in back," John said, adding, "It's safe," in a conspiratorial whisper.

Warden wasn't sure why they were going behind the African Studies building or what it was safe for, but he followed like a puppy on a leash. In the dream, it was almost dusk. The other buildings were cut off from view by tall trees. A thick carpet of leaves covered the ground. Warden shivered as they stood facing one another in the liquid darkness.

Warden reached out to John, who lifted his hands at the same instant as though in a mirror. They touched. Warden felt a jolt of energy beneath his skin. He sensed his body expanding, streaming outwards as it divulged secrets of the most exquisite pleasures. Of beautiful birds nesting on cliff tops, the arcane knowledge of moonbeams and blizzards and the joy of swimming naked at midnight. Warden fell head-first onto the leaf-blanketed lawn, oblivious to everything. He lay there a long time. Through the branches he watched the planets whirl by in their mysterious circular configurations to the sounds of tinkling glass and dying leaves.

* * *

The day he left was cold and bright. It had snowed lightly the night before. Beatrice came downstairs in a nightgown and slippers and stood perched on the front step, as though that were the farthest bounds of safety of her world. She watched as they took his luggage

15

to the car.

She hugged him. "Please be careful, Warden," she said. "We'll miss you, so write. Have you got everything?"

"Yes."

"Money?"

"Yes."

"Have you packed enough clothing?"

"I think so."

She released him. He moved to the car door.

"Warden..."

He turned. She wanted to say something. To caution him against something, but what? The nebulous, unformed dangers that haunt a mother's mind. And life itself, she imagined. She smiled at the handsome young man standing patiently before her. It seemed as though he were someone else now.

"Bye, Mom — see you sometime. Try to get out a bit."

"Goodbye, Warden — send us some pictures of you when they show up in the magazines."

* * *

Unknown countries floated below him now. He tried to imagine what they were. He was waking with the taste of hot coffee and the somewhat-premature celebratory glass of champagne he'd ordered to the surprise of a sleepy-eyed stewardess. This was followed by a piece of hard, bitter chocolate, affecting him now with the collision of competing substances in his bloodstream. At that altitude he felt an enviable freedom he'd never known before.

It was in this state he caught his first glimpse of the Alps. Jagged peaks brooded in the distance among broken patches of cloud, resurrected out of a gothic existence. Sun glinted on powdery peaks in the thin air as the plane's shadow rolled across a great sea of silver and black. It was as though the rag ends of creation had been dispersed over a staggering emptiness, ringing the horizon in a colossal granite disguise.

A stewardess wandered down the aisle picking up empty trays and discarded napkins. Outside, the sky was lowering.

"Where are we right now?" Warden asked as she picked up his tray.

"We are almost in Milano," she said. "Ciao, bello — welcome to Italia."

2

At customs, the lethargic guard didn't bother to feign interest when Warden offered his passport. The man inquired as to the duration of his stay and whether he intended to work while in Italy. Warden was about to say yes, then thought he might require a work permit. Perhaps the agency had arranged it. Was his name on a list somewhere? Calvino hadn't mentioned it. In any case, he didn't want to have to explain this to the guard whose recalcitrant cap had crept down over his forehead and whose accent was barely decipherable. Warden hesitated, then finally said, "No." He heard a quiet thunk as his passport was stamped and returned.

The airport lobby was nearly empty. He purchased a map of Milan at a kiosk and walked to a bus stop where others waited to be taken to the city. The bus arrived and he climbed aboard. As it pulled onto the highway, Warden turned to watch the tail end of the Alps recede, the sky blue and seamless beyond.

The driver was a garrulous man given to shouting out the names of landmarks in a tortured, though not unrhythmic, English. He turned the radio volume up full to provide a background for his animated narration. The landscape outside the window was full of light, the barren earth breaking into springtime pastures imbued with a magic quality of infinite richness common to foreign lands. Across the aisle, a dark-haired girl his own age smiled at him.

"Hi! Where're you from?"

"Toronto."

She sighed. "I'm from Boston. It's been so long since I've been home."

The pack under her seat bulged. She wanted to know what was happening 'back home'. He told her whatever he could remember of North American domestic affairs. She seemed lost in nostalgia. When the ride ended outside a massive stone fortress in the middle of the city, he said goodbye and debarked with his bags.

From the station, a cab driver who spoke no English took him to the address scribbled in his date book. The vehicle pulled up beside a four-story stone building. He paid and got out. Inside, he heard voices. American. Footsteps pounding down the stairs.

"What's happenin', dude?" a voice called out.

Six or seven energetic young men in sweaters and jeans bounded through the doorway and scattered like minnows. Warden shouldered his bags and climbed the flight of stairs. A small boy crouched on the landing with a plastic truck, zooming it back and forth on its wheels, making sounds appropriate to such activities.

"Ciao," said the boy, looking briefly at him.

"Ciao," Warden said, and continued upwards.

On the next landing he came to a desk sporting a rack dotted with dozens of pigeon-hole slots. The wall behind it was covered in a collage of four-by-six cards featuring the eager faces of dozens of young men like the ones he'd just passed. Warden set his bags down and rang a bell. A dark-haired woman emerged from a doorway, drying her hands on a towel. She scrutinized him without coming to any conclusion as to his presence before her.

"Ciao."

"Ciao," he said. "Do you speak English?"

"Yes. How may I help you?"

"Is this the Albergo Sirtori?"

"Yes."

"I'm from Maura's Model Agency. Sr. Calvino sent me."

She flipped through a register on the counter in search of something that might verify his statement while her face registered skepticism. She looked up. "You are Sr. Fields?" she asked cautiously.

"Yes."

"May I see your passport, please?"

He handed over the document.

"We were expecting you tomorrow," she said, frowning as she studied it. "Sr. Calvino is not very precise about his arrivals."

Warden shifted nervously. He wondered what he would do if she told him to come back in the morning.

She looked up. "Never mind. It cannot be helped," she said, her voice softening. She offered her hand to shake. "I am Irena. Come — I will show you your room."

She scooped a key off its hook and led him down the hallway past rows of numbered doors. He heard music coming from some of the rooms.

"I have put you in with another American boy. You will have to share for now. His name is Jimmy. He has gone to Firenze for a show tonight but he will be back tomorrow." She clucked her tongue and looked him in the eye. "There are no girls allowed in the rooms after ten o'clock."

She opened a door and switched on the light. The room was small and unadorned, but clean. Two twin beds took up most of the space. A set of wooden doors opened onto a balcony. Warden thanked her as he set down his bags.

"I hope you enjoy your stay," she said simply, and went out.

He examined the room. A night table separated the two beds. At the far end, a sink and a portable wardrobe. Suitcases peeked out from under a collection of shirts hung hastily beside an assortment of dress pants. A pair of worn running shoes waited expectantly at the foot of one of the beds. Discarded clothes draped themselves everywhere.

On the table, an inexpensive lamp. A book of Italian phrases, a Bible and a cheap romance novel leaned against it. A handful of pop music cassettes lay scattered nearby, some of his favourites among them, Warden noted. An ashtray on a lower shelf contained a smattering of unusual coins.

A stack of modelling cards presented a freckled face with a friendly grin. The name Jimmy Caitlin across the top, logo of a New York agency in smaller letters on the bottom. Real American stock, Warden mused.

Following his absent roommate's example he unpacked, storing his deflated bags in the wardrobe. He stepped out onto the small balcony overlooking a courtyard in the low light of afternoon. Rooftops connected to neighbouring buildings with courtyards of their own. By summer they would afford an abundant green beauty. Right now the branches were barely in bud, red tips of hope.

He stared at the view, wondering what was concealed there waiting to reveal itself to him. He wanted something to offer a hint of why he'd travelled so far, and for what. It had all happened so fast. It wasn't hard to believe he was there, he realized. What was hard to believe was that this place was any different from the one he had just left.

Warden stepped back in and closed the doors. He washed his face and hands at the sink, then lay on the bed staring up at the cracked ceiling trying to recall the events that led him there. His eyes closed. When he opened them again the light at the window was dimmer.

The air was cool where it drifted in from an open window. He pulled on a sweater and went out into the empty hallway. A pungent smell met his nostrils. He heard children's voices as he approached the reception desk. In a well-lit room he saw the young boy who had greeted him on the landing sitting at a table beside another boy and a girl. They waited expectantly as Irena ladled a steamy broth into bowls. He passed the simple gathering and went down the stairs.

From the streets below he heard voices in the falling darkness. The sounds were unfamiliar, yet comforting. Twilight overtook him as he drank in the sights and sounds of the city, its newness engraving itself on his consciousness more deeply than the half-habitual memory by which he had come to know his own home on walks there.

He wandered awhile, arrived eventually at a crowded piazza at the city's heart. The space opened before a giant cathedral. He gazed at the massive shape rising above the square, heights lit with a greenish glow illuminating the stiletto spires of stonework. Across the piazza, contrasting the old world with the new, a neon billboard gleamed with electric intensity. It struck him, as he stood there, that in the whole country there was not a single person who knew him. Loneliness touched him like the wave of a hand.

Back at the albergo, which had been empty when he left, he discovered a gathering of young men surrounding the parlour TV, their figures draped and folded over sofas and chairs. He wondered if they all spoke Italian well enough to understand it, but it turned out to be a program of English music videos. He sat at the edge of the room where the faces crowded listlessly around the TV, too tired or too vacant to turn their gaze away.

Not all were American, he soon discovered, though most spoke English. There was a Norwegian boy named Jörn and a French boy named Jean-Luc, as well as those of several other nationalities. They were all varied and all good-looking. Warden felt as though he'd landed in a roomful of specimens of the prototypic male. He watched their wan faces in the light of the pale blue screen. They accepted him freely, without curiosity as to his presence among them.

Someone conquered inertia long enough to change the channel. Warden chatted a bit, then said good night and went back to his room. Taking paper and pen out onto the balcony, he sat with his arms pulled inside his sleeves so only the pen point protruded in the cool air, and began to write his mother a letter. A low, salty moon hung on the horizon like a stepping stone into the galaxy.

3

He woke from a sleep that was deep beyond any remembrance. The albergo was empty except for a maid going from room to room cleaning and changing the linen.

Warden showered and shaved, then dressed to meet Sr. Calvino. His roommate had not returned. He left a note on the bed opposite: "Howdy, neighbour. I hope you like company, because you've got some." He signed his name on the bottom.

He tried phoning the agency to find out when they expected him. Once he'd made his travel arrangements there had been little communication except for an odd exchange with Calvino who urged him only to "Come soon, baby," though he couldn't have come any sooner. He tried calling several times from the room phone but the line was busy. He was becoming restless. There was a pay-phone in the café downstairs, Irena told him. He could also get breakfast there.

The café was small with plenty of morning sunlight. A handful of customers sat around drinking coffee. He chose a seat near a window and stared at a menu written completely in Italian. At the far end of the room a jukebox spewed current American love songs. When the waiter came he asked for 'un cappuccino' and hoped he was getting coffee.

He found the phone and attempted to call again. Still busy. He dialled the two other numbers in his day book with the same result. He tried several times until the waiter arrived with a steaming cup piled high with stiff white foam. A whiff of dark coffee hit his nose.

"Grazie," he said, one of the handful of words he'd memorized from the phrase book the night before.

"Prego," the boy said, and wandered back over to the counter.

Warden drank the coffee and listened to the music. In a few minutes he tried the phone again. A woman's voice answered with an Italian accent.

"Maura's Models. Pronto."

"May I speak to Sr. Calvino, please?"

"But he is on another line. You will please have to call again very soon. Thank you. Grazie."

The voice hung up. Warden tried several more times in the next half-hour. Busy again. He ordered another cappuccino and managed to indicate to the waiter to bring him some pastry. When he finished he tried calling again. Finally it rang. A different voice answered.

"Maura's Models. Please hold."

The line clicked to a hollow hum. He heard ghost voices talking faintly on the wires. On the jukebox, a country singer crooned something about a lost dog. The waiter wandered among the tables, clearing up. Finally, the voice returned.

"How may I help you?"

"I'd like to speak to Sr. Calvino, please."

"He is very busy. Can you call back?"

"No!" Warden shouted before he realized the voice wasn't going to hang up on him. "I've been calling for nearly an hour," he said, trying not to sound whiny.

"He's very busy right now," the woman insisted.

"Would you please tell him Warden Fields from Toronto is calling and I'd like to speak to him before I have a caffeine attack."

"One moment."

The line clicked off. In seconds it was picked up again.

"But darling... you should have told me it was you!" gurgled the warm, salty voice he'd first heard over the line at Christmas. It sounded much closer, no longer drowned under a sea of water.

"I've been trying," Warden said. He visualized an overweight, middle-aged man sinking into a plush office chair in a spacious boardroom in the middle of the city.

"Where are you right now?"

"I'm downstairs at the hotel you sent me to."

"You're not at the American Hotel?" he asked suspiciously.

"No, why?"

"Never mind — it's not a good place for you."

An odd answer. He didn't pursue it.

"I'm at the Albergo Sirtori."

"Well, get here as quickly as you can."

"Where?" Warden interjected, still afraid of being disconnected suddenly.

Calvino gave him the agency address along with a command to appear soon. "Ciao, baby. And take a streetcar — the taxis will take you the long way around and charge you too much."

He hung up abruptly before Warden had a chance to say anything more. Italians were a hurried race, he thought.

He looked around for a streetcar, wondering which one to catch. He wandered for several minutes, aware he was incapable of asking directions in Italian. He couldn't even see a taxi. Finally, he recognized a face from the albergo walking towards him. He asked how to get to the agency.

"Turn left here and take the number five streetcar at the end of the street," the boy said, pointing.

"Thanks."

"No problem, dude."

At the stop a small crowd stood waiting as a car rolled up. Warden boarded and asked the fare in English. The driver scowled and said something in Italian. Warden pulled out a thousand-lira note and offered it to him.

"This much?"

The driver scowled again and threw his hands in the air.

Warden pulled out two more bills. "This much?" he asked, thinking the cost was quickly becoming exorbitant or else he was being taken advantage of because of his inability to communicate.

The driver turned to the carload of passengers. Warden heard him use the word 'Americano' in a surly tone. People were laughing. A young boy came towards the front.

"He say you have to buy a ticket," the boy informed him.

"How much is it?"

"You cannot buy here. You must buy it in a... " the boy hesitated. "You must buy it in a storm!" he finished proudly.

"In a store?" Warden asked.

"Yes, in a store!" he agreed.

The driver barked something at the boy.

"Come!" he said, taking Warden by the hand and pulling him off the streetcar. "I show you."

The car rolled away from them.

"He doesn't like for you to make stop the streetcar," the boy explained.

Warden followed him to a corner store. The boy paid for a ticket with the money he offered. It cost less than he expected.

"Now we go back," the boy said.

They waited for another streetcar. When it came, the boy showed him how to use the punch clock in the middle of the car.

"Now you can ride for this much of minutes," he said, showing Warden the number 75 stamped on his ticket.

Warden thanked him, complimenting his English as they rode along. The boy blushed.

"I am learning in school," he explained.

He showed him the agency address written in his book. "Do you know where this is?"

"Yes," the boy said. "It is three stops ago."

Warden got off and walked back till he found the street. He saw the number '17' in brass figures on a new stucco building and entered a lobby incrusted with iron filigree. A grey-haired woman sat knitting at a desk. She glared at him over her glasses, raising a finger to her lips as though he might break into a loud racket at any moment.

"Due piano," she said, pointing above. "Second floor."

"Grazie."

Warden went up the stairs. He found a nondescript door with an opaque window and a small sign that read 'Maura's Models — Avanti'. He opened it and found himself in the middle of a busy room. Faces moved in every direction, clutching portfolios, envelopes and photographs.

In an office across the room three women sat speaking quickly into telephones, banging receivers down, then answering again. As they spoke they pencilled notes on large desk calendars. They hardly noticed the swarms of young people parading in and out of the room. One of the women waved a sandwich in the air as she exclaimed into the mouthpiece.

A face that looked oddly familiar went by in the chaos. It belonged to a tall, gangly youth clad in jeans and a sweatshirt.

"Excuse me, are you Jimmy Caitlin?" Warden asked.

A straw-coloured head of hair turned towards him.

"You bet!"

"Hi. I'm Ward Fields. I'm your new roommate."

The boy's face metamorphosed into a grin, scattering freckles.

"Good to meet you, Ward," he said. "I was wondering if they'd turfed me out yet. I haven't been home in three days."

"I just got here yesterday," Warden explained over the noise. "I haven't even met Sr. Calvino yet."

"He's not here. Talk to Maura," Jimmy said, pointing to the woman with the sandwich. "She'll help you out. Hey, Maura!" he yelled.

The woman looked up. Jimmy pointed at Warden.

"Gotta go. I'm late for a go-see," he said. "Catch you later, Ward."

Warden watched Jimmy's wide shoulders move through the crowd and out the door. Maura screamed one last phrase in Italian

24

and slammed the phone onto its cradle.

"I tell them always not to call at lunch time and they call always at lunch time!"

She looked up at Warden and smiled.

"Yes, how can I help you?" she asked, her voice suddenly pleasant and courteous.

"I'm looking for Sr. Calvino."

The phone rang and she picked it up, answering in Italian. A woman approached and placed an envelope in front of her. Three photographs of a girl in jeans and a skimpy blouse. Maura flipped through quickly and pointed to the middle one, all three coming perilously close to being spread with mustard from the omnipresent sandwich.

"Questo — this one," she said.

The envelope vanished from under her nose as she nodded into the phone.

"Si, si — ciao!"

She hung up, and looked at Warden.

"Sr. Calvino is not here now," she said. The phone rang again. She picked it up.

"Pronto. Maura's Models..." Her eyes flamed. "Why do you call me now?" The hand with the sandwich went up into the air. "I told you never to call me when it's busy!"

She slammed the phone down and looked back up.

"Sr. Calvino has gone for lunch. He leaves me when it's busiest and expects me to look after everything!" she complained, as though the two women beside her did not exist.

"I'm Warden Fields," he said. "From Toronto."

"Warden? Oh, yes, I remember. You're late. One moment," she said as she answered the phone again. The caller was put on hold. "We were expecting you much sooner."

"I had some difficulty getting here."

"Sr. Calvino was hungry — he couldn't wait. I am Maura," she said, extending a hand over the desk. Her face bore a smile that could have killed a cat. Both hand and smile vanished in the same instant, retreating somewhere behind the desk. "Sr. Calvino went next door to buy a panino," she said, indicating the rolled-up sandwich. "He will be back in fifteen minutes. In the next doorway is his office. You can wait there."

She pointed the way. The phone was ringing again. Warden went out through the lobby to the next room. It looked identical to the one he'd just left except it was empty. The walls were cluttered with photographs and calendars. A wooden rack displayed a collection of faces and bodies on four-by-six composite cards, a catalogue covering the spectrum of human features. Warden wondered if they had all been summoned by the salty voice offering to lay continents at their feet.

He sat and leaned his head against the coolness of the wall. Feeling as though he'd walked into a cologne factory with a myriad of smells swirling in the air vying for his attention. Alone now in the office, everything seemed to slow for a moment.

Shadows passed over the opaque windows. He expected any one of them to walk up to the door, open it, and he would find himself in the presence of the plump, middle-aged man who belonged to the gushing voice that had beckoned him across continents. He could hear Maura on the phone in the next room. More shadows. Noises. His watch ticked.

"He's waiting in your office," he heard Maura say.

Footsteps. A single, thin shadow approached. The door opened to admit a slim young black man with his head completely shaved.

"Man, I thought you got lost," he said, coming over to shake Warden's hand.

"Sr. Calvino?" Warden asked in surprise.

"Yes baby — ciao!"

Behind him a crowd of six or seven heads had formed and stood at the door to his office. He turned around to them.

"Out, out, out!" he yelled, waving them away. "I have to talk to the new boy from Canada."

"I need to know where the M Agency is," a young man shouted from the doorway, as if afraid of being hung up on.

"The M Agency! What's that?" asked Calvino, stiffening at the continued affront.

"You told me yesterday I had an appointment there at noon today," the face explained. "I can't find it on the map."

"I told you before to ask Maura these things," he said, taking hold of the door.

"She told me to ask you!" protested the boy.

"Well, ask her again," he said, shutting out the offending face. The noise and confusion settled like dust in the room. Calvino turned his attention to Warden.

"What took you so long?" he asked.

"I had some difficulty getting here."

"Well, never mind that now, darling. Let me see your card."

Warden hesitated. "I — I don't have a card."

Calvino looked shocked.

"You have to have a card, baby. Who told you you could come here without a card?"

"You did."

"I told you you could come without a card?" he asked, incredulous that anyone should suggest such a thing. "Well, you can't," he said, flatly contradicting his own authority. "You must have a card. We will send you to a photographer tomorrow. You will have a card by next week. Now stand up."

Warden stood while Calvino looked him over.

"You're too skinny," he said.

"I'm sorry, I... " Warden said.

"I want you to go out and eat. You have money for food?"

"Yes."

"Good. And get some sun, too. You're too pale. You look sick."

He ran a hand through Warden's hair.

"Very fine. We will have to see how it holds up. Remind me to send you for a haircut."

He walked back to his desk. As he did so the door to the office opened a crack. A perky face peered in. Hair standing straight up.

"Hiya, Mr. C! How's it goin'?" said the face. "Hi," he said, nodding to Warden.

"Hi," Warden replied.

"I need to talk to you for about five minutes, Mr. C," the boy said in what sounded like a Brooklyn accent.

"Not now, Joseph," said Calvino. "I'll talk to you in a minute when I'm finished."

"I'll be waiting."

He disappeared out the door. Calvino turned back to Warden.

"Now, darling, what do you know about modelling?" he asked.

"Not a lot."

"Then we will have to begin at the beginning. Now watch me."

He began an elegant, ballooning stride with shoulders held back, carrying him gracefully across the room. He stopped just short of Warden, turned with a whirl and wafted back to his desk.

"That," he said, "is how you walk when I send you to a go-see appointment."

The shoulders slumped. He sighed and sat facing Warden in

the desk chair.

"Basically, darling, they don't care. You've got the face. That's all that matters. Just say yes to everything and if anybody asks, say your cards were held up at customs. It happens sometimes if they think you're trying to come into the country to work illegally."

Warden remembered the guard who'd questioned him at the airport.

"You mean I'm working here illegally?"

"Of course, darling. Don't worry — nobody cares," Calvino said, waving away the question. "It's only a problem if the mafia get involved," he said cryptically. "But that hasn't happened for awhile."

Calvino had him fill out a form of body measurements and particulars. He proffered a small booklet across the desk.

"This is your list of regular clients," he explained. "You have a map of the city?"

Warden nodded.

"And a day book?"

"Yes."

"Good — take these down."

Calvino rhymed off a short list of names and addresses of designers. Most of them meant nothing to him, but a few he'd heard of.

"They are all in your book. Try to see as many as you can this afternoon, the rest you can see tomorrow. Call in at least three times a day for your appointments."

His face grimaced.

"Not at lunch — it's too busy and Maura gets upset. Tomorrow when you come I will tell you where your photography appointment is. If you need to know anything else ask the other models. They will tell you."

Calvino stopped and frowned in a way that reminded Warden of the concierge at the desk downstairs, as though the two practised making facial expressions together.

"You're not staying at the American Hotel, are you?"

"No — I'm at the Albergo Sirtori."

"That's good. And remind me you need to get a haircut."

Calvino stood. Warden understood the interview was over. He was now among the ranks of fashion hopefuls. Calvino went to the door, opening it for him.

"Just remember, always be polite. Improper behaviour will make you known in this business but it won't get you work."

Calvino looked him up and down and clucked his tongue.

"Please eat, darling — and get some sun," he admonished like a world-weary mother.

Half the lobby seemed to be trying to get into his office at once. "One at a time!" he heard Calvino scream.

Out in the lobby, Joe sat grinning in a chair near the door.

"First day?" he asked, as Warden approached.

"Yes."

"It doesn't get any better, but you'll get used to it."

Warden grinned back. "Do you think so?"

"You might even come to like it."

Around them, the lobby walls featured photos of some of Maura's models, past and present, an agency hall of fame. The faces stared down from the frames as though viewing him from another world.

"That's where everybody wants to be in this place," Joe said. "If you're up on the wall, you know you've made it."

Warden looked over a few of the faces.

"What's the American Hotel?" he asked.

"Bad news, dude. It's where all the party animals stay. It's one big celebration from dusk to dawn every night. Are you into drugs?"

"Not really."

"Then you're not missing a thing."

"Joseph!" Calvino's voice screamed from the office.

"Gotta go," he said, jumping up. "Good luck."

Downstairs the concierge was still knitting at her desk as Warden left, glaring suspiciously as if people were trying to sneak past her constant vigil.

4

Warden located his first appointment and found himself in the foyer of an ordinary office building that might have been his father's back home, nothing of the glamour or prestige of the fashion business suggested by its appearance. After a few minutes, a door opened and a young man much like himself came out, nodded at Warden and left.

He was ushered into a room laid out with tables covered in soft, uncut folds of cloth. A dozen expensive-looking dress-suits hung on large mobile racks. Warden stood quietly as his measurements were taken by a thin man making hurried markings on a card. They were watched by a bearded man with a worried expression.

"You are from Maura's Models?" the bearded man asked, consulting his appointment sheet first.

"Yes."

"And do you have a card, please?"

"It was held up at customs," Warden said, as he had been told. "I should have a new one out next week."

"Yes, yes — very good. Make sure I get one," said the man, apparently satisfied. "And you have done shows before?"

"Yes," said Warden, remembering Calvino's words.

The thin man placed a large hat on Warden's head, adjusting it, standing back, then adjusting it again before taking it off.

"Write your name here," the other man said, pointing to the card with his measurements scrawled across it.

He did so.

"Thank you. Grazie. That is all," the man concluded.

Warden thanked them and left. Two young men just like him sat where he'd been waiting as though some mass-reproductive principle were secretly at work. Warden nodded and went out.

At his next appointment the clients spoke a guttural Italian directing the models. Amongst themselves they spoke German. No one spoke any English. When his turn came, Warden stood before a video camera as the lights were turned on. The entire room was soon laughing at his inability to understand what was required of him until an impatient young woman came up and physically directed his movements. First one profile, then the other. Finally a full frontal shot with a smile which she indicated by pulling her mouth into a wide grin with her fingers.

"Grazie," she said when he had finished.

Warden left, embarrassed and glad to be done.

At his final appointment he found himself in a long line of people winding up a flight of stairs. He heard sudden enthusiastic greetings of friends inquiring of one another where they'd been and where they were staying. He saw now what the camaraderie around the television at day's end was about. Like himself, they were transplanted from other lands with natural and social barriers all around. For this they substituted what they could of friendship as casually and quickly as it came.

As the line moved up the stairs, Warden heard a shout from below. "What's happenin' here, dudes?" a voice with a heavy Texan accent inquired.

"Gucci casting," someone yelled back.

"Oh, no! Not that shit again!" the voice bemoaned. Footsteps tromped back down the stairs.

"Plenty more where that came from," someone quipped, followed by laughter.

The line up moved quickly as they entered a long, narrow room, hurriedly arranged in rows of seven abreast. Each row walked the length of floor to a loud pounding beat. As one line advanced, another formed to take its place. Occasionally, someone was taken aside and asked to try on a piece of wardrobe. The model's name and agency were noted and the others sent on their way. A table near the door was littered with discarded composite cards.

When Warden's turn came he marched in step across the room. The boy beside him was asked to walk again and taken aside. No one asked Warden his name, nor did they ask for his card. He hadn't seen anybody walk like a balloon either, he mused.

Outside, he headed back towards the albergo. It was nearly four o'clock. He felt weary and tense with excitement. It was a whole other and amazingly active world of which he'd just become a part. He'd had enough adventure and newness for one day and wanted to rest.

As he walked up a narrow one-way street a white sports car slowed and stopped. The driver rolled down his window. The man wore sunglasses and a white cap. His mouth formed a practiced smile as he offered his hand.

"Ciao!" he said. "I am Mario."

"Ciao, Mario. How's it going?" Warden asked, taking the hand.

One of the assistants at the Gucci casting had been named Mario. He wondered if this were the man. Still shaking his hand, the driver motioned for Warden to get in the car.

"No, thanks, I'm just going around the corner."

"Would you like a cigarette?"

Traffic began to pile up. A horn beeped.

"Thanks, I don't smoke."

Warden tried to pull his hand free but the man hung on tightly. "Your eyes are the colour of the sea," he said. Three more horns joined in the chorus behind them protesting the slow-down. "I love you," Mario said, inexplicably.

Warden tugged his hand free of the grasp.

"Ciao, Mario — gotta go!" he said, and ran along the road in the opposite direction.

The flood abated. Warden's blood was pounding by the time he reached the albergo.

* * *

That evening Jimmy took Warden with him to eat at the neighbourhood trattoria. Warden told him about his experience with the driver of the sports car. Jimmy laughed.

"It doesn't mean a thing," he said. "He was just saying he likes you. Things like that happen everyday. Everyone's a little crazy in Italy. 'Poco loco' as they say. Once you've been here awhile nothing seems too far out any more."

Jimmy ordered for Warden in broken Italian when the owner came to the table.

"You don't always know what you're getting, but the food here is awesome," Jimmy said.

"'Awesome'. That's American for 'good', isn't it?" he joked.

"Awesome means it's pretty great," Jimmy agreed. He smiled. "Where are you from, Ward?"

"Toronto."

"That's a city, isn't it?"

Warden laughed. He'd heard of the geocentric attitude of Americans.

"It's trying to be," he answered.

"Isn't that where the Blue Jays are from?"

"There's a little more to it than baseball, but you're right. How about you?"

"Marion, Indiana," he said. "It's a great place to be *from*, if you know what I mean. You know the scene — small-town America with a main street, a movie theatre, a couple of schools and three churches for democratic choice. All the kids hang out after school practicing their rim shots on the basketball court and everyone grows up to marry his childhood sweetheart and work at the same plant as his dad."

"I get the picture."

"At the age of ten I was rescued when we moved to New Jersey. That's home now, I guess."

"Jimmy from Jersey."

"That's me. Haven't seen it for awhile, though."

"When was the last time you were home?"

"I was home for two days at Christmas. That's it. If you get caught up in this business it keeps you pretty busy. I'm planning to go back for the whole month of August, if I make it."

"Do you miss it?"

"I miss it like crazy when I have the time to stop and think about it. And that's one thing you should never let yourself do because then you miss it too much."

Jimmy's girlfriend, Corrine, was also a model, Warden learned. They'd met on a shoot the previous summer, but hadn't seen each other in more than two months because of conflicting schedules. It was just occurring to Warden that people lived this sort of life for months on end. Friends greeted one another on the steps of client offices or during chance meetings in studio and agency lobbies, while lovers met on the fly between location sets.

After supper they walked down Corso Buenos Aires, a wide main strip with a centre meridian. The air was cool. Shop doors were closing as lights came on in the dusk.

"Now what do we do?"

"Now we're free till morning. There's a movie house where they show films in English. If you want a drink there's Bar Magenta. It's an American hang-out."

They turned down a side alley where the buildings appeared drenched, underwater in the glowing darkness. The city seemed suffused with a quiet vitality. The streets were narrower, the pace slower, as though life were lived on a more intimate scale than the broad spectrum of North America.

Outside the albergo Jimmy took out his cigarettes, offering one to Warden.

"I guess you really have to enjoy this life to keep it up for so long," Warden said, shaking his head at the offer.

A match flared. Jimmy lit his cigarette.

"I used to think I liked it," he mused. "But it's true what they say — it chews you up and spits you out when it's done with you. I've seen it. And there'll be no one there to wave goodbye when you leave. Remember that, if you remember anything."

They leaned against the building. Others passed in and out through the door as they stood at the bottom of the stairs.

"You're lucky to be starting so early," Jimmy said. "I've been at it for two years now. I figure I'm good for another four at most. By then I'll be thirty and ready to go home, settle down and forget this crazy existence. You've got a few solid years ahead. Make the most of the time you've got, Ward. You won't be able to later on."

It hadn't occurred to Warden he might be doing this beyond the summer he was spending there on what seemed like a lark and had never thought of seriously. Upstairs, they passed the parlour where a crowd had already gathered around the TV screen like a bedtime ritual.

"Hey — what's happenin', dudes?" a voice rang out.

There were one or two new faces in the room. They had flown, bussed or taken trains from various places and sat trading stories of jobs, countries and personal encounters — the lingua franca of fellow travellers spoken brusquely in a world of hurried effects and blurred edges.

According to Jimmy, the season's transmigration had yet to begin in earnest. When it did, the faces changed daily in a shuffleboard game of fashion shows and hotel rooms. Little wonder it was no big deal when he arrived. New faces were routine — one met and forgot them as quickly as they came and left again. There was always a retinue of suitcases and bags at the door. It would amount to a great deal to be enthusiastic about every new face that came and went through it.

* * *

In the morning, Warden watched the others skidding in and out of the shower wrapped in towels as he waited his turn. They had flawless faces and bodies to match the ideal forms of the ancients. He felt like a pretender, a fraud who had passed in unnoticed and was holding his breath lest someone spot him and point out his illegitimacy to their rank. He let the cool water splash over his head, waking him and tingling on his skin.

Back in the room, Jimmy watched him struggle with his hair, trying to coax it into place.

"Here — try this," he said, tossing him a tube of gel.

"'Natural style support'," Warden read from the label. He squeezed some onto his hands.

"Just think of it as a bra for your hair," Jimmy quipped, pulling on a sweater.

"Thanks — I think," Warden said. "If you have any more tips, pass them along. I'm going to need all the help I can get."

"Nothing to it. Study the magazines. Check out the poses. Take the ones you like and reproduce them for the clients. You'll catch on. You've got what it takes, so don't worry. The rest you can fake."

"That's what everybody keeps telling me."

"You'll learn. It's a crazy business and we're in one of the craziest agencies around. They don't call it 'Maura's Noodles' for nothing. Just keep your head on straight and you'll be okay."

Jimmy picked up his portfolio. "Ciao," he said. "Catch you later."

Warden dressed and walked to the agency. The lobby was nearly empty. Calvino was in his office alone and opened the door when Warden knocked. He looked him over and frowned, squinting at his hair in a vaguely disapproving manner. He waved a list of items in one hand.

"I have set up your appointment with the hairdresser at ten o'clock and for the photographer at two o'clock. In between, you can go to the other addresses you didn't go to yesterday," Calvino said. "The hairdresser is first because we want you to look good for the photographs." Another squint at his hair. "Don't say anything to her. Just let her cut it how she wants. When you see the photographer, don't worry about clothes. He will have what you need. Everything comes out of your paycheck at the end of the month so you don't need to pay anything now."

It was all pre-arranged, sight unseen. Calvino handed him the list with both addresses.

"How was Sr. Ferré?"

"Who?"

"Gianfranco Ferré — the big bearded man I sent you to see yesterday. Didn't you see him?" Calvino asked suspiciously. He was constantly cross-examining his models to make sure they followed orders.

"Oh, him. Yeah, I saw him — he didn't say much."

Calvino looked at him with his best look of astonishment.

"Darling, you were in the presence of fashion royalty. Don't you know who is Gianfranco Ferré? What have I brought over from Canada? I send Ferré only my very best. Don't disappoint me. Didn't he say anything at all?"

"He took my measurements and asked me to write my name down. Oh — and they made me try on a hat."

Calvino looked reassured. "That's good. Now go to your appointments."

He looked up as Warden reached the door.

"Get some sun!" he growled.

The hairdresser turned out to be an unsmiling young woman whose features suggested much rumination on unfulfilled desires. She took him in at once. While she cut his hair she expressed her opinions on a wide range of topics. Americans she liked very much, she said, assuming him to be one. She had once visited Manhattan with her sister and there had been no end to the flowers arriving at their hotel suite. The English, though, were quite another story. She disliked them because they were cold. No emotions. No passion. Perhaps they had not sent enough flowers to assuage her disappointed desires. In any case, she did not like them.

She cut quickly as she spoke, her thoughts lending speed to her fingers. Suddenly she whirled him around to face the mirror.

"You like, yes?" she asked, not leaving him the option of an alternative opinion.

It was a good cut, despite its duration. He looked refined compared to the scruffy, unkempt style he usually sported.

"Yes — it's very nice," he agreed, remembering Calvino's admonitions.

The cutting session over and opinions spent, she whirled him back again. He thanked the sombre young woman with her preference for Americans and left. He spent the next two hours in a line-up waiting for a single casting only to have the search cut off right in front of him.

He grabbed a coffee and panino on the run before meeting with the photographer. He caught a streetcar and rode a very long way. The address turned out to be one in a series of row-houses. A concierge let him in when he pronounced the photographer's name.

"Terzo piano," said the old man, pointing to a stairwell.

He headed to the third floor. He'd resolved to learn Italian as well as he could, memorizing the numbers up to a hundred from Jimmy's phrase book before going to sleep. A small, neatly-lettered sign announced the photographer's studio where a tired-looking face ushered him in.

Warden followed the figure along the hall to a studio set up with tripods and flashes amid an intricate architecture of metal and wire.

"Please," the man said, indicating he was to sit. "Sr. Calvino say you need to make portfolio. You have nothing?" the man asked, shaking his head as though it were scarcely to be believed.

"I didn't know I needed to bring anything."

"Don't worry. We fix it."

The man tinkered for awhile, talking as he worked.

"Sr. Calvino is very big model himself many, many years ago. He coming from Trinidad, very poor. Now very..." He stopped to let his hands describe something round and large in the air. "Now very big man, I think."

The photographer reached out and took his chin deftly with his fingers, turning his head from side to side.

"Mmmm," he pronounced mysteriously.

"It's a bit stiff," Warden said, remembering the cut.

"Don't worry. We fix it."

He went to a wardrobe crammed with men's clothes. A couple of suits hung shyly in the back.

"We make simple for today," he said, pulling out two shirts, one caramel-coloured, the other purple with blue shell-like patterns. "Right now one, maybe two shirts is good."

"Sounds great. What do I do?"

"Please, this way," he said, indicating a set of French doors.

They stepped onto a tiny balcony flanked by a row of dirty windows and a rusting metal fire escape. Warden hadn't known what to expect — perhaps not runways with dozens of blazing lights, but certainly not this four-by-six cement balcony. It was far from the magic world of fashion he'd expected. There was nothing splendid or glamorous about it. Another expectation shot down.

The man indicated Warden was to sit in front of the fire escape. "Now, just relax."

He followed the man's instructions, given largely with his hands. Chin up. Head left. Eyes right. Lean against the wall. "Very good," he would say. "This is nice." Encouraging him with each shot. Nothing of import seemed to be happening. It was too easy, Warden thought. What could come of such small movements on the balcony of a suburban apartment?

The camera clicked. Warden followed instructions. The man stopped and offered him the caramel-coloured shirt. Warden stood to unbutton the one he had on.

"No," said the man. "Not to wear. I want you to make love to her."

"What?" Warden looked at him quizzically.

"This shirt is a beautiful woman. Be nice to her. Talk to her."

He crouched and held the shirt up to his cheek, feeling the softness of the material. He smelled the warmth and fleeciness of fresh cotton.

"Yes, this is good. Just relax now."

Warden found himself changing his pose and expression with each shutter snap, forcing himself to relate to the cotton garment. The material fell back to reveal a Ferré label. He smiled, thinking of the bearded man he had met yesterday and Calvino's horrified look when he had all but admitted he didn't know the name.

"Wonderful!" the man said.

Rain began to fall, lightly at first, then with force. He thought they would stop, but the shutter kept clicking. Warden responded by changing his position with each frame. His hair began to fall down, tangled and limp across his forehead. He wondered why the man didn't stop. Why he didn't notice what a mess he must look.

"Now is even more wonderful!" he heard the man exclaim.

The picture taking went on for another ten minutes, long enough for Warden to be thoroughly drenched and chilled. The photographer called the session to a halt when he noticed his teeth chattering.

"I think is enough now, yes?" the man said with a laugh.

He sent Warden inside to change.

"When will they be ready?" Warden asked, returning in his dry clothes.

"I think, uh... maybe tomorrow," the man answered, as though unsure. "You coming to Sr. Calvino and you see then."

"Great. Thank you very much. Grazie."

"Prego."

It was not yet four o'clock when he left the photographer's studio. Outside, a false dusk had come on with the rain dripping through the leafless trees. Warden pulled his jacket close as he stood by the streetcar tracks watching the silver rails flash down the avenue. He felt the tiredness settle in his bones and wondered briefly, once again, what he was doing in Italy. It was a long, slow ride back. All the warmth of the afternoon had been washed away in the rain.

He got off at Corso Buenos Aires and walked to the agency. The office buzzed with spent activity as the afternoon wound down. Even the telephones rang only sporadically. The few models there were taking a break between the hectic rush of go-sees and the nightly videos and eventual sleep that claimed even the most resilient at the end of the day.

Calvino's office was closed. As he walked past, the door lurched open. Calvino came out, not floating like the balloons of yesterday as though his life were still lived somewhere out on the model ramparts, but surging forward, arms ahead as though to ward off contact with any stray bodies that might be drawn into his orbit while his feet carried him quickly across the room.

"Hi, Sr. Calvino. I just finished my shoot with the photographer... " Warden began.

"Not now, darling," Calvino said, his line of flight carrying him past Warden toward Maura's office. "A big, big star has just arrived. Come back later."

Calvino went in and the door sailed to a close behind him. Warden chuckled. Already, after one day, he was just one of the others. Oh, well, he thought, what could you expect?

The door flew open again and a receptionist emerged carrying a file folder. She smiled at Warden, leaving the door ajar. Inside the office three large suitcases took up most of the floor space while a figure sprawled across Maura's desk, laughing and talking loudly. Warden recognized his distinctive features. He had seen the face a hundred times before on magazine covers, billboards, even on television.

Calvino, Maura and the others fawned and fussed over their star, making a great occasion of his presence. Everyone seemed especially light on their toes, as though animated by his arrival. The receptionist with the folder returned with three more like it, still smiling.

"It is a very big star, yes?" she asked Warden excitedly, going back into the office and shutting the door behind her.

"I guess," Warden said, looking up at the faces surrounding him on the walls.

5

At the trattoria that evening, Warden and Jimmy were joined by Joe and Mike Blum, a model from an agency called Ugly People. That was the best name he'd heard yet, Warden thought. Mike and Warden had already crossed paths on an afternoon go-see. Mike was friendly and asked questions other than the ubiquitous, 'What's happenin', dude?' that neither expected nor required a response.

Afterwards they went to Bar Magenta, a local establishment that transformed itself nightly into a fashion industry watering hole. The tables were filled with a casual, vagabond crowd whose looks were as diverse as their languages. It was not unlike the crowded campus pubs Warden frequented at home, he thought. Yet the faces that perched on seats, gulping beer, laughing and gossiping like other mortals had sprung from the glossy pages of magazines.

They glowed with the particular and the abstract all at once as they assumed lives apart from the cool distance of photographs. It was a select network of youth crowded into hotel rooms in a handful of cities, responsible for creating standards of looks around the world. And he had become a part of it.

Jimmy hailed a tall, dark-haired man coming towards them. He was already known to Joe and Mike, who nodded. Warden shook hands with him.

"Derek and I were roommates two summers ago," Jimmy explained. "Where are you coming from, Derek?"

"Paris. We finished the new Gaultier show last night. Absolute rubbish, it was."

He spoke with a faint English accent, as though its borders had been broken down by international travelling.

"Ward's from Canada."

He felt himself regarded with critical intent.

"Ah, a Commonwealth member — that's admirable. We've got to keep up an even distribution between the Yanks and the natives."

Derek spoke with an air of disdain, as though he carried a smug contempt for everyone he met. As he spoke, a waitress in a tight skirt passed by. Derek nudged Jimmy.

"I wouldn't mind a piece of that," he said. "What do you say we hit on a few while we're in town? I'm ripe for some action."

"Sorry, Derek, I'm a married man now."

"Oh, yes — I forgot. You're still with that little chickee of yours?"

"Her name's Corrine."

Derek smiled scornfully, but said nothing more.

A door swung open at the front of the bar and an ebullient threesome entered. They stopped and regarded the surroundings with curiosity, as if their erratic wanderings had brought them there by chance and might take them elsewhere at a moment's notice.

Warden recognized one of the three from the albergo. He'd mistaken him for an American when the boy greeted him with the usual 'What's happenin', dude?', extending the greeting into a butchery of syllables.

"Only a Yankee can turn 'dude' into a three-syllable word,"

Warden joked, but the Yankee turned out to be an Australian who took exception to the slight against his identity.

"I'm from Australia, mate," he said coolly, in an accent totally different from the one Warden thought he'd heard.

The second boy he hadn't seen before. The third was the loudest of the three, his face an unrehearsed portrait of darting eyes and dancing hair. It was Calvino's 'big, big star' from that afternoon. His presence seemed to cleave the air as they barged into the room.

"Oh-oh, it's the immorality squad," Joe quipped.

Derek turned to look. "I should've known they'd be in town. I guess Milan isn't safe tonight."

"You were asking about the American Hotel," Joe said. "Those guys run it. They breeze into town every couple of months and turn the place upside down. That's Eric Nevada in the middle. He was on ten magazine covers last year."

"I saw him at the agency," Warden said. "They were making a lot of fuss over him."

"Yeah — I saw it, too," Joe said. "Iron filings cling to a magnet with more sincerity."

The unholy trinity surged forward in its rampage, greeting everyone they knew or seemed to think they should know. The group stopped before their table.

"Dudes! What's happenin'?"

"What's up, Eric? I heard you got back today," Jimmy said.

"Hey! News travels fast. The boys and myself are lookin' to hoover a little toot. I hear there's some good Peruvian in town. Help out those third world economies and all."

"He's a real jerk," Joe hissed into Warden's ear.

Eric's hand held an unlit cigarette, taken out before a series of greetings had temporarily caused it to be forgotten. He raised it to his lips.

"Hey, Joey — got a light?"

"No, Eric. I still don't smoke."

"Well, hey! Don't you think you should carry a lighter for guys like me who do?"

"Right. And vegetarians should carry pork chops to feed hungry carnivores."

Warden watched incredulously as Eric pulled a small handgun from his pocket and aimed it at Joe. He pulled the trigger and a flame shot out the barrel.

"Bang, bang," Eric said, lighting the cigarette. His group of supporters sniggered. Unable to muster any real excitement, they moved on, enlarging the circumference of their circle as they went.

"Those jerks are everywhere," Derek griped.

"They're alright," said Mike. "They're just a bit loud."

"Don't you wanna be like them, Derek?" Joe asked. "They get all the good-looking girls and the best work in town."

"Ah, you know what they say," Derek said. "Today's face is tomorrow's fishwrap."

"I wouldn't mind a chance to stink of fish a little more," Joe retorted.

"Speaking of which, I can't figure out how your ugly mug manages to turn up so often in my morning reading," Derek replied with a sneer.

"Only my booker knows for sure," Joe said. "And she don't speak your kind of English, dude."

"Go on — we all know you're the boss's boy," Derek said, pushing Joe's face away with his hand where it leered at him over Warden's shoulder. "You're too ugly to get all that work without selling something."

"I may be the boss's boy, but I'm not his bum boy."

"I don't mind kissing Calvino's ass once in awhile," Jimmy broke in. "The only problem is he expects you to wipe it for him afterwards."

They all laughed and the conversation turned to other topics.

It was late by the time they returned to the albergo. The lights were off in the hallway as they crept in. The television was still on in the lounge, flickering silently in the dark. The faces that gathered around it had gone to bed, each one silent behind his door, dreaming in the listless darkness.

* * *

The next day Warden had a half-dozen appointments and spent the morning travelling all over the city. By mid-afternoon he found himself in the centre of a well-lit studio. At the door, a woman handed him a slip of paper with an Italian phrase on it. "Che buon sapore di latte," she pronounced with a flourish of hands. "You must say this to the camera." She made him repeat it till she was satisfied, then sent him to the waiting room.

Joe was sitting on a bench.

"How's it goin'?" he whispered.

"Great," Warden replied. "What's going on?"

"Video casting — we're just waiting our turns."

A group had formed, lining up against the wall. Every few minutes someone else came down the stairs, paper in hand. Warden recognized another face from Maura's. He was introduced to Cody, a moody Stanley Kowalski in contrast to all the swell-guy Americana around them. Cody's face was strikingly masculine, with short black hair and stubble that miraculously reappeared on his cheeks an hour after he shaved.

Cody grunted his acknowledgment when introduced. Warden was to recall him two years later when he was arrested in Paris for the murder of his girlfriend, a celebrated prêt-à-porter runway model, casualty of a fast-paced, unstable lifestyle, achieving a macabre sort of fame in the end.

"What's this shit for?" Cody growled, waving the paper in his hand. "I ain't sayin' this."

"You gotta say it, Code — it's for a commercial," Joe said.

"What's it mean?"

"It means 'the great taste of milk' in Italian."

Warden laughed. "North Americans selling milk to Italians — now that's funny."

Each had his turn before the cameras, pronouncing the rippling phrase for its analytical eye. Warden stumbled and had to repeat his. Cody's came out sounding more like garbled American than Italian. The client showed no further interest and they all left together.

Outside, the trees were beginning to take on a fat, budding appearance. Cody had another appointment to meet and caught a streetcar. The sun was warm as Joe and Warden walked back to the agency.

"You know, this is something I would never do in New York," Joe said.

"What's that?"

"Walk."

Warden laughed. Joe asked how he came to be in Italy and he related the tale of his one TV commercial and Calvino's beckoning call. Joe told Warden he'd been spotted by Madonna dancing in a New York nightclub. She hired him for a video. From there he'd made other contacts.

"I think she's a genius for changing personalities. No one really knows who she is," Joe said, as though that in itself were an accomplishment. He held up a ring with a miniature hand-gun engraved on it. "She gave me this ring. I traded her a set of Bernini vases for it. Who likes glass anyway, right? I mean, it's too ornamental. It just breaks. Violence is more symbolic of life, don't you think?" Warden was amused by Joe's concept of life.

"I met William Burroughs, too. You know — the writer? He's a cool guy. We used to hang out together in New York."

"What did you talk about?"

"Well — not writing, actually I didn't read his stuff. It's too much like poetry, you know? We used to play darts and hang his washing out on the roof. He had a cool view of the harbour."

Warden thought of them on a rooftop in Manhattan, hanging sheets as they knotted and caught in the wind, emblematic cloth rising and floating above the streets like fleeting hieroglyphs.

They passed a fortified stone fortress erected to house the emperor Napoleon on his conquering tour of Europe. The intricate stonework attested to years of arduous labour, a monumental achievement in its time. They walked through the entrance and over the earth-covered courtyard at its heart. On the other side, Joe looked back for a moment's reflection.

"This is, like, a really major thing, isn't it?"

"Pretty major, I would think." Warden laughed at his summary of the centuries-old monument, the way Joe's mind reduced all things to essentials.

At the agency they ran straight into Calvino.

"Hiya, Mr. C," Joe said.

"Joseph — you're late. Why weren't you back half an hour ago?"

"You told me I had no more appointments till three-thirty, Mr. C," he answered cheerily.

"Never mind what I told you. You should always check. Now you have to go straight to Via Spiga to see Versace. They have requested to see you."

Joe rolled his eyes at Warden as their director talked.

"It's for a big campaign they are doing. They will tell you what you have to do there."

"Yes, boss. Ciao, Ward — I'll catch you later. Thanks for the walk."

It was the first time Warden had seen Calvino since the hurried episode the previous afternoon. He expected the same casual brusqueness he'd received then. Instead, his director was courteous and attentive.

"Darling, come into my office," he said, opening the door. "Your photographs have arrived."

Warden had almost forgotten the photo session the day before.

"No one is to disturb us," Calvino said imperiously in the direction of Maura's office.

They went inside and closed the door. Calvino went to the desk and picked up a large envelope.

"This is wonderful," he was saying. "We have an excellent selection to start your book with. I have already prepared your card for the printer."

He spread out a handful of photographs on the desk.

"I told you I would lay all of Europe at your feet," Calvino said excitedly.

Warden inspected the photographs. He recognized the imprint of someone like him, who must have been posing in a body like his, having the same thoughts as his at the time the shutter clicked. But it was someone so nearly perfect, someone who did not — could not — exist. It was someone other. Yet it was himself.

"I can't believe they look so good," he said.

"Darling, they are not just good," Calvino intoned. "They are wonderful! You are a natural. The camera loves you."

Warden took the photographs into his hands, examining the brilliant colours — silver skies, caramel and purple cloths of the shirts. The rusted bars behind him blurred into an ethereal reality, suggesting not a tenement fire escape but something finer, eloquent and out-of-the-ordinary.

Best of all were the shots of his rain-sprinkled face glowing with concern for a simple piece of fabric. Caressing, embracing, entwining himself in it like a new skin while his hair hung in brash, petulant strands belying the softness of his face and the expression in his eyes. It was the magic he'd been looking for, breathed into it, bursting up like a bird given flight and condensing like the rain on his hair and skin.

6

Warden's first job came unexpectedly. The same afternoon, he learned he'd been requested to work in the Ferré show. Calvino was ecstatic over his young protégé for a few minutes, then promptly got over his excitement and went on with other things.

When Warden arrived at the casting that would give him his first taste of success he was confronted by the usual waiting-room scene. A dozen cream-of-the-crop blonde American surfer types, most of whom turned out to be Scandinavian or German. Cleft chins and broad shoulders were the order of the day. He was sure he'd never be singled out among all those muscular, easy-going dudes greeting one another as they came and went.

The clients huddled together in a corner wearing long, white smocks as the models paraded up and down the room. They looked each one over, evaluating their results on clipboards as though observing some curious, inoffensive disease. Warden handed over his newly printed card when he was called upon, thinking it would all be done soon and he could get on to his next appointment. They left him standing while they conferred in Italian. Finally, one man turned to him.

"What is your agency, please, Warden?"

"I'm with Maura's Models."

"Very good. I will tell them we would like to use you and they will tell you where and when."

The man smiled as though to conclude the agreement. They had found their choice, their cure. And it was him.

"Thank you — grazie," Warden mumbled, unsure what to say.

The line-up moved and the search continued. He left feeling lighter than when he arrived. The video tests, the go-sees, the wardrobe fittings, had up till then satisfied with their novelty and excitement. Now he had an actual accomplishment to flaunt. Outside, he jumped in the air and let out a spontaneous whoop before realizing he was being watched by curious bystanders. He chuckled to himself and went off to his next appointment feeling exultant.

The clients who chose him told Calvino he was the most natural-looking of all the models they'd seen. Many of the others had pumped up their muscles until designers were complaining they looked more like body-builders than real people. But it was not only his physique that made him their choice — there was a naturalness to his presence that appealed to them as well.

The session happened the next afternoon. It was a simple shot on a crowded sidewalk. Carefree young man wearing a casual suit, trenchcoat slung over his arm, walks along as passers-by turn to stare at the impelling strength of his image. Warden enjoyed it, keeping in mind what he had learned working with the photographer who took his first shots. Afterwards, he was thanked for his cooperative manner and told to expect more work. The results would be in print within the month.

* * *

Jimmy and Warden's suppertime appearance at the trattoria became a regular occurrence. They were frequently joined by others seeking company as much as nourishment. The mistress of the restaurant had begun keeping a table for them. It was her express pleasure to be feeding what she considered an exceptional gathering of youngsters.

She kept the table piled with baskets of warm rolls and generous helpings of home-cooked meals while her husband seated anyone who came in. The woman's father, cranky and hard of hearing, stood nightly behind the tiny bar in a wrinkled white shirt and suspenders, sleeves neatly rolled to his elbows as he oversaw the dispensing of beverages.

It was not uncommon for his son-in-law to give him a verbal remonstrance if he felt the service was too slow. Then he would wink over at the table of young men as if it were a joke for their pleasure. The old man would shout something back in a thick dialect, a small cloud of fury rising and settling just as quickly again.

On any given day, the group consisted of Warden and Joe, Mike Blum, Jimmy and his friend Derek, as well as one or two others. At some point they were nicknamed the InternationalTable because of their collection of accents and nationalities and ready acceptance of all who came by.

Politics, Warden discovered, was a topic of almost comic vehemence in any gathering with Americans present. They espoused a patriotic viewpoint at all times, placing their land of birth somewhere between heaven and earth in magnitude of importance and their president somewhere between their mothers and God. Unlike the Americans, members of other nationalities who shared their table seemed capable of offering a more-or-less objective outlook on world events. Others may have known, but Americans *felt*, and feelings went a long way towards their understanding of the world. Mike Blum, alone of the Americans, was willing and able to look at the world from an unbiased point of view.

More than politics, however, conversation in the trattoria carried an overriding regard for the fashion trade. Who was in and who was out of this season's trade shows. Who was working for or sleeping with which famous designer. Who was making it big and who was heading for a burn-out, a fiery flash on the spiralling ladder to success and its constant other, oblivion. The rumours swelled and rippled.

One agency owner, a jet-setting celebrity whose bottomless pockets extended into the agency till, was said to live in Rome on weekends with his wife and 12-year old daughter, and in Milan the rest of the time with a beautiful 13-year old protégé whose parents were aware of the arrangement. Another fashion maven was rumoured to hold exclusive after-hour shows where the models took off their clothes and left them off for the duration of the evening. Tickets to those events went for $1000 plus.

Of the fashion business itself, reports had it that any day the entire industry would dissolve in a cloud of mist, taking its exotic wraps and accoutrements with it, no longer able to sustain the illusion of originality in a world where the new was either old the moment it was unveiled, or had simply been done before.

In any case, it was common knowledge the ridiculous outfits on most of the runways were there for the shock value and promotional advantages offered only by notoriety. Who would buy a silver-lamé G-string? And where would you wear it?

According to Jimmy, who looked on Warden with the concern of an older brother, a model could choose between two lifestyles. The first succeeded because they worked hard. They took themselves and their work seriously. They were there to last. The second type wasted their earnings, squandering their time and looks on drugs and all-night parties at an all-consuming pace. These invariably burned out in a year or two at most. No one on that kind of collision course could stand the pace.

Warden noticed the majority of his American colleagues exhibited little interest in speaking Italian. Whatever fragments or phrases they attempted came out with a sublime inflective indifference. They learned as little as possible, apart from what was necessary to obtain such essentials as food, alcohol and proper directions. Greetings, however, were an exception to this steadfast rule of refusal and 'ciao' was the one word taken up by the Americans with gusto. It was their token attempt to break through language and cultural barriers and was quickly added to a list of stock expressions, including 'howdy' and 'what's happenin', dude?'

One evening, on arriving at the trattoria, one of the models saluted the group in a mistaken mixture of Italian and American, and thus was born the accidental Americanization of 'ciao' into 'chowdy'. Upon hearing it, Mike rolled his eyes at Warden while the others at the table broke into laughter.

"Maybe if we make everything half-Italian and half-American it will be easier to get them to speak the language," he said.

The table adopted it as their password. 'Chowdy' caught on and soon sprang up unannounced through the halls of the alberghi and the agencies. Eventually, it found its way into casting offices and from there went out into the streets, causing more than a few uninitiated Italians to turn their heads at the sound of it.

At night after eating, the group would disband, each going his own way to enjoy the remaining hours before returning to the albergo to sleep. Proper rest was becoming a must, for work was coming in consistently.

As summer drew closer it became increasingly clear Milan was about to become one of those hot, dirty industrial towns that, but for its fashion trade and a world-famous opera house, would be almost unknown. Occasionally on his daytime rounds Warden ran into the big, big star looking as if he'd been spending one too many late nights carousing rather than plying his trade.

"No one can tell a success what to do," Jimmy sermonized. "Just be glad you and I have better sense."

Although he was working frequently, the payment he received for his labours — or his leisures, as he thought of the lounging act he did on the merits of his cheekbones and other superficial aspects of his person — had been far from the overflowing coffers Calvino promised. For every paycheck earned, his director came up with new expenses to cut it by half — hair-styling, photography fees, management costs. By the time he received it, the resulting pay resembled something closer to a form of indentured servitude than anything like freelance work.

As well, he had yet to see the results of work in print. The Ferré show was still to come and his image had not seen the light of publication. The only tangible evidence thus far was the card bearing his name and four photographs of himself, which he promptly sent home when he got it. The clients who hired him were unsure how to use him. They liked his looks, recognizing his natural appeal, but a definitive statement was still to be made by someone prophetic, or imaginative, enough to define the plastic material of his presence.

One evening as he arrived at the trattoria, a magazine was being passed around the table. "Hey, Ward!" Jimmy shouted. "Get over here! I've got something for you to see."

The magazine he held was *Per Lui*, a young men's fashion bible and trade staple. Jimmy turned a page and held it under Warden's nose. He saw himself in muted tones of blue and grey, a trenchcoat trailing from one arm, striding casually along the streets of Milan as admiring passers-by looked on.

"Hey! That's me!"

"Say, that's pretty good," Jimmy quipped. "You figured it out all by yourself! You sound more like a real model everyday. Bend down and let me see if I can look through your ears yet."

"Let's see," Warden said excitedly, picking up the magazine. "Wow! I can't believe it!"

He turned over the page. There was Derek on a bicycle wearing a tweed jacket. On another page, Cody leaned against the hood of a car, his chest covered in grease and sweat, a tire iron in one hand. A dark-haired woman in an evening gown was offering him a drink. 'A Franconi Woman Needs Her Man' was written across the top of the page.

"Sexist crap," Mike carped.

Warden flipped quickly through and saw a young man in boxer shorts with eyes made up to look as though they had been blacked out.

"Hey, Joe — is that you?"

"Sure thing, Ward. Funk and punk. Pretty awesome, huh?"

"What page are you on, Jimmy?"

"All of them," someone shouted. "He's in there at least six times."

"Page 34," Jimmy replied, grinning.

A full-page photograph showed Jimmy in a turquoise shirt and rust-coloured sports jacket against a background of brick, hair whorled above like a flame. Underneath, simply, 'Lubiam — Italia'.

"Nice," Warden said.

The mistress of the trattoria came over to the table. Jimmy showed her Warden's picture.

"Very good, Warden," she said. It was the first English he'd heard her speak.

One at a time, they dutifully turned over the pages to reveal themselves, recounting vignettes of the images printed there. These were things they would remember, tales to relate on their return home. Look here... I was famous... we had fun... see this photograph.

* * *

It was late when Warden got back to the albergo that evening. The light was off under the door. He crept in so as not to wake Jimmy. He smelled smoke and saw the arc of a cigarette flash in the dark.

"Chowdy," Warden greeted.

He began peeling his clothes off wearily, kicking his sneakers into a corner.

"Chowdy, pal," Jimmy said. His voice carried a well-worn edge of sadness.

"Have a good evening?" Warden asked, feeling out whether Jimmy wanted to talk.

"Alright."

There was a pause. After a moment Jimmy spoke.

"How 'bout you? Did you have a good time this evening?"

"Pretty good. Joe and I went to Magenta and then to a video arcade for an hour. I've only got one casting tomorrow. I'm worn out, though. Really looking forward to the weekend."

The radio was playing faintly. Warden could just make it out.

"I'm a stranger far from home... " a lonesome voice crooned as though it saw them lying there.

He left his clothes in a pile on the floor. Normally Jimmy would chastise him for it and Warden would reply that he already had a mother, thanks. Now he said nothing. Warden slid in under the cool covers, the sheets caressing his aching muscles, making him groan with pleasure and pain. The cigarette glowed and swung back again. Smoke rose like a nimbus in the darkness.

"Can't sleep?"

"No," said Jimmy. "I've been thinking."

"Ooh — that could be dangerous for all of us. What about?"

"Home. Family and shit."

"Homesick?"

"Yeah. And lonely, I guess. I keep telling myself it'll all be over soon and I can go home. I try to convince myself one day Corrine and I can get married and settle down. But right now I'm sick to death of foreign cities and travelling around the world. And every time Derek arranges a date with some girls he's just met I go out and have a boring time, or else I sit and think they're just another couple of whores. But they're not, I know. They're just lonely, like me and everyone else."

Warden looked over, but couldn't make out Jimmy's face in the darkness.

"I'm sorry you feel that way," he said.

"Ah — don't listen to me. I'm just griping. It's the price you pay. I know it."

Warden didn't try to console him any further. He'd been in Italy two-and-a-half months at that point. He knew what Jimmy was talking about. They lay there, letting occasional remarks funnel out into the darkness till they both fell asleep.

7

Warden soon found himself working two or three times a week. The remainder of his days were spent trekking through the hot Milanese streets from casting to casting. At some point he lost track of how many jobs he'd done, never sure where he might encounter his own image next.

Weekends were spent recapturing leisure hours. Summer was in full swing, brimming over in a constant surge of activity. At Bar Magenta it was the usual Friday night crowd, sipping beer, relaxing and complaining about the heat. Jimmy and Derek were soon arguing and Joe had wandered off. Warden got up to stretch. The sidewalk was mired in a squabble of tables and chairs and parked motorbikes. The smell of cologne and cigarettes hung in the air like meandering moonbeams. Warden stood in the doorway absently looking out.

Across the street, a figure stood framed in a pool of light. Long dark curls blew across an oval face, leather jacket slung over one shoulder. Jeans with rolled-up cuffs and a white T-shirt completed the uniform. The young man seemed to have stepped onto the street corner from a different world, and stood waiting as though anchored at the foot of the stars.

A group staggered out of the bar and Warden felt someone brush against him. He turned to see the face of a boy he'd worked with earlier in the week, now off in search of unknown pleasure.

"Sincerely sorry," the boy said, turning, then recognized Warden. "Hey, Ward — how's it goin', dude?"

"Great, Kent — looks like you're off for some fun."

"Gotta make the most of the weekend, man! Hafta face that old sidewalk come Monday morning."

He gestured vaguely toward his companions who had stopped,

drunkenly watching the exchange like prisoners out on leave for the weekend, uncertain how far to take their new-found liberty.

"Catch you later, then."

"Awesome, man — keep well."

The group staggered into the street, oblivious to passing cars and other mortal dangers. When he looked around again, the boy with the leather jacket stood next to him. His lips were wrapped around a cigarette which he removed from his mouth and let fall to the ground.

"My name is Valentino," he said.

Warden stared into two eyes framed by a dark grove of lashes.

"You don't know yours?" he asked with mild sarcasm.

Warden laughed awkwardly and extended a hand.

"I'm sorry — it's Ward."

"Piacere. Pleased to meet you." Valentino pointed across the street. "And that is Paolo."

Warden looked over but saw no one.

"Where?"

"There," he said. "My motorcycle is called Paolo." He looked slyly at Warden. "If you are free, Paolo and I will take you for a ride later."

Warden liked his humour. He was drawn to the boy's dusky presence. In the bar, Warden introduced Valentino to the others who took him for a model.

"I am a student," he corrected them. "I am studying architecture."

Valentino related stories about Italy and asked the others in turn about their backgrounds. He and Joe exchanged formidable-sounding anecdotes about mafia activity in Sicily and Brooklyn. Around them the bar was crowded to capacity, the air filled with affable talk and easy laughter.

"You are free to go for a ride now?" Valentino asked.

"He's not free but he's relatively cheap," Joe piped up.

"What does this mean?" Valentino asked.

"I'll explain later," Warden said, chuckling, as they stood to leave.

"Make sure you're not out late, Ward. You know how we worry," Jimmy said.

"Yes, Val, we want him home by midnight," Joe added. "We'll be waiting."

"Don't worry, guys — I'm in good hands," he said. "Ciao."

Valentino slipped on his jacket as they crossed the darkened street. They passed a fence topped by dangerous-looking spikes constraining a flowering garden. Valentino took a penknife from his pocket, reached through, cut a blossom free.

"What's the rose for?" Warden asked.

Valentino looked at it as though he had just discovered the blood-red flower in his hands.

"I think it is for you," he said, handing it to Warden.

Warden put it through a buttonhole in his vest. "In my country boys don't give other boys flowers," he said.

"This is not your country. It is mine."

Valentino stood over the motorbike and gunned the starter with his foot. It roared and shook with life.

"Climb on!" he yelled.

Warden slid a leg over the seat and sat unsteadily behind. Valentino turned to give him a sarcastic stare.

"If you sit this way you will fall off. You must put your arms around me. Are you afraid?"

"I'm not afraid."

He put his hands around Valentino's waist, feeling the other boy's ribs through his jacket. The bike rolled onto the pavement, picking up speed. Warm wind lifted his hair as they sped through the city, passing beneath stone archways and along winding streets. The grey facades of ancient granite buildings flew by until they seemed to have left the twentieth century behind, vanishing into the cool face of antiquity.

Warden gripped Valentino tightly. Smooth leather grazing his cheek as they wove in and out of traffic. Eventually, the bike veered onto a narrow roadway following a shadowy canal and stopped.

"There is the naviglio," Valentino shouted over the noise of the engine.

They dismounted. Valentino jumped on the kickstand, leaving the bike standing upright.

"Now I will take you to my favourite bar," he said, leading the way along a dark, cobbled street, pursued by the echo of their footsteps.

The canal rippled off to the right, reflecting pale street lamps lining its edges. They came to a building with a flashing sign — Scimmia Jazz — lighting up the block. Inside, the bar bristled with music.

"What's it say?" Warden asked, looking up at the sign.

"Shee-me-yah," he pronounced. "It means the animal that lives in the trees and likes bananas. How do you call it?"

"A monkey?"

"That's it, Jazz Monkey."

As they entered, a saxophone made clipped squawking sounds like coins tossed across table tops. A singer poised in a pinspot of light broke into melody as though she had been waiting for them, her wafer-thin voice reaching out to greet them.

"I will buy the beer," Valentino said, taking out his wallet as a waitress came up balancing a tray.

Valentino held up two fingers and she placed two glasses on the table, pushing them forward along the water-beaded surface. He fanned a collection of bills at her, allowing her to pull several from between his fingers. He winked and put the rest back in his pocket. She said something rapidly in Italian. Valentino turned to Warden.

"She says you are a very handsome boy."

"Grazie," Warden said. He removed the rose from his vest.

"May I?" he asked Valentino.

"Of course."

He laid it across her tray of glasses.

"Per me? Grazie," she said, laughing as she went on to the next table.

They sat back and relaxed. Valentino laughed when Warden explained Joe's parting comment at Bar Magenta.

"I did not think you would come with me," he said. "Most American boys do not talk to the Italians."

"I'm not American — I'm Canadian."

Valentino shrugged.

"Is it not the same thing?"

"Not to a Canadian."

"You are quiet and more polite."

Warden laughed, thinking of his mannerly, order-loving compatriots back home. How happily they queued up for anything. How politely they behaved even when they went on strike or protested the government.

"But you have the same country. The American president is your president, no?"

Warden shook his head and laughed again. "We share the same continent but we're a separate nation with our own government."

"Who runs your government, then?"

"We have a prime minister. Technically, the Queen of England is our head of state."

Now Valentino laughed. "You are joking me," he said in disbelief. "The Queen of England does not run your country."

Warden tried to explain but Valentino remained skeptical.

"What is it like to be a Canadian?"

"It's very clean. We believe in fairness and respect for the individual and protecting the environment. It's... " He couldn't think what it was exactly, unable to define the very place he came from. "It's a big country, so it's a lot of things," he said with a shrug.

"What is it like to be Italian?"

"The best, of course!" he said, laughing. "Italians have passion and we love beauty and our country. But you are a lucky country, I think. It was never a big war in Canada."

Warden remembered the week before having seen the ruins of a bombed-out building rise up startlingly in an urban neighbourhood, unchanged in nearly half a century. He also recalled the great station he had arrived at the first afternoon, a long, crypt-like monument fronted by prancing stone horses built to celebrate the glory of Mussolini and his Fascisti.

The bar was crowded with a garrulous mixture of locals and holidayers indulging in a timeless atmosphere. The music flowed, metamorphosing with the shifting moods of the crowd. Each time the elegant singer appeared her costume changed, becoming more and more extravagant. It was well past the oasis of midnight when the band stopped playing, disregarding the stamping and cheering of the noisy partyers hoping to extend the night for just one more number that might possibly stretch on to eternity.

Outside, the cafés and restaurants had dimmed their lights, the revelry put away as the crowd drifted home, only half-conscious their laughter and jubilant manners were at odds with the echoing stillness telling them to save their exuberance for another day.

It had cooled slightly from the day's oppressive heat. The evening was deflating like a balloon whose air escapes in small degrees. They mounted a foot bridge over the naviglio and stopped midway. The moon, exactly half-light and half-shade, reflected soggily on the water, rippling with the slight breezes that had arisen.

They leaned on the railing, staring out over the water. The silence was comfortable. Occasionally their eyes met. Warden was reminded of the dream about his former classmate, John.

"It's nice here," Warden said, his gaze following the river winding through the city.

"I think to myself you will like this place," Valentino said. "It is more quiet."

The air was filled with night sounds. Street lamps traced an ephemeral path along the canal. Warden pondered Valentino's face framed by its dark ringlets. They watched one another in silence.

Valentino reached out and touched Warden's cheek. A smile flickered, faded. His face moved closer. Breath held, lips open slightly. Warden shivered as their lips touched, moist, warm. Then parted.

He stood there, mouth agape, as though becoming vaguely aware of certain things. The taste of salt in his mouth, the fragrance of flowers in the air, the infinitesimal distance between stars. Things that had been there all along which he had never noticed before. It was like looking over the garden wall into the unknown.

He had never been kissed by another man before. In the world he had inhabited until that moment it would have been impassable, like Gulliver's distance. Tabu. But there was a boy in a black leather jacket wearing a white T-shirt with curls fawning around his neck. Valentino's lips pressed forward again, retracing their eager route.

Warden felt a sense of trepidation, as though he had broken an inviolable rule. He pulled back. Valentino's face wore a look of intoxication.

"I think this is another thing the boys in your country do not do with each other," he said.

"No — none that I know."

"I had to kiss you — you were so beautiful." Then, almost apologetically, "I do not kiss other boys very often," he said.

"You could've fooled me," Warden said.

Valentino grinned impetuously.

"You have a problem?" he asked.

"No," Warden shook his head. "Not any more."

They laughed at the same time.

"Come, I must take you home," Valentino said, heading back to the motorcycle. "A photo-model must sleep so he is as handsome in the morning as at night-time."

They sped through the empty streets in the coolness of the approaching morning. It was nearly three a.m. when they drove up to the albergo, the motorcycle's echo roaring in the air around them.

"What room are you?" Valentino asked.

"Twenty-two."

"You are free later this week?" he shouted. "Or do I say 'cheap'?"

"For you, I'm always a bargain."

"Thursday I will come at seven," he said, and drove off in a roar, leaving a cloud of exhaust hanging in the air.

Warden jaunted up the steps. Most nights the door was locked at midnight, an old-fashioned form of curfew imposed by pious hotel keepers in the land of love. Latecomers had gotten into the habit of wedging a piece of cardboard in the doorjamb to assist the next latecomer who, it was understood, was to do likewise. It was in place that evening and Warden slipped quietly inside. He did not turn off onto the second floor, but continued up to a rooftop patio ringed in by walls on two sides and a sloping tiled roof on the third. He lay in a hammock strung up in one corner.

He remembered Valentino's kisses, how his lips felt, and the touch of their bodies gently nudging together. He listened to the stillness between his heartbeats like the silence that follows a sound in the dark. Then he fell asleep, feeling like a thief in the night.

8

Warden stopped in at the agency one morning later than usual. The lobby was a circus of comings and goings as lunch hour approached. Calvino fluttered around him like an excited butterfly, chiding him for his lateness. He stopped short to say he'd had a favourable report from a photographer who'd been into the agency looking for new faces and had seen Warden's card on the rack. "Who is this boy with the spiritual face?" he'd asked, picking up the card. He had 'oohed' and 'aahed' over it, making a fuss until Calvino had to ask him to leave to make way for a long list of appointments.

"This could be very good for you," Calvino said, rubbing his hands over his head as if in memory of hair. "Many models have been discovered by photographers who give them the chance which makes them famous. He said yours was a face 'to die for'."

A look of suspicion came over him as though the encouragement might not be an altogether good thing for a model who was already showing signs of losing self-discipline.

"We work so hard for you and you think you can just come strolling in at a quarter to eleven. You're getting lazy," he warned, shaking a mercurial finger at him. "That is every model's downfall."

He recited the photographer's address, admonishing Warden to go immediately before he'd wasted the entire day. Then he held him back a moment, hesitating to say something.

"If you work very hard, you could be up there," Calvino said, looking up to the rows of celebrated faces on the lobby walls.

* * *

At the studio, the receptionist smiled and asked his name. It was not unlike dozens of offices he'd seen as one more hopeful face in an endless trail of go-sees over the last three months. He sat and looked at the walls hung with photographs featuring male models. They looked, he thought, like a lot of young boys running around trying to act like men.

The door opened with a sigh as a beaming, effusive man came towards him, hands extended. A shapeless smock draped over his features made him resemble a large teddy bear. He pushed a gorse-growth of shoulder-length hair away from his face, which had the all-accepting look of an idiot or a saint.

"You have come at last," he said. "I am Andreo Oliviero."

The hands extended towards him were not intended to shake so much as to define the air around him. He crouched down to where Warden sat on the sofa, holding Warden's index card up as though to compare the original with its image.

"When I saw your face I told Sr. Calvino to send you immediately," he said, eyes blinking on and off like a stoplight. "Yes, yes — I knew you were the one I wanted. It is such a spiritual face."

He stood there swaying, hands clasped as though in prayer.

"Come with me, please," he said. "I would like to show you my work."

Warden followed him to a well-lit studio space. There he handed over a portfolio, something other photographers had not done. Between its covers Warden recognized celebrated advertisements he had seen countless times in places he couldn't begin to remember.

Oliviero's style was distinctive as much for its personality as for its beauty. His models glowed with the languidness of gods. Each photograph bore the mark of a master, unique and immediately recognizable, as if it could belong anywhere — between the pages of a high-quality fashion magazine or plastered over billboards on a street corner.

"Your work is beautiful," Warden said. "I've seen a lot of these ads before."

"Thank you, I'm so glad you like it," he said excitedly. "Because I would like very much for us to work together.

Warden wondered if the photographer were selecting him, or he the photographer, whose hands were busy defining the air again.

"I would like to use you for a series of things. Individual pieces — some interesting, some not so interesting," he explained. "Once the clients know your work with me they will see what I can do with you. Then we will see what we will see. But don't worry. Basically they let me do what I want."

He smiled and rubbed his hands together like a child faced with a choice of desserts.

"You see," he began, "there is something special about you. I feel it. For every decade there is a face that captures the imagination. In the eighties there was Jeffrey Aquillon. Do you know him?"

Oddly enough, Warden did remember the man with the blue eyes and handsome face who had been called the world's most beautiful man.

"He was famous! Everybody knew him instantly — he got fan letters. So far there has been no face to appear to dominate the male fashion world in this decade. That face could be yours."

Warden listened to this wizard of photography making success sound like child's play.

"When shall we start?" he asked, anxious to begin the fun he was contemplating.

"Any time," was all Warden could think to say.

"Good. Tomorrow, then." He clapped his hands in joy.

* * *

Warden's head was buzzing. When he wasn't thinking of Andreo's pronouncements, he thought of Valentino. The memory of his touch stayed with him all afternoon, through a blur of appointments and castings.

At the International Table that evening Mike, Joe and Derek were there as well as a new model from France. While they were eating he told them of his meeting with the famous photographer.

"Wow — that's great!" Mike exclaimed. "He could do wonders for your career. You could really go places with somebody like that behind you."

"I worked with him once," Joe said. "It was in that ad for Lust Perfume that everyone got so upset about. You remember the one with all those naked guys in a blue haze making love to the woman in the centre? I have my head pressed to her thigh in the bottom right corner. When I arrived at the studio he said, 'I don't need your face but I do need another body'."

"What's he like?" said the French boy, momentarily disengaging an all-consuming interest in his food.

"Sort of like an Easter Bunny — you almost expect him to be wearing a big pink suit and hopping everywhere," Warden said jokingly.

"I hear he's pretty pink," Derek quipped.

"In your mind a guy could risk ruining his personal image by ordering the wrong drink," Joe said.

"Your friend Valentino seemed like a decent guy," Mike said, changing the subject.

"Watch out for those Italians," Derek blurted out. "You never know what they're after."

"Warden's pretty capable of looking after himself," Mike said to disarm his friend's social ineptness.

* * *

Valentino was sitting on the steps outside the albergo when Warden returned, his motorcycle parked nearby.

"At last!" he exclaimed. "I am afraid you will forget me."

"Not a chance," Warden said, smiling at the figure in chinos and blue-and-white striped shirt. "Just let me drop this off in my room," he said, indicating his portfolio, "and I'll be right back down."

When he returned Valentino said, "We will walk to the Giardini Pubblici. It is very nice in the evening."

Along the avenue vendors sang the praises of their wares, fresh-cut crescents of watermelon and jumbled pyramids of coconut shell stacked under trickling silver fountains. Insect sounds heralded the emergence of stars as clouds rolled coolly away in massive, twilight shapes. Earth's polarity reversing itself. Everything suspended by daylight was awakening. Changing. As though an account of the day's activities were being taken before entering the soft contradictions of night.

They walked the darkened garden paths lit by glowing lamps like stars in a terrestrial universe. Warden told Valentino of his meeting with Oliviero.

"This is indeed fortunate for you," Valentino said. He put his hand lightly on Warden's shoulder to keep them in step.

"In Italy, Andreo Oliviero has a big reputation. He gives a good image of what this country is."

Their bodies brushed up against one another, then drifted apart again as they walked. Valentino's hand felt natural, not forced or uncomfortable. He sensed a new language at work, one of touch and physical affection. So far from the crisp, clean sanitation of his own emotions. It hinted at the possible amalgamation of passion and reason.

"When I am kissing you last weekend, I hope I am not making you angry," Valentino said.

"N-no," Warden said, stuttering. "I think... I liked it."

"I think you are liking it, too," Valentino said with a grin. "I love beauty," he said, as though to explain his actions. "Just like your photographer, Oliviero. I want to hold it to my soul like a candle."

They both laughed at his poeticizing.

"Sometimes I would like to make in love with you," he said, treating the felicitous phrase as a noun.

"You mean you would like to make love with me," Warden corrected.

"Yes — I would," Valentino agreed.

Warden laughed.

"Why do you laugh? Is it not possible for you to make in love with another man?"

Warden laughed again and tried to explain what he had meant.

"You do not want to make in love with me?" Valentino asked, pouting.

"It's not that. I mean... I don't know."

They stopped and looked at each other.

"What don't you know? I will show you," Valentino assured him. "When I make in love with a girl it is one thing and when I make in love with a boy it is different."

"You make love with girls, too?"

"Of course — you have never been with a girl?" He laughed. "Ah, you are a bambino, my friend."

"What's it like — I mean, making love to another boy?"

"It is solid and strong, like a hard rock or a tree."

"You make love to girls and yet you make love to boys, too?"

"Yes," Valentino said. "Do I shock you to say such things?"

"I guess a little bit."

Valentino's hand squeezed his shoulder. He felt bewildered. So many things that had worked without effort now seemed to be running in opposite directions. He felt poised over an abyss, a step between being and doing. It frightened him.

Warden looked at Valentino's boyish face. He felt something metamorphosing inside. An old identity slowly becoming part of a new landscape. He was drawn into the centre of it as he confronted the notion that everything changes, that time is not tricked by the imperceptible slowness of life but that slowness is in itself the trick. While everything is pulled everlastingly onwards.

"You have a problem?" Valentino asked.

"Not one I won't get over."

They walked back to the albergo, night winds breathing in and out of the trees along the streets. At the door, Valentino seemed prepared to say goodnight, as if afraid he might be pressing his welcome.

"Don't go yet," Warden said. "We can sit on the roof for awhile."

"I am glad," Valentino said, smiling. "I am afraid maybe I am too honest and you will want me to leave."

The rooftop was lit by a ring of candles in bottles winking mutely into the night. The smell of smoke and wax hung in the air as they sat overlooking the darkened courtyard with the city spread before them. Cool twinge of night breezes on their skin. Valentino pressed against him as they looked out across the heat waves rippling the unreal distance.

Warden felt comfortable, sitting there like teammates after a game or friends camping on the banks of a river far from home. The moon was rising.

"La luna," Valentino said, watching his gaze. "The moon is a woman."

He took Warden's hand into his own.

"La mano," he said, squeezing it and winking. "It is nice to hold."

Warden pointed to a drinking glass glistening in the moonlight.

"What's that?"

"Un bicchiere."

He pointed to other items shivering in the darkness gathered at the outskirts of the circle of flames. Valentino named them as Warden repeated the words. A mosquito landed on Warden's bare arm. Valentino's palm slapped over it.

"Zanzara," he said and they laughed together.

Valentino rested his head on Warden's shoulder. Slowly, Warden reached up to his face and caressed it, fingers catching in a tangle of curls. A sigh broke from his lips, futile protest against his confused emotions telling him he could not be doing what he was doing. Valentino stirred.

"You must soon go to sleep," he said.

"I'd stay here all night with you if I could."

"Some night we will stay together when you will want me to."

Warden opened his mouth to answer.

"When you will want me to," Valentino said, pressing a finger over Warden's lips.

They went downstairs and stood on the front steps.

"Paolo! You have waited for me," he said comically to his motorcycle. "You see — I have a boy to go home with every night. You will have to be my second friend-boy."

"Boyfriend."

"Yes."

They said goodnight. Warden listened to the engine fade in the streets as he went upstairs. The light was on in his room. Jimmy was home.

"Chowdy," Warden said as he came into the room. It seemed like ages since they'd had a good chat about 'life and shit', as they referred to their talks.

"How's it going?" Jimmy responded.

"Awesome, man! Just awesome!"

"You sound more and more like a Yank every time you talk," Jimmy said. "You sure you don't want to come back and live in Jersey with me someday?"

"Hey — I'd follow you anywhere, pal. You know that."

Jimmy was folding shirts and socks, laying them on the bed as though he'd been doing laundry.

"So, what's up?"

"Valentino came by and we went for a walk in the gardens. He just left."

"I like that guy," Jimmy said, nodding. "He's down to earth, unlike most of the assholes we work with. I'm glad you've found a friend."

"He's really a great guy. I hope I get to know him better."

Warden pulled his sweater over his head.

"And that's great news about Oliviero, by the way."

"How did you... ?"

Jimmy laughed. "Everyone was talking about you at the agency today. We'll all be pretty jealous in a few months when you're hitting the covers of every hot fashion mag. You're a very lucky guy, Ward."

"I know it. First shoot tomorrow morning. I'll put in a word for you, if all goes well."

"Thanks. That'd be great."

Jimmy continued to fold. He went over to the closet and took several more shirts off their hangers, bringing them over to his bed.

"What are you doing? Got an out-of-town gig somewhere?"

Jimmy straightened and turned to him.

"I've got some news, too, Ward," he said quietly. "I wanted to tell you earlier but I never got the chance. I got some work, too — it's in Australia. I leave tomorrow."

Warden stood, mouth open, tongue moving dryly. It was so unexpected. "Ah, fuck... " he said finally. "I mean, that's great, man. I'm really glad for you."

"I know," said Jimmy. "I know it. But when you're called, you gotta go. You can't miss out on that opportunity. And this could be something really big."

"Ah, shit... well, that's great, but it's just so sudden. You mean you're not going to be here for the July fourth show?"

" 'Fraid not."

"I was really looking forward to working with the great Jimmy from Jersey."

Jimmy smiled ruefully and gave a faint shrug, turning back to his shirts.

So this is how it ends, Warden thought. With an impetuous toss. Not a slow unwinding, but a sudden break. He was stilled by the feelings of having shared the last four months of his life in a small, cramped room with another man in the bed next to his own.

"Hey, don't worry. We'll see each other next spring," Jimmy said optimistically.

Warden disliked the thought of running into Jimmy in a line-up at a casting and calling out, "Hey, man! How's it going? How've you been since the last time we saw each other?" as he had seen so many others do.

"It's a great job," Jimmy said as he packed. "Guaranteed five spreads over the next seven issues of a classy Australian bridal magazine."

"I'll miss you. The International Table won't be the same without your sparkling American personality."

Jimmy looked up almost fearfully at this successive sharer of the homeless life. He straightened in a manly, military sort of way.

"It'll be okay," he said. "It's been nice to live with a decent guy for once, Ward — I really mean that. It's been a fucking pleasure."

"Awesome, man."

Chowdy.

Part II:
Fabiano Boy

9

After Jimmy, Warden had a succession of roommates, none of whom stayed for more than two or three days. Although he missed Jimmy's reassuring presence, he felt he had at last gotten into the swing of things. Go-sees continued and he worked with Andreo regularly. One afternoon Warden returned to the albergo to find his latest roommate had gone and not been replaced.

"Nobody has come," explained Irena with a shrug, as though apologizing for the empty bed. "If there is no one by tomorrow evening, probably then no one comes until next week."

It was a rare respite to have the room to himself that night, rolling over to see the empty bed across from him. That hadn't happened since the first day he'd arrived. Lying there in the dark, he thought of his family and friends at home. He remembered something Jimmy had told him about feeling lonely and sleeping to escape the loneliness. You dream of work, you dream of going home, and you dream to escape it all, Jimmy had said his first week there.

The next day Warden went to a wardrobe fitting for the Ferré show. He stood patiently, letting the dressers and fitters fret and fuss over him, muttering under their breaths in Italian about last-minute changes and other unknown worries that constituted dark clouds on their private horizons.

Afterwards the models gathered in the auditorium where they were told the basics of show etiquette — no talking, no smoking, no fooling around. They were walked through the show step by step with music cues and choreographic arrangements as outfit changes were timed between alternate sequences.

Coming back from rehearsal he dropped into the agency, oddly tranquil now at the end of a busy week. Calvino was on the phone and waved from his office as he entered.

"Any work?" Warden mouthed.

"Monday," Calvino said, covering the phone with his left hand.

Warden checked the agency mail box. There was nothing for him.

"Yes, darling, I know, I know... " Warden heard him say soothingly into the phone as though smoothing the feathers of some ruffled cockatoo.

Outside the afternoon billowed like a slowly slackening sail. He walked to the albergo and showered, then went to the trattoria. He had avoided the International Table since Jimmy left, robbed of its biggest, most amiable clown. Now, for the first time, no one else showed up. The shows which had commenced that week had so disrupted everyone's schedule that no rules of logic or regularity applied.

He sat and chased a cluster of twisted fusilli around a bowl with barely enough interest to eat it. He hated eating alone. A short plump man at a far table puffed on a black cigar, punctuating his conversation with the old man at the bar. At times like this, he thought, it might help if I smoked. He got up, leaving his meal unfinished.

Back at the albergo the halls were empty. He turned on the shower at the end of his floor and stood for a long time under the running water. He was changing in his room when he heard a motorcycle's roar in the street followed by footsteps running up the stairs.

"Ciao, Warden! Are you here?" he heard Valentino call.

"Ciao!"

He pulled on a jersey and went out to greet him.

"How are you, my American friend-boy?"

"Very happy to see you. And you?"

"I am happy as well," he said. "And Paolo, also. He misses you. All week he asks me when you are going for another ride. You have had a busy week?"

"Yes. Very busy. I had my fitting for the Ferré show today."

"Ah, I like Ferré!"

They went outside, where the sun was setting. A golden hue hung in the sky and mingled with the awakening lights of the city. Valentino's face glowed.

"You look very handsome," Warden said.

He protested. "You are the handsome one," he said. "And very sexy. I don't know if I can stand to have you sit behind me on Paolo tonight." He winked.

"Don't you trust me?"

"Oh, I hope not," Valentino replied, laughing as Warden climbed onto the back of the motorcycle.

They headed along the broad avenues joining a leisurely flow of traffic. Valentino swerved into a brightly lit piazza where a crowd milled about and vendors sold souvenirs to every taste. They headed directly across the square towards a flock of pigeons feeding on spilled popcorn. The birds broke upward, panicking, away from the marauding motorbike. And then they were off again, jumping curbs and roaring down narrow alleyways, the wheels beneath them barely touching pavement.

"Are we going to Scimmia?" Warden yelled.

They approached a red light. Valentino waited till they had stopped before answering.

"You are dressed much too nice for Scimmia," he said, turning to face Warden. "We will go to Plastica, a very nice club. It is alright with you?"

The light turned green. Cars on either side began to inch forward.

"Anywhere's fine with me."

"You are sure?"

Drivers behind them honked their horns. Some moved up and around, slowing to shake their fists. Valentino ignored the scene they were causing.

"Sure I'm sure."

"You have a problem?"

"No, but if you don't get going I'll give you one."

"I hope so," he said, gunning the accelerator.

They sped past cars, gliding in and out of traffic till they arrived at a bright pavilion under a grove of trees. Inside, the air was luminous with figures twisting softly on the dance floor as they entered its vacuum. All around them was a world of beautiful, androgynous youth. The muscular chests of men and the firm breasts of women seemed the same at a distance.

Valentino introduced Warden to a group of friends. He shook hands with the two boys, then offered his hand to the girls. They looked at him shyly and giggled, finally shaking hands with him.

"Let's dance," said Valentino, taking him by the hand and leading him to the dance floor.

"Is it alright to dance together?"

"Of course! This is Italy."

"Why did your friends laugh when you introduced us?"

"They want to know who is my handsome friend. I tell them, 'This is my American friend-boy'."

Warden looked back over to the girls who were watching them curiously.

"I think they are jealous," Valentino said.

"Good," Warden said.

He leaned forward and kissed Valentino, grinning at the surprised look on his face.

"You have a problem?" he asked.

They danced, returning to Valentino's group of friends. Later, they went up to an outdoor terrace where the cool air refreshed them. They sat and joked, balancing on a railing facing one another. Warden yawned and rubbed his tired eyes.

"You have had a long week. I should take you home soon and put you to bed, bambino," Valentino said.

He took Warden's hand in the friendly manner he had assumed all evening.

"Come — it is time to leave now anyway."

They walked towards the exit where they had to make room for someone coming in. It was Jimmy's friend, Derek. Warden hadn't seen him in several weeks. Derek looked at them cooly, barely acknowledging Warden as he brushed past. Warden stopped and looked after the retreating figure.

"I'll be back in a moment," he said to Valentino.

"I will go to find Paolo."

He followed Derek through the crowd, catching up with him at one end of the bar.

"What's up your ass?" Warden asked, grabbing his shoulder.

Derek looked startled.

"Nothing. Why?"

"You just pushed right past me without saying a word back there."

"I thought you might not want to be seen in here. You know — image and all."

"What's that supposed to mean?"

Derek laughed awkwardly. "Well, you know," he said vaguely, waving an arm in the direction of the entrance.

"No, I don't know," Warden said. "I've just spent the last four months having supper with you almost every week and now you pretend not to know me."

Derek looked nervous.

"I just thought you might not want to be spotted in here. The place is full of wops and fags."

"And which did you come for, asshole?" Warden retorted, brushing past the other boy who looked after him in astonishment.

Valentino sat waiting outside. Cool drops of rain splattered on the dry streets as they made their way back to the albergo. The smell of moist earth and fresh air caught their nostrils. Outside the albergo, Valentino cut the motor. The sound drifted away into the night.

"I shall come up and sit with you on the balcony for awhile?" Valentino asked hopefully when they dismounted.

"You can come up to my room if you like."

"I thought the signora does not allow visitors after ten o'clock."

"It's just girls she doesn't let in. Are you afraid?"

Valentino grinned. At the top of the stairs all the lights were out except for a small lamp over the reception desk. Warden reached over and freed his key from its hook. He took Valentino's hand and led him down the hall. He unlocked the door and looked in. There was no one in the other bed. Nor was there any luggage deposited on the floor at its foot. The room was unoccupied, as he'd hoped.

They entered and Warden closed the door behind them. As they stood in the darkness their lips met in small, experimental kisses. Valentino's fingers explored his face, moving over his cheeks and closed eyes. Valentino pulled back.

"What if your roommate comes?"

"We'll just say we were out dancing. You have a problem?"

Valentino laughed quietly.

"No. No problem."

Warden unbuttoned Valentino's shirt. It slid over his bare shoulders onto the floor. He pulled his own jersey over his head. They stood outlined by the light coming through the balcony doors. Smooth skin and taut muscles crushed together.

They wrestled their way onto the bed, edging over one another, scraping shins and elbows. Smothering sudden impulses of laughter as they remembered their sleeping neighbours on the other side of the walls.

Warden's hand moved across the broad warmth of a belly. He felt the easy grace of Valentino's body, the lean silkiness that contradicted his senses. He searched until he found the object of his curiosity, brushing it quickly aside with embarrassment borne of inexperience and desire. He breathed in the smells in the blind areas of his body as they rolled and tumbled over one another in a way he had been led to believe only a man and a woman could do.

10

Warden worked closely with Andreo for the rest of the month. At each session he was greeted as effusively as he had been on their first meeting, as though Warden were the celebrity rather than the photographer himself.

Andreo had started as a photojournalist, fond of the daring and cleverness required for work as a war correspondent. By the age of thirty, with his person still intact and facing a diminishing reserve of bravado, he suddenly gave up the thrills of fear-seeking as easily as he had taken them up. On returning home, he was assigned by an editor with a peculiar sense of humour to cover the aggressive postures and stances on the battlefields of fashion. An instant love was born.

As they worked, Warden began to grasp Andreo's vision. His photographic eye sought to find the absolute in everything, as though life were a pathway between a series of fixed images. Like the sulky blue boys of Calvin Klein with their star-spangled visions of American youth, or the fabulously-tinted European montages of Claude Montana, his photographs created a feeling of solidity amid the peripheral drift of fashion, with power to remain long after their fashion statements had vanished as vital forces.

Where some photographers survived by executing the same successful picture over and over again, hired and re-hired for their safe predictability, Andreo chose not to console but to confront. He offered change and challenge in place of comfort, becoming more and more daring in his pursuit of imagistic truth. Those who once praised him began to damn him for shocking their sensibilities.

"My vision is vital, but it is not meant to be transgressive," he would say with a gentle smile. "If I offend some, perhaps they need to be offended."

He chuckled as Warden sat listening on the studio floor.

"My first crime was many years ago. For a series of ads I used clerks from the stores where they sold the clothes. Smiling, happy people, instead of frowning models. Real clothes for real people — how extraordinary! It had never been done before. The campaign went over very well. The agency directors all hated me because I had pointed out the emperor's new clothes."

He shrugged.

"My latest scandal was over a model I used for a very famous dress designer. She is a young girl who works the streets here in Milano. A beautiful little ragamuffin. 'Oooh, she is so sexy,' they said. Later, when I told them she was a prostitute, they pretended to be horrified with me. 'Why?' I asked. 'What is the difference between what she does and what a model does?'"

He looked over at Warden who sat laughing.

"Pardon if I offend," he said with a faint smile.

Andreo walked over to a desk obscured beneath piles of paper. He looked down and sniffed, wrinkling his nose at the inscrutable mess. He spoke briefly to his assistant. The man reached in and retrieved a folder from among the sheaves of notices demanding attention.

"Let's see, what have we for you today?" Andreo adjusted his glasses. "Fabiano fall campaign — very nice. And... oh, yes, you will like this. You will look wonderful. Francesco will prepare you," he continued. "His English is minimal, but let him do what he wants with you."

He was led to a tiny drawing room.

"Prego," said the man, motioning him to enter, holding a wool suit over one arm.

Warden changed into the suit, following Francesco's directions to occupy a chair in front of the make-up mirror where his hair was sprayed with cool mist from an atomizer. The man ran his fingers nimbly back and forth over Warden's head, arranging the damp locks to his satisfaction, drying the excess water around his temples with a cloth.

"Prego," he said again, indicating for Warden to follow him back to the studio.

"Wonderful," said Andreo when they returned. "Francesco knows always what I want without having to be told.

He indicated a backdrop.

"The Fabiano people like their backgrounds very simple," he said. "We will use one or two colours and play with the lights for contrast."

Warden stood in front of the backdrop. He knew his first course of action in any situation was to look as though he knew exactly what he was doing, but he decided to risk asking.

"What do you want me to do?"

"Do what you do best, my dear one — just be you," Andreo said, fixing his eye to the camera. "One must remain neutral in front of the camera. Let us fill it with our fantasies and give it a purpose while you simply give it a presence."

He looked up at Warden.

"The most important thing is for you to look good wearing the clothes. The model is of secondary importance, if you will forgive me. You see, Warden, I can make anyone look beautiful. For me, everyone can be a model. But don't tell that to your Sr. Calvino because it would make him lose sleep over his precious agency."

As he spoke he took several shots.

"To me, there is no difference between naïve beauty and beauty of a conscious design. One may be as valid as the other. I do not want to describe something idealistically so much as show how it makes me feel. The beauty comes from within. It is only through images that we can make sense of our world."

They went through an assortment of shots as Andreo coaxed him to relax and be at ease with himself. He changed clothes several times.

"I'm bored," Andreo said suddenly. "Let's jazz it up a bit."

Andreo had him change into a suit of fine beige linen, classic in its simplicity.

"Madonna mia! You were born to wear that suit," Andreo declared, when he saw the result.

He spoke to Francesco who scurried off and returned with a trumpet. Andreo placed the brass instrument in his hands while Francesco slicked back his hair. Andreo took off his own glasses and handed them to Warden.

"Glasses for a more serious, studious look — all part of the business of selling the product. People will believe anything if you present it right. We can say you're in a pop band and that you agreed to pose for a promotion gimmick," he joked, looking up from the camera. "We'll call it the Yellow Submarines, tell the kids you're the newest pop star. Soon you will be getting offers for recording contracts. People will follow you in the streets asking for autographs. What do you think of that?"

He laughed at his own mischievousness.

Warden turned his body in a three-quarter profile to the

camera, looking out with a steely gaze of self-assured calm as he raised the trumpet to his lips.

* * *

There had been smaller shows all week. At the height of it, Milan reached a pitch of excitement as new collections were unveiled each night and fireworks exploded in the sky. That evening's special presentation included a gathering of some of Italy's pre-eminent designers for a gala showing in aid of a newly formed fashion design council. Feuding competitors had put aside their pins and cutting shears and come armed only with their most glamorous creations.

The models assembled in the dressing rooms like so many prize blossoms as dressers and make-up artists fluttered from one to the other making sure each fold, each crease, found its proper place. Warden was not in the first segment. That portion belonged to Gianni Versace. Gianfranco Ferré, the younger of the two statesmen of fashion, claimed the second. Warden waited until the first group of models was led out before taking his place at the make-up tables.

Outside the dressing room, the pounding music and cheerful permapress creases of the announcer's voice commenting on the collections meant the show had begun. Within moments the models from the first group were back, inserted in and out of their exits and entrances between brief changes and the soft fluttering of applause.

"She is magnificent!" he heard one of the assistants exclaim. The man was peeking at the runway from behind a curtain. "Brava! Brava!" he cried, wringing his hands.

Warden knew the excitement was over Tamarra, a star whose face frequently appeared on the covers of the glitzy fashion magazines and whose lifestyle and personality were reputedly even larger offstage. According to Joe, Tamarra was actually a transsexual from the slums of Brazil.

He was distracted by the hands that reached out to brush his hair and dress his body. His stomach fluttered. The second group was herded out of the dressing room and checked as they lined up for the parade down the runway. Warden took his place backstage waiting for the introductions, voice booming in his ears.

He looked around. Joe stood up front, hair slicked down and in place at last, still looking like a mischievous teenager under his conservative adult garb. Behind him was Cody, slate-eyed and steel-chested. Warden waved. He nodded back, unsmiling.

He looked around for Mike, finding him at the opposite end of the line-up alongside several women from his own agency. Mike looked over. "Good luck," Warden mouthed. Mike smiled, giving him the thumbs-up sign.

One of the assistants fluttered around, waving his hands and pulling his lips apart in a wide grin, making hideous faces until they were all laughing, all those beautiful men and women conscious only of their nowness. As though that were all that mattered.

They were let out of the narrow confines one at a time, the pounding beat propelling them down the celebrated catwalk. A door opened and they entered a different universe where the stars had reassembled, taking their proper place inside the pavilion for the night.

Warden watched the models ahead of him spin down the run-way ramp one after the other as though across an abstracted horizon. Formations turned and scattered, reassembling instantly as taut lines and dagger-sharp curves plunged the eye into a brilliant substitute existence. They seemed to re-invent themselves with every step, scarcely aware of the extraordinary fuss they were causing.

Warden stepped onto the catwalk, caught in a trembling light. At the far end of the stage was the 'magnificent' Tamarra and Eric Nevada. They turned in perfect unison and swept back up opposite sides of the ramp. Tamarra floated along ethereally, nothing in her graceful movements suggesting she had ever been anything other than what she was right now. Eric, all quivering nostrils and effervescence, strode up the far side, darkly luminous like a nervous racehorse.

These were the two models who were magic that year. Somewhere someone had decided as much and given the stamp of approval. This was the look, the stance, the face of what constituted the here-and-now.

Flashes went off like timed explosions around the room, as if to touch with ethereal hands the face of beauty. Warden felt a surge of power as he glanced out over a sea of admiration for the vibrating forms whirling past like magnetized matter. The room was filled with fleeting subtleties, the routes of suggestion upon which the lightness of illusion travelled. This is what it looks like, Warden caught himself thinking.

How temporary it all was. Beat, look, model. Worlds winked

out in quicker-than-the-eye changes. High cheekbones, pure skin tones, slender, supple bodies repeated themselves endlessly. Retreating behind glossy curtains to be transfigured and melted down in an infinite array of guises.

Warden felt magnified by the attention surrounding them. It was a kind of marriage, an ecstatic union, being so close to these others. The flashes of light caught on their skin like tiny smiles of adoration. He rose, porous with ecstasy while the Lilliputians looked on.

The end of the show exploded into an American tableau in honour of Independence Day. Models dressed as guards of honour carrying long-bannered flags flanked both sides of the ramp. Down the centre paraded Tamarra in a vermilion evening gown leading a Siberian tiger cub on a leash. She looked as sleek and tawny as the cat itself. The cub was not in the best of humour, spitting and snarling with each synchronized flash as the show ended in a splurge of colour.

And then it was over. Lights dimmed and the fanfare converged to a distant hum. The public, press and friends rose to follow the oracles of fashion to the reception. The spectacle was over. It was time to let the effects of the show gain momentum, taking it off the runway and into the streets.

Inside the reception hall, a vast arena of marble and tulle that might have passed for the lobby of some giant multinational corporation in North America, the models reappeared one by one to mingle with the public. Standing with the designers and posing for the photo-hungry. Finally, the stars entered, Eric followed by Tamarra. She stood for a moment at the top of the stairs as though caught by surprise when the flashes started again. She descended, elegant and ever-lovely, with a smile that seemed to say to everyone in the room 'Ah, there you are at last!' but which really said 'Here am I'.

The reception went by in a blur. Between the excited introductions and brassy greetings, the brilliant talk and bitchy gossip, small quantities of cocaine began to be dispensed furtively among the glasses of champagne. Warden watched with curiosity as it went around until Tamarra herself came over to offer the drug of the gods to him. She smiled benignly and lifted it up on the plastic back of a credit card.

"Here's to it," she said, wrinkling her nose. "Up the spout."

He had one quick snort of the cold whiteness up each nostril

77

and felt a numbness descending his throat. Gianni Versace passed by with one of the show's coordinators.

"You were wonderful, my darling!" he said, taking Tamarra's hand and kissing it lightly.

"Gianni, Antonio, I'd like you to meet Warden," she said. "Warden is with Maura's. We'll have to get him in our show next year. He's going to be very good."

They spoke briefly in English, then switched to Italian. Tamarra laughed at something he couldn't understand. Crowds surrounded them. Tamarra and the famous designer drifted off in a haze of smoke and camera flashes, followed by the coordinator.

The music in Warden's ears had begun to sound peculiar. Everything sparkled, as though the room were being strewn with delicately-petalled flowers. There was a glittering edge to it all, outlining the gathering in an air that was fabulous yet vaguely insidious.

Cody went by with a woman on either arm. A waiter passed carrying a tray that floated towards him and he picked up a glass with an amazingly long stem. He watched as Calvino went through the crowd, a blur with an anxious face. After awhile Tamarra reappeared. For a brief instant, he thought he saw traces of blood and bone emerging beneath the skin, her celebrated cheeks eroding as she stood chatting and laughing, ignorant of her own impending demise. He shook his head as though clearing an ear blockage. The nightmarish vision disappeared.

"This place is getting too fabulous for words, darling," she said, shaking her vivacious hair at him. "Some of us are going somewhere to dance and we think you ought to come along."

And then they were clambering into one of several cars with a dozen or so others who had taken part in the show. Mike was there and he felt reassured. He watched as parts of Milan flew by he'd never seen before. Out of a general buzz of conversation he heard Tamarra speaking.

"This one needs taking care of," she said, patting his head.

He was aware of a face leering at him from the front seat.

"I'll help," he heard the man's voice say.

"No, you won't," said Tamarra. "You keep your hands on the steering wheel and off of this boy. He's an innocent among us wolves."

Warden smiled and suffered her attentions while the car drove through warm streets with its top down. Eventually, they arrived somewhere and piled out at a park where outdoor celebrations were taking place. There was music and dancing and occasional fireworks like ersatz stars dissolving in the sky.

After an appropriate amount of time the night began to move off in search of more adventure before dawn. Warden found himself in an all-night dance club where everyone looked as elegant and beautiful as the runway models. He felt as though he'd walked into the centre of a diamond, everything moving in a din of white lights and beating sound.

The man who'd driven them came over and put a drink in his hands. Warden was thirsty and downed it quickly. The man said he was a photographer. He told Warden he was very beautiful and wanted to make him a star. He asked Warden to come and live with him.

"I will provide you with everything," the infatuated man said, trying to kiss his lips.

Warden pushed him away.

"You probably couldn't afford me," he said, repeating a line he'd heard someone else use once, and went off to dance.

He swayed back and forth like a feather in a breeze. Around him faces gleamed, radiating haloes and receding in the distance. The music had become a dull roar and he knew it was very late. Someone took him by the shoulders and ousted him from the club as though waking him sharply from a dream. Outside, someone else wrapped him in a jacket that looked surprisingly like one he had been wearing God-knows-where in another time and place. Then he found himself on the street, gravel crushing under his feet like peanut shells.

"Can you look after him, darling?" he heard Tamarra say, as hands pushed him gently into a taxi, unable to shut the door behind him as he lay stretched out on the seat.

He heard Mike answer something about 'sticky pearls' which made him laugh, feeling as though veils hung inside his head while he watched Tamarra stumble away from them. He struggled to sit up in the seat trying to think, to remember where he was or how he got there.

"Oh, my God!" he heard Tamarra say. "I can't believe it! I've got a Gucci show in three hours and I've still got my Versace make-up on!"

He watched as a long, black limousine rolled slowly up to the curb like a hearse. Tamarra went over to the driver's window.

"Darling, have you got any cocaine?" she said.

A door opened and she stumbled inside. It was the last thing he remembered in the lavender night.

11

Warden woke with the beginning of a hangover bursting in his head. He remembered an appointment for 10:45 and reached out to grab the clock beside his bed. His cheek stuck to the pillow.

"What the fuck?" he mumbled to himself as he stumbled out of bed. His pillow was smeared in blood. He looked in the mirror and shivered.

Dried, caked streaks of red ran from his nose across his cheeks. His hair stood up straight while his face glared with sullen puffiness. He washed his face and rubbed a handful of gel into his hair, combing it through with his fingers. He threw on his clothes and looked in the mirror again. A slight improvement, he thought. Then he put on sunglasses to cover the circles under his eyes, grabbed his bag and left.

By the time he found the street where his appointment was located he was already twenty minutes late. He walked along, searching for the address on the paper Calvino had given him. He passed a warehouse at number 17. He followed the street to the corner, but it did not continue. He checked his sheet again. He clearly read 23 in Calvino's long, looping scrawl. He found a phone box and dialled the agency.

"Hello, this is Warden. I have an appointment with *Amica Magazine* but I can't find the address."

He heard the receptionist flipping though her schedule.

"Yes, Warden, we have you listed for 10:45," she replied finally.

"I know, but I can't find it. What's the address?"

"Number 17, Via Scarsellini."

"Thank you."

He hung up and walked back to the warehouse, locating the magazine in the directory listing. He was now half an hour late. Not good form, he told himself. An elevator took him to the third floor where he stepped out into an empty hallway. Every door he passed was closed. He heard a typewriter in the distance and followed the sound to the room it was coming from.

"Scusa?" he said, poking his head inside the doorway.

The woman behind the desk removed a pair of dictaphones from her ears and scowled at him. Warden removed the glasses from his face which had started to feel slightly less puffy. He tried to smile but his face muscles stiffened.

"Si?"

"I have an appointment with Sr. Gustavo."

"You look like shit," she said impatiently, as though it were of importance to her. "And Sr. Gustavo's not here."

"But I'm supposed to be working with him right now."

"They are shooting," she said. "But not here."

He must have looked so distraught she began to soften.

"You should be here," she said, and wrote down an address on the other side of the city. "Your agency should have told you this."

She shook her head sympathetically, whether for his appearance or for his bad luck, he couldn't tell. "You cannot get there in time, though. Even by taxi it is almost half an hour away. But don't worry," she said, brushing the matter aside. "There will be others."

He wasn't sure if she meant other models to take his place or other jobs for him in future. He thanked her and left, replacing his glasses as the daylight hit his eyes. That's Maura's Noodles for you, he thought, remembering Jimmy's nickname for the agency.

He stopped at a pharmacy and bought some aspirins. He swallowed four as he huddled into a phone booth. The same receptionist answered at the agency and he explained what had happened.

She laughed. "It's not a problem," she said. "You have no other appointments this morning. You can go home to sleep."

He rolled his eyes. Life was so simple to the Italians. Either one had a problem or one didn't. That was all.

"Grazie, bella," he said and hung up.

He headed back to the albergo and sat in the café, ordering a cappuccino. The caffeine surged through his body, expanding the vessels in his head as though a sluggish drain had begun to empty. He went upstairs and lay on his bed. When he woke again, the pain was nearly gone. Valentino was looking in from his doorway.

"Hello, superstar American photo-model," he said.

Warden sat up.

"The show was a big success," he said. "Your picture is in all the papers."

Valentino sat on the bed holding a newspaper. He pointed at a photograph of Warden.

81

"It is very exciting," he said.

"It was pretty exciting last night, too. What I can remember of it. My head still hurts."

"Poor bambino," Valentino joked, tousling his hair.

"Ouch!"

"To make you feel better, Paolo and I would like to take you for a ride to the Riviera, if you are free this afternoon."

"The Riviera? I'd love to!"

Warden called Maura's to book himself off for the afternoon, a standard procedure for any model engaged on a shoot or otherwise unavailable. He relayed his message to the receptionist, expecting her to say 'grazie' and pass the information on to the bookers so they would take no further appointments for him that day.

"Moment," she said.

He was put on hold. In a few seconds Calvino's voice came on the line.

"Warden?"

"Hi, Sr. Calvino."

"What are you doing, darling?"

"I'm booking off for the afternoon."

"But, darling, why? What are you doing that is so important?"

"I'm going to the Riviera with a friend. I didn't think it would be too busy after the show yesterday."

"Think? Who told you to think? You don't know when we might need you. Don't you realize it's almost the end of the season? We have to get you in to every last appointment. Why are you wasting your time? How important is your work to you?"

"I'm sorry — I just wanted to get away for the afternoon."

"Never mind that. I need you to go to see a photographer who wants to meet you for a testing. I told him you would come this afternoon."

"Just a testing? Can't it wait till next week?"

"No. He's going to Paris tomorrow early. This is the only day he can see you and it is very important. You are becoming so lazy, Warden," he chided. "Now take this address down, darling. I need you to go right away."

"Alright."

Warden wrote down the name and address of the photographer.

"And make sure you call me back once he's seen you."

Warden hung up and called the photographer's studio, telling the receptionist who he was and asking if there were any later appointments.

"Of course," she said. "He is not busy. He can see you any time tomorrow or next week."

Warden hung up and grabbed a shirt, barely stopping to wonder if Calvino had lied or simply been mistaken. He ran down the stairs. Valentino sat waiting on Paolo.

* * *

They roared off following traffic single file out of the city. The road widened as the buildings became sparser and the landscape flattened into Byzantine perspective. They pulled up behind a flashy red sports car. Valentino honked and drove past, the surge forward momentarily suspending the motion of the car. Warden felt as though he'd left his body behind. Catching up with time.

They went north into the hills. Deep blue-green valleys opened alongside them, the ruins of stone buildings perched on cliffs above. They emerged from the mouth of a tunnel, rounding a final summit. Below, like a vision of ancient civilization, pink, orange and salmon-coloured walls incrusted to the valley sides, glittering in the bone-white light like a mythical city.

"Genoa," Valentino shouted back as they passed the birthplace of Columbus, no different then than now, as though the new world still lay waiting to be discovered.

They raced downwards through the intense afternoon sun that bleached and flattened everything into an ethereal nothingness until the spectral blue of the Riviera opened up on the horizon. Following the coast they reached a harbour of brightly-coloured boats bobbing on the water. At a small cantina they purchased a basket, filled it with food and wine.

At the beach, Valentino rented a rubber dingy with life-jackets and spare paddles. They loaded up and he started the engine with one pull, manoeuvring among the tethered boats until they reached the open sea. Haze shrouded the hills of the coastline. They puttered by stone buildings built into cliffs and within minutes edged past an ephemeral town in a flat blue bay that looked like something out of a dream.

"This is Portofino," Valentino said. "It is very famous."

He pointed to the top of a hill. Warden looked up to see a tall villa crested in black and gold.

"It was the villa of Rex Harrison," he said. "You know the American superstar movie actor?"

"He was British," Warden replied, laughing at how willingly Valentino Americanized anything foreign. "Nice place, though."

"One day we shall live in such a house as this," he said. "You and me and our wives."

Warden laughed. The merry-coloured town floated away like a carnival as silhouettes of trees dotted the hills above. They rounded a jutting escarpment and Valentino slowed the boat. A matrix of masts filled a tiny harbour like rows of crosses.

"This is San Frutuoso," said Valentino. "It is a fishing village. There are no roads over the mountain so it may be reached only by boat."

He stopped the engine and let down an anchor. The rope slid quickly between his hands.

"I hope you can swim," Valentino said sheepishly. "I forget to ask."

Above them rose a sparse, tree-dotted mountain, rheumatic and inaccessible. A tiny collection of buildings rooted to its slopes comprised the whole of the village. In contrast to its colourful neighbour, Portofino, the buildings were unadorned, built in a uniform grey stone.

"I want to tell you this place is sacred," Valentino said quietly. "Once there was a very big storm when all the men of the village were out on the sea. Everyone thought they would drown. When they all returned home safely and did not drown they wanted to make a sign of thanks to God for answering their prayers."

They glanced wonderingly at the silent shores before Valentino continued.

"Under the water is a large statue of Gesú Cristo. He is made of gold and very, very tall. He stands on the bottom blessing the boats that pass out to catch fish. You can see him if you dive down far enough."

"Cool! Where is it?"

"It is over there somewhere," Valentino said, pointing to an area that took in half the bay. He handed over a pair of swimming goggles. "Take these and you will be able to see better."

Valentino stretched his arms and pulled off his T-shirt. He dove deftly into the water leaving the dingy bouncing from side to side. Warden followed, trailing Valentino's head as he bobbed away from the vessel. After a minute Valentino stopped, scanning the shore as though to get a bearing.

"Put the glasses on and dive," he commanded. "You will see it."

Warden fitted the goggles over his head and dove. Schools of fish swam beneath him. Above, he saw the bottoms of nearby boats. Here and there the water was split by shafts of light in the soft gloom. He swam further until he could see the sea floor. There was nothing that looked like a statue, only uneven sand and a few rocks on the bottom. He kicked back up and broke the surface, gasping.

"I can't see it," he said between gasps.

"No. I remember now! It is over here," Valentino said. He was moving away from the other boats.

Warden followed him, then kicked his legs and dove again. To his right a silhouette reached up from the sea bottom. He swam down till he saw the golden-skinned statue. Face turned upwards and hands lifted in blessing. There was an eeriness about it down there, submerged and surrounded by long green shafts of sunlight transformed into a chalky transparent moonlight. Folds of robes seemed to sway in the silent currents.

Warden kicked down farther. A dull weight pressed in at his temples as his hand reached the tip of an extended finger. There was a surprising mildness to its touch, as though it might warm him in the cool depths. He turned and pushed upwards, exploding into the air, coughing and spluttering.

"You have seen it?" Valentino called from a short distance.

"Yes!" he choked out.

"It is beautiful, yes?"

"It's wild!"

"My turn," Valentino said, swimming over.

Warden handed him the goggles and he went under. Other searchers had reached them, diving excitedly, coming back up slightly subdued from the experience.

They headed back to the dingy, splashing the black rubber skin with water to cool it before climbing aboard. They rested awhile as the sun dried their bodies to a crusty saltiness. Valentino was the first to stir, grabbing the oars and guiding them towards shore with curt sawing motions. As they reached the rock face of land Valentino stepped out, grabbing the basket of food.

"We must take the oars for someone not to steal the boat," Valentino said.

Warden hoisted the oars across his shoulders as they trekked up the mountain. After twenty minutes they had nearly reached the top when Valentino called a halt to the climb. Warden laid his burden down and turned to look back. Around them small, twisted trees extended branches of fattening figs and ripe olives. The buildings of the village were laid out below like tiny seashells. Farther down lay the harbour, its waves like frothy clouds set out in diminishing perspective. On the horizon the sky and sea poured into one another with an indistinguishable blueness while a sea of branches knotted hands and raised its arms around them.

They settled in under the shade of a crabbed fig. Valentino opened the basket, uncovering a trove of pungent-smelling food and passing it to Warden. They looked at one another and began to laugh, their faces and limbs coated with salt, hair sun-dried and dishevelled. They sat eating, happy with the exuberance of being young and at leisure in a beautiful place.

The sun moved overhead and the shade shrank around them. In the distance straight lines melted with the heat until everything looked distorted. Warden rubbed a hand over his torso, grimacing at the sharp, dry sensation on his chest and stomach.

"I'm getting a burn," he said.

"You are not used to our sun," Valentino chided. "You are only an honourary Italian, my friend."

Valentino had not burned. His chest was bronzed and smooth as he leaned back on his elbows. Warden felt the weaving of delicate desire in the air as he gazed at the glow on Valentino's skin and the dark hair falling over his shoulders.

Valentino reached into the basket again, removing a bottle of wine and a small flask of olive oil. He pulled the cork from the wine with his teeth and handed it to Warden who took a mouthful and passed it back.

Valentino sat up, stomach muscles contracting like a cat's. He lifted his head and drank until the wine ran out his mouth and down his neck, spilling over his chest. He looked slyly over at Warden. His cheeks expanded and spewed a shower of red at him. Then he laughed. Warden wiped his face and chest and held out his hand for the bottle. Valentino passed it to him. Warden raised it to his lips, sipped from it. He swallowed, then turned the bottle upside down, pouring a stream of liquid over Valentino's head. The two burst into laughter.

"Now we are baptized!" Valentino exclaimed.

Within minutes the sun had dried them both, as though its

86

merciless kiss could tolerate no moisture. Valentino picked up the flask of oil and poured a thin flow onto his hands. He rubbed them together, placing them on Warden's shoulders. Warden smarted at the touch. A pungent odour rose around them as fingers kneaded his flesh that beaded and knifed with pain. Warden leaned back. The air was dense with scents and the sounds of insects and birds. Amber flowers nodded their heads with potency among the greenness and the solitary murmuring of bees.

Valentino allowed the oil to dribble over Warden's shoulders and across his chest where it rolled slowly, abundantly downward. He leaned forward and traced its path with one hand, soothing the burning skin. The other hand pulled Warden's face toward him, oil and lips mixing and slipping apart. Warden felt an unravelling, stitches loosening inside like a bolt of fabric. He was aware of himself lingering in the darkness of his friend's eyes as he felt the warmth of sun and oil on his skin. Above, purpling fruit hung like dark flesh under the coronal of a fig tree.

He felt Valentino raise him until he half-stood, half-knelt over his body. At that distance, the other resembled a coastline beckoning, calling him down to his horizon. Warden felt himself slide awkwardly forward as Valentino laughed at his clumsy efforts.

"No, like this, bambino," he whispered, grasping Warden and guiding him into himself, unfisting him once he was secure.

Warden fell backwards into a cornucopia of mouthings. He could feel Valentino hugging him, bucking, gripping with his arms and legs against his back. It embarrassed him and excited him as he felt a sensation like an iris dilating. The sky leaned forward, clouds dissolving into blue as everything stopped for a moment. Then time began its ineluctable spread around them again, inconspicuously, in tiny, endless waves of consolation.

12

One night near the end of July Warden arranged to meet Valentino in Bar Magenta before going on to the American Cinema together. He sat waiting for more than an hour, well past the starting time of the movie, an unusual occurrence where his normally-punctual friend was concerned. When Valentino finally arrived his face bore a look Warden could read as trouble before he even sat down.

"I am sorry I am late. It is my father, he... " He stopped, unable to voice what he had to say.

"What is it? What's happened?"

He took a breath.

"My father has signed me up for the military duty."

"What? He signed you up for the army?"

Valentino shook his head, as though uncertain how to explain. "It is something every boy must do in Italy. Everyone must go to the training camp. I want to wait until after I finish the school, but he says I must go now... "

"But why now?"

"He thinks I am ruining my life. He says I run around too much and go to parties with girls all night long," he answered with the trace of a smile.

"Why didn't you tell him otherwise?"

Valentino looked at him askance.

"Do you really think it will help? I think this way perhaps is better," he stated.

"And will you go?"

"I must."

"But how can you just... ?"

Valentino interrupted.

"In Italy, a young man must listen to his parents. I try to talk to him but he will not listen. He is very angry that I should argue with him. I ask also my mother to help me speak to him but she says she cannot interfere with his wishes. I must do what he says."

Warden sat looking at Valentino across the flat surface of the table.

"Then there's nothing you can do?"

Valentino looked up disconsolately and shrugged, shaking his head. "I must go."

"How far will you have to go?"

"I am not sure. It will probably be to a small town... "

"Can I see you at all?"

He shrugged again. "It will be difficult. You cannot stay overnight, but I will be allowed one weekend pass a month."

He looked sadly at Warden, eyes begging him not to make him more miserable than he already was.

"How long will you be gone?"

"A year... possibly more."

"A year!"

"I know. It seems forever to me, too."

Warden realized there was no use arguing the point. They went to Plastica and danced. Neither of them enjoyed the evening. They gave up and sat at a booth by themselves where Warden again brought up the subject of trying to change his father's mind. Valentino snapped at him.

"It is not possible!" he said. "You don't know what you are asking."

Warden looked at him for a moment. "I'm going back to the albergo," he said.

He stood and grabbed his jacket. Valentino did not offer to drive him. Warden left the club, walking all the way to the hotel. His emotions cooled as he walked, realizing he was being unfair to Valentino. Just as he arrived at the door, Valentino drove up.

"I am sorry," he said. "Please — we must talk. Come with me for a short time."

They walked to the public gardens and climbed the metal fence. Inside, they lay on the grass in the darkness, swollen branches of trees arching overhead. Talking was difficult and they soon gave up. Valentino cried and Warden tried to console him. The moment of tenderness led to a hard, angry sex, each trying to immolate his desire for the other and the sense of impending loss they both felt.

* * *

At the train station a week later, Valentino stood surrounded by his family. His father and mother, dressed stiffly for their son's leave-taking, stood proudly side-by-side. A younger brother watched indifferently alongside a pretty little girl of seven or eight. Her heart-shaped face was a replica of Valentino's in miniature.

Warden purposely arrived late and stood to one side, watching. Valentino called him over and introduced his family. He shook hands with Valentino's father and nodded to his mother.

"Piacere," he said.

"Da quanto tempo è qui?" his mother asked pleasantly.

"Da sei mesi," he replied before Valentino had a chance to translate.

Valentino raised his eyebrows at him. "Show-off. Since when are you speaking Italian?" he asked with a half-smile.

A train whistle sounded.

"Take care while you're gone," Warden said.

Their riotous emotions and the awkwardness of the situation

weighed heavily on them. After a quick hug, Valentino picked up his bags and turned to him.

"My friend, I will see you again," he promised.

*　*　*

Later that afternoon Warden strolled into the agency, his portfolio tucked under an arm. Before he got halfway across the lobby an angry voice began screaming at him. It was Calvino saying he'd missed an appointment that morning.

"What do you mean? No one told me I had an appointment this morning."

"Where have you been? I call and call and call and you are nowhere to be found! How can I run a business if I can't find my workers?"

Calvino continued, his voice unabated in volume and without the silky pacifying tones he normally engaged in between bouts of temperament. He told Warden he was getting spoiled and lazy and said he hadn't worked in more than a week.

"What are you talking about?" Warden said heatedly. "I had a fitting for a show two days ago and I worked with Oliviero twice last week!"

A small crowd had gathered in the lobby, listening to the exchange. Warden caught Joe's face out of the corner of his eye.

"All night you are running around at parties and these dirty clubs. There is no drugs, no anorexia, no diseases here! I'm not interested in unhealthy, skinny models!"

When he started to protest, Calvino called him a 'stupid whore'. Warden was startled. He wondered if this had anything to do with Valentino. Calvino began screaming the agency's reputation was at stake. In his rage, he jettisoned his sleek, Italianate manner and began spitting words in a halting Trinidadian accent. His anger was well matched by Warden's. Sensing his young protégé was beginning to get overheated, he began to back down.

"Now, darling, don't you be giving me trouble — I always say you Canadian boys are better behaved than the Americans."

Warden was having no pangs of conscience on behalf of his country's reputation.

"You have to always be so careful, darling," Calvino cooed. "The agency's reputation is at stake with all our clients." The sleek tone had come back into his voice.

"Agency's reputation! You can't even get your appointments straight!" Warden yelled. "And how do you expect me to do *my* job properly when you send me all over the fucking city to find an address that doesn't exist?"

"Don't be upset, darling... " He was running out of words. "We'll make another appointment for you."

"Forget it!"

Warden stomped across the lobby and slammed the door. He was shocked by his own outburst. Outside, he slumped against a wall. A moment later Joe came down the stairs looking for him.

"You okay?" he asked.

"I'm okay."

"You were very angry," Joe said with a grin. "Just like an Italian."

"I think I need some time off," Warden said. "I need a vacation from this place."

"Don't get me wrong, Ward, but I saw your paycheck. They don't pay you enough. When you come back tell him you're very hurt and you're thinking of leaving the agency. He'll offer you twice as much. But where are you going for now?"

"Wherever the first train leaving the station when I get there takes me."

Joe grinned.

"I always knew there was a fire somewhere under that cool surface," he said. "Ciao, Ward. Take care."

Warden packed a few clothes and told Irena he would be back at the end of the week to pick up the rest of his belongings. He considered making a plane reservation home right then, but thought better of it. He scarcely had enough cash till the next payday. He decided to leave it till his return.

"Ciao, Warden. I will look after your things for you," Irena told him.

On the way to the station Warden dropped in to see Andreo at his studio. The photographer was engaged in a shoot but he stopped when Warden entered.

"Ciao, bello, I am so pleased to see you!" he said. "Take a break everybody," he said.

The models broke their poses while Andreo led Warden to his desk. He picked up a large file-folder and opened it, papers falling onto the floor. Warden bent to pick them up.

"Leave them — we will always get more."

He laughed and gave Warden's face an affectionate squeeze between his big hands.

"How are you, my lovely boy?"

"Bene. Va bene, maestro."

Warden watched as he spread a pile of photographs on the desk. He saw himself wearing a suit, then a sweater and cotton trousers. Smiling, then pensive. The stance was confident and self-assured, with a look that drew in and kept out at the same time.

"Go ahead — say it," Andreo said. "They're exquisite. Did I not tell you it was a face to fall in love with?"

Warden stared at his image, feeling as Narcissus might have, drowning in a pool of his own making. There was a naturalness and ease with which he stood, as though contemplating the world from a pinnacle of potency. Where others aggressed the camera, he acquiesced to it, drawing it after him. Andreo clasped the back of his neck with one hand.

"And this, my beauty, is going to earn for you more praise than all the others combined."

He turned over the final photograph. It was the beige suit, his body in three-quarter profile, head turned towards the camera with the trumpet flying from his grip in a gesture of victory. Warden remembered his insecurities over the powerful-looking men all around him when he first arrived and realized how unfounded they had been.

"Very nice, don't you agree?" Andreo asked, watching him. "I am very pleased."

Andreo closed the portfolio.

"I tell you a secret," he said with a grin, eyeing the other models lounging around the studio. "You are my best model."

"You're my best photographer," Warden said, grinning back.

Andreo laughed.

"I must get back to work now or they will become impatient with me," he said, sniffing as though it were distasteful that a photographer's actions should be at the whim of a model. "Next week I will have some work for you," he said. "Come and see me after this weekend."

"I will, I promise. I'm going out of town for a few days. I'll drop by when I come back."

In the station he stood looking over the schedules where he had bid farewell to Valentino a few hours earlier. There was a train leaving for Florence in the next five minutes. He remembered

Valentino's saying Florence was the most beautiful city in the world. He had also spoken of Isole d'Elba, a small island in the Mediterranean just to the south, as his favourite vacation spot.

Warden bought his ticket and hurried upstairs where the nose of an engine pushed up against the loading dock. Thick, greasy smoke rolled out among the wheels and giant gears covered in dirt and soot. All along its length people were rushing to get on board, as though to do anything in Italy before the last minute might be a mistake or a sin. Faces peered out of every available window to watch others clambering aboard or say farewell to those left behind.

Warden slung his bag over his shoulder and hurried down the track and up the steps as the whistle blew. Inside, the air was stifling. The slight breeze caused by the train's motion when it rolled out of the station felt as warm as the air it had disturbed. He walked along the passageway peering into each compartment for an empty seat. Every place was filled. The passengers sitting in compartments stuck their heads out of the windows to cool off and watch the city move past.

Along the passageways people were eating and drinking beer, their luggage piled beside them. In the vestibule at the head of the car most of the passengers were young. They were comfortable and content there, sitting on the floor with an air of cheerful vagabondage. Warden lowered his knapsack and sat. A breeze from the open doorway between the cars provided the coolest relief he had felt so far. Florence was just three hours away.

13

Under the canopy of night, Florence glowed like a music box built with tiny bejewelled fingers. The sky stretched overhead like a net covered in thousands of tiny fish, their scales winking and twitching as they strained to be free. With no schedule and no appointments to keep, Warden had a choice of any direction as he left the station and stumbled into the tourist quarter. The sky glowed purple as twilight tarried amongst the noise and confusion of the merrymakers thronging the streets.

His anger now completely spent, he felt a little foolish for having come. Still, he reasoned, he needed a break from Milan and Maura's Models. He wondered where he would stay that evening as he searched for signs of an inexpensive hotel.

Along dark, steamy side streets, lamps flickered like pale blossoms on insubstantial walls. A bevy of teenaged girls sat perched on the steps of the first place he passed. One of them gave a low, salivating whistle that attempted to pass for unbridled lust. He smiled as he walked up the stairs past the refractory group, their heads turning to watch him. In the lobby an elderly signora looked him over as he came in, shaking her head.

"Finito," she said, briskly sweeping both hands back and forth in front of her before he could speak.

"Grazie, signora," Warden said with a nod.

The girls on the steps watched him come back out.

"Finito!" cried several of them, mimicking the hand motions of the signora.

"You can share my room," said a bold voice. This elicited several gasps and the shrill treble of pubescent giggling.

"Thanks. I'll keep it in mind, but I'll try down the street first," Warden said, amused by her audacity.

"They're all finito," one of the voices informed him. "All the school tours are in Florence this week. Next week it's Rome."

He watched their curious faces wearing too much make-up and smelling of heavy perfume as if gentle breezes had stirred an odd nocturnal floral arrangement on the stairs.

"Besides, you wouldn't like them anyway," one of the girls continued. "They all have midnight curfews."

The group groaned with teenage rebellion. Warden thought of the Albergo Sirtori and its cardboard night-latch.

"Well, we can't have that," he said. "Where do you suppose I can find a reasonable place without a curfew?"

"You can't — the whole town's full. We just told you that."

More giggles. Warden hoisted his pack onto his shoulder again.

"So you don't think I can get a room anywhere?"

"No, but you can try."

"I guess I'll have to do that."

"Good luck," someone called as he headed back down the stairs.

They had told the truth, at least about the hotels in that neighbourhood. They were all full. As he wandered in search of a vacancy it was fast approaching curfew and he knew with a house full of schoolchildren the suspicious signore would be reluctant to open their doors to him. The 'no vacancy' signs began to thin out as he approached a well-lit pedestrian concourse.

Crowds had gathered on corners around street performers.

Mimes clowned and light-soled dancers moved as though walking on air. At one walkway, a fire-eater's flames stopped foot traffic for the duration of his act. The air snapped with spontaneous applause. Coins flashed into inverted hats and open guitar cases like wishing wells on the ground in front of the performers.

Warden walked till he came to a large, nearly empty piazza. He sat on the stone steps and looked at his watch. It was past midnight. A man approached him from the far end of the square, flickering in and out of the shadows, his movement a slow-motion film of barely completed actions. He stopped to light a cigarette then crept up to where Warden sat.

"Hello, Yankee-boy," he said softly, glancing around as though afraid of being overheard.

"I'm not a Yankee," Warden said out of habit. "I'm Canadian."

"You are looking lost," the man said.

"I'd believe it."

He seemed to take this for encouragement.

"Why are you out here so late?" he asked. "I thought all good Yankee boys had to be home in bed at this hour."

"I just got into town," Warden said. "I'm looking for a place to sleep."

"Yes, I am thinking so," the man said, peering at him from the shadows.

He came closer, smiled. Teeth rotting and stained. Face decrepit and wrinkled. He held out a hand as though to touch the boy sitting alone on the steps.

"You can to sleep with me," he said, laughing softly. "I will pay. How much are you?"

Startled, Warden looked up.

"I'm not for sale," he said.

"That is too bad," the man said, laughing again, sloughing off his refusal with a gesture reminiscent of the hotel-keeper's 'finito'. "You would be beautiful to sleep with."

"Do you know of any parks near here?"

"Parks?" the man said, a quizzical tone in his voice.

"Parchi."

"Ah, si! Yes, I know — there is the Piazzale di Michelangelo. Why do you want to know where is the park?"

"I need somewhere to sleep," Warden said, wishing he would go away.

"You would be better to sleeping with me," he said. "In a nice, soft bed where I can touch your smooth skin."

Warden shook his head. The man shrugged.

"Is no problem — the park is that way. Across the Ponte Vecchio."

The man disappeared into the shadows of the piazza.

Warden found the famous bridge where it sat like a honeycomb of lights stitched across the canal. A few vendors' booths were still open with their exhibitions of silk and jewellery for curious tourists who marvelled at having found in the shimmering apparition a real structure.

He crossed the bridge. Further along the road he found the park entrance guarded by a single-tiered tower and followed where it led up in darkness. An occasional car passed him, its faceless occupants slowing as the glare of their headlights picked out his figure. A stream spilled noisily over the face of unseen stonework as the road wound upwards. The sky opened to admit him to a flat summit where he found himself overlooking the city, its twinkling lights engulfed by darkness.

A series of trident lamps followed the edges of the piazza laid out with marble benches. He chose one, put his pack under his head and lay back. The surface was smooth and cool. Sounds came over the wind like fragmented radio waves, uniting finally into the strains of 'Guantanamera'. Somewhere in the distance some homesick Cubanos were singing of their lost land across the sea.

The curious stars faded above and he fell asleep, waking occasionally to rub away an annoying mosquito. Sometime before dawn he woke thoroughly chilled. The temperature had dropped considerably. His watch read a few minutes past five. Even the mosquitoes had left him alone. He shivered as he pulled from his pack the single sweater he'd brought, pulling it over his head.

A chocolate bar tucked into one of its sleeves fell to the ground. He picked it up and tore it open hungrily, thinking of food for the first time since he got off the train. The only sound was his breathing as he ate. He looked up at the statue hovering above which he'd earlier failed to recognize as a giant replica of Michelangelo's David, the body green and weathered with time. No wonder Italians are so unabashed, he mused, looking up at its giant proportions, remembering Valentino's boldness.

A shadow came slinking towards him, a lone dog or perhaps even a wolf, he couldn't be sure. He didn't know whether or not there were wolves in Italy. It slid along, nose to the ground, guided more by smell than sight. The creature sniffed its way towards him. It froze as it sensed another presence and stood trying to pierce the darkness to discover what other life form was sharing its hilltop kingdom uninvited that morning. Warden bit off a piece of chocolate and threw it to the creature.

"Here you go," he said softly.

It sniffed suspiciously at the offering before accepting it, then slithered off into the shadows like primordial mist.

When he woke again his watch read 7:30. The air was warm once more. He sat up and looked east where a red glow had caught hold, snaking along the waters of the canal whose banks he'd followed to the park the night before. Now he saw Florence for the first time by daylight, a jazzy mosaic of red tile roofs and white sand walls surrounded by blue skies. Small gold domes glittered in the hazy distance and palm trees fleshed out the streets as though he'd gone too far south and hit Morocco. It was a city of sublime if earthly beauty, shaped with the reverence of a sacred engraving from some medieval text, ringed round by illusory-looking mountains. These seemed connected more to the clouds above than the earth below, a great grazing herd of cattle that at any moment might pick up and move on. In the centre of it all, rising above sleeping houses in cathedralic resplendence, sat the great cap of the Duomo, chaste and sunlit, gleaming in the rising light like the unimaginable eye of God.

He made his way back to the city, already thronging with tourists. There he found a café and went in for breakfast. When he was finished he asked directions to the Accademia Belle Arti, home to the real Michelangelo's David. He cut back across the tourist section, the deep shadows of narrow streets strangely reminding him of home.

While Copernicus was discovering the universe and Columbus the new world, Michelangelo Buonarotti was discovering the perfection of human form in an older world, achieving the perfect blending of classical antiquity and nature, the one becoming the measure of the other. Inside the academy, Warden stood before the colossal statue of cool Florentine beauty, hair dishevelled, pack slung over his shoulder in unconscious imitation of its massive musculature. Two teenaged girls, noticing the statue's fleshly counterpart, nudged one another and giggled. Others were silent, moved by the pale contours as though in the presence of something beyond ordinary comprehension. The statue's gaze doubled them back, liars with sunglasses and cameras, as they stood mutely before it.

When he had seen enough, Warden made his way to the train station. He sat and wrote a postcard home, feeling very much alone. Something was missing, he knew. He wanted to be sharing all of this with Valentino. He'd already decided not to spend another night in the unreal beauty of the city, leaving the park to the dog and the homesick Cubans.

While waiting for the train, he went into a public washroom to change. He was startled by his image in the mirror. His locks had turned into dense vines curling around his temples while his face was streaked and coated with the dust of a long day and night under the stars. His clothes were creased and wrinkled from the knapsack he carried them in. He thought of the fastidious look of horror that would overcome Sr. Calvino if he could see his young protégé now.

14

Warden watched the hills of Florence slide past with the pale resonance of an apparition. Resisting a temptation to think how tenuous his life was at the moment, he drifted off to sleep, lulled by the dull chugging of wheels beneath the train. He woke to a porter shaking his shoulder, letting him know his destination was approaching. In the seat across from him, two women who had not been there when he fell asleep sat grinning behind their hands to conceal their amusement. One of them said something in Italian.

"Cosa?" he asked.

She made a noise to indicate he'd been snoring.

"Capisco," he said, smiling back.

The train slowed as they approached a handful of buildings clustered around a dock. A dozen passengers got off carrying bags and luggage and made their way to a ferry, the only boat in sight. As soon as they boarded the vessel embarked. Two hours later they were moored at the base of the sloping black hills of Isole d'Elba.

Once off the boat he boarded a bus that carried him into the mountains across terrain as beautiful as it was unfriendly, up to a height where he could see falling all around him the dark edges of the tiny continent-world spreading out into the sea. As they descended again, the driver pointed out a villa where the deposed Napoleon once lived under house arrest. It could not have been such a bad existence, Warden thought, noting the red tile roofs and the lush gardens surrounding the building, even if he had exchanged an empire for a quiet, anonymous villa.

Soon after, the bus stopped at a spot where six or seven meandering routes converged as at the midpoint of a wheel. Warden disembarked, knapsack in hand, and walked to a beach where dozens of masts sat tethered in green water. A campground nearby swelled with the colourful movements of canvas tents. At the far end of a horseshoe-shaped bay lay the town of Marina di Campo, walled in by a thin line of silver sand stretching between the sea and the mountains.

Warden walked along the boardwalk until he found a café. He went in to eat, hours having passed once again since his last meal. He took a place at a table overlooking the beach feeling dirty and dishevelled, but no one else seemed to notice. In the distance, white jet currents of boats spread out like ghostly ribbons. Lights were beginning to come on around the bay as the sun sent a cascade of rays over the hills.

In the evening, he strolled among tourists in airy white linen like picture postcards approaching and dissolving in the sweet distance of evening. In cafés and along the shore people sat drinking a translucent turquoise liquor. He bought a wedge of watermelon from a stand near the beach and walked across the sand.

In the centre of the darkened beach a building sat like a burning vessel, light and sound spilling through open windows, echoing from its wooden porches. Smiles greeted him like flung confetti as he entered. The music blaring from the loudspeakers was a familiar collection of pop tunes. He felt as though he'd come home. Three identical-looking blonde boys leaned on a wooden railing, the picture of Aryan youth. The middle one saluted him, raising his beer. He shouted across the bar asking if he were 'deutsch'. Warden shook his head as the young man approached.

"What are you then?" the boy asked in English.

"Canadian," Warden said. "But one of my grandfathers was German."

"Yes, you are one of us," said the boy, identifying him with their particular aesthetic.

Matthies, the boy who'd spoken, introduced Warden to his two friends, Hans and Oliver. They sat in a circle up on the wooden deck while below a series of searchlights played over the water, illuminating its dark surface. Small schools of fish gathered, turning and flashing, attracted by the dazzling lights. A crowd on the beach below threw chunks of bread out into the water.

The boys asked him what he did, what part of his recondite country he came from. Others soon joined them, expanding their circle in the pursuit of momentary joy while they laughed and talked and lingered. For a moment he was lost in the lamp-lit revels on a beach on a small island he'd never heard of before that summer. Suddenly Matthies pointed out to the broad sweep of light across the water.

"Look," he said, as the others clambered around pressing against one another.

At first all Warden could see were the floating chunks of bread tossed out to the fish, bobbing up and down on waves like calcified sea foam. Then he saw what Matthies had been pointing at, a long scaly body moving in and out of the water like a fabled sea serpent crossing the patch of light-filled water.

"What is it?" someone asked.

A drunken Italian girl, seeing nothing but the shredded bread afloat on the water, answered a bored, "È pane."

"Pane — it's bread!" someone shouted as a howl went up among the group of temporary, cross-legged companions.

The night seemed to outlast the limits of ordinary time. At some point someone noticed day had begun, pointing out a shivering patch of dawn like an intruder as the partyers moved to make their way home.

"Where do you sleep, Warden?" Matthies asked.

He explained he hadn't made any arrangements.

"Then you must share our tent. We are staying at the camping ground. Let us find Hans and Oliver and we will go."

* * *

In the morning they washed and trekked back to the beach. They found it populated by hordes of bathers and sun worshippers who spent their time oiling and stretching their golden limbs, as if the entire beach were posing for a family snapshot.

Matthies and his friends had brought bathing suits; Warden hadn't. Without looking around, he lifted his T-shirt over his head and stripped to his underpants. They were amused when he said that with all the half-naked bodies around no one would notice he was running down the beach in his underwear. He grabbed the waistband of his cotton shorts to prevent them from jettisoning their cargo as he dove under, coming up gurgling and splashing. He felt revitalized as the salt sponged away all the aches his muscles had gathered since leaving Milan.

They spent most of the afternoon on the hot sand or in the cool water. Sleeping and waking in the sun. That evening they went to town to eat, the four of them like blood brothers. Afterwards they passed along the darkness of the beach to the bar where they'd met. Again they stayed till dawn was not far off, saying goodbye to their island friends, making promises to return the following summer. Hans had to be disengaged from the embraces of a girl who'd succeeded in enrapturing him after a week of sly courting. That night Warden shared their tent for the final time.

In the morning he woke to a raw pinching. Barnacles gripped the skin on his arms and chest and legs where they'd been exposed to the sun the day before. He was amazed to see the hue his skin had taken on, never having been so dark before. After a breakfast of instant cereals out of packs he helped the boys pack their tent and belongings. They exchanged addresses, promises to keep in touch. He said goodbye, going with them as far as the crossroads. They turned and headed for the far side of the island.

Not wanting to spend another afternoon on the beach, he decided to explore, following a trail up into the mountains. He found a pole, using it as a staff on his climb over terrain more desolate than anything he'd seen. He was surprised to find, hundreds of feet up in the dry air, a gravel road cutting across his path, disappearing among the twists and turns ahead. There was no other sign of civilization. All he could see in any direction were mountains. Beyond that, cool sparkling water. Looking across the horizon he felt as though he could jump effortlessly from one hilltop to another. Far below, a handful of offshore rocks took on the appearance of stepping-stones. The backs of giant, grey-shelled turtles.

He left the road and cut straight down to the sea, stumbling and sliding, the staff preventing his falling. He passed layers of rock, folded, sliced open to reveal startling colours. Stigmata bleeding from stiffened veins in an anxious journey to the water. At the bottom he stepped onto a stony beach. In the tidal pools lay the small islands he'd seen from above, the largest no more than twice his body length.

Warden stripped off his clothes. Laying his staff aside, he swam out toward the islands. Beneath him, clinging to rock, the black amorphous outlines of sea urchins. Churlish-looking, spiked carapaces.

On the largest and farthest of the islands he climbed precariously out of the water, grasping at slippery footholds, scrambling onto the dry surface. He lay back, spreading his arms and legs, sun drying his skin, shook the water from his hair, rubbing the droplets across his chest. He felt his flesh stained by the air and the light, veins singing in a language he could barely understand. As if he'd never before existed so fully in the moment.

The water had risen when he raised his head again. It swept over the tops of the rocks nearest the shore, submerged and inaccessible as the sea multiplied itself. He dove in and began to swim. The sea urchins had swelled in number as well until their army covered every shelf and ledge underwater. They hovered beneath him like black angels. Nearing the shore he felt a cramped wrinkling of pain in his foot, as though he'd connected with flint and a spark had entered his flesh. He crawled up out of the water and hobbled over to a rock where he examined his appendage, pulling the detached spine from the sole of his foot. A trickle of blood fell, swept away by water washing over the stone.

He pulled on his clothes and picked up his cast-off staff, walking back along the shoreline quickly vanishing beneath the rising sea. He came to a small alcove where the rock split into striated steps. The waves obliterated the path ahead of him and he could go no further. He climbed up to a clearing which hid the vacated remains of a stone dwelling. A door half-stood, half-fell off into the gloom of the interior.

In the overgrown yard surrounding the house, a garden of cacti and tall bushes burst with clusters of red flowers. He made his way past them and through the doorway onto the silent earth floor like a padding of suede beneath his hushed footsteps. Rotting timbers had fallen through the roof, leaving a vacant hole staring down from above. The floor he stood on was charred by a history of makeshift campfires, the coals of which had been used to decorate the walls in a profusion of languages.

Tendrils of plants crept in over decomposing brick and soil, inheriting the spoils of this improbable abandoned kingdom. Walls, cracked and peeling, supported the last fragments of a roof. They stood ornamented with the vernacular of decay inscribed by pilgrims to the abandoned sacristy, rich with graffiti and hieroglyphics on the tiny Easter egg of an island.

Warden sat on the doorstep, overlooking the harbour spread out below like a rippling pond, toy boats criss-crossing the waves, tiny ant figures on the beach just beginning to pack their insect belongings and migrate back to town. He pulled pen and paper from his knapsack and wrote a letter to his mother, trying to describe the beauty of the place, to encode the essence of what he felt in words and capture his emotions like the preserved flesh of fruit, dried and crystallized.

In the grove of self-assured cacti and cypress surrounding him, Warden could easily imagine Apollo's golden son, Phaëthon, hair aflame, a luminous star falling through the sky. Or Icarus landing with a thud among islands such as these. Even Absalom, suspended from black boughs by his hair: all the fallen sons of yore. He felt the capriciousness of his own existence as fragile as the caps on the waves glinting on the sea below, sun and sand the only witnesses to his presence.

The sun set as he watched the nearby hills cascade into hills farther off. The stepping stones of Titans. The translucent light falling on the horizon seemed beyond such temporal qualities as joy or despair. Shadows stitched up the spaces around his feet, as if aware of a presence they had not felt for a long time. He became conscious of the forces within pulling him forward like a long dull ache dragging itself to life, to growth. He felt the differences inside him between the boy and the man like the amorphous light of twilight with its rushes and flares of impurity and the pure, clear darkness that follows.

Lights came on like a series of constellations around the bay. He heard the ironic scrape and slap of surf and sand like a mad dance in the sepulchral twilight, the great expanse of night paring down. The sound of the waves reached him like the stroke of a bell followed by the exquisite nothingness between each crash in the instant of fullness that marks the moment of passing when we awake and are no more.

Time rose, luminous, shuffling off to find one more beginning in the dust among the offerings of blood and bone, between the unobtainable poles of wisdom and innocence, not quite human till we have betrayed its urges. The night came on one star at a time. A vast dynasty of perfection under the awakening dome, the trees and the island burning into blackness, stiffening in the Mediterranean night.

* * *

When he arrived back in Milan, wandering into the agency offices like a returned truant, he allowed himself to be scolded and pampered by the office secretaries. They had worried. They had missed him. They remarked how dark his tan was. He'd changed his dirty, ragged clothes for clean pants and shirt and combed his filthy hair, but his hollow, sleepless eyes were filled with the enchanted fictions of sunrise and the disembodied dreams of dusk. He was prepared to encounter a deluge of abuse from Calvino who was being informed of his presence. A door opened and his director came out.

"Darling, welcome back!" he said with a magnanimous wave of his hand, coming over as though he would embrace the prodigal son on his return. "The Fabiano people called yesterday. They want you for a major campaign — billboards, ads all over the country!"

Part III:
A Fever in the Marrow

15

The Fabiano people had seen Andreo's rush shots of Warden. His quiet dreamy presence suited their image. They wanted to use him in a comprehensive campaign for fashion magazines and billboards.

In August he thought of going home for a week, uncertain of his itinerary because of the projected campaign, but each time he tried to make plans he found himself with unexpected work. It was just enough to keep him occupied. Calvino had warned him fall would be busy.

Following the appearance of his photograph with the trumpet people began to recognize him in the streets. One day a group of teenaged girls followed him in the subway, advancing with him stop by stop. When he noticed them, one of them held an imaginary horn to her lips in imitation of his pose and played a few mute notes on it. They all laughed. Other passengers looked around to see what was happening. He felt embarrassed.

At the next station he tried a feint, ducking out the door and back in just as it was closing. The nearest of the girls shrieked a warning to her fellows, forcing the door apart as they clambered back inside. They stayed on, giggling all the way to his stop, following him right up to the steps of the albergo. He turned with a smile and waved as he went in.

When the billboards appeared at the end of summer he watched the larger-than-life images replicate themselves around the city, his face blossoming like a clear pool of joy in the air. His image seemed poised on the brink of an everlasting present, looking down from the realm of an alternate, perfect existence.

When he saw the sum on the first instalment from Fabiano he had to read it twice to be certain of the amount he held in his hands. All that for having the right cheekbones, he thought, tucking the cheque into his pocket.

One afternoon Warden arrived at Andreo's studio for a follow-up to the original Fabiano campaign. The model who was to be his female counterpart had not shown up. Warden dressed and Andreo took a few solo shots. After a quarter of an hour the photographer began to fidget. His shooting schedule was hectic and he hated to waste time.

"I wanted to use this young lady because she looks like she could be a sister to you, but she is very temperamental," Andreo explained. "She has stood me up before."

"Can't we get someone else or just shoot around her?" Warden suggested.

Andreo looked at his watch.

"It's too late to call an agency to send someone over," he said. "What else can I do?"

He snapped his fingers.

"Of course — I tell you what we will do," he said excitedly. "A simple double-exposure. It has been done a million times."

He went over to the set and turned the backdrop lights off.

"Francesco!" he called.

His assistant came rushing out as though he'd been waiting for his master's call.

"I need something very special of you today," Andreo said. "Our handsome young man here is about to become a beautiful young woman."

"What!" Warden cried.

"Trust me, dear one — it will be wonderful!"

Warden protested but Andreo would not hear of it. "No one will ever know, I promise you," he said, laughing. "It is the photographer's art to dictate what is seen. Believe me, you can sell anything if you try hard enough."

Warden sat before a mirror and watched as Francesco filled in his cheekbones, investing them with a feminine grace. Under the assistant's skilful contrivance appeared a beautiful young woman. Altering his identity. Usurping the one thing he'd thought most unique and inviolable about himself.

When Francesco finished, Warden moved his mouth slowly as though unused to it. He watched the face in the mirror, surprised to see it move with his own.

"Madonna santa!" Andreo exclaimed at his incarnation, clapping his hands together. "You have been radically feminized."

"Father, you use me ill, I fear," Warden replied, looking in amazement at his ivory cheeks.

"So serious," Andreo said mockingly.

Warden stared at the pantomime in the mirror that followed his every action.

"Who do you think we're going to fool with this?" he asked.

"Why, everybody, my dear. Francesco — what do you think?"

Francesco scrutinized him as though Warden were a work of art he might consider purchasing.

"Beautiful! She is magnificent!"

"There — you see? And Francesco loves beautiful women."

Andreo moved behind the camera and began to shoot his bewildered subject.

"It will be alright," he said encouragingly. "No one will ever know. You see, we all have this innocent belief that the photograph cannot lie... "

He paused to take several rapid shots.

"The photograph may not lie," he said smiling, "but the liar can take photographs."

He stopped to laugh at his own joke.

"That is because what the world desires, my dear Warden, is not truth, but flattery wrapped in an image of itself."

Andreo's camera clicked as Warden found himself stiffly responding to the shutter.

"Totally loose, my dearest one. Be at ease with yourself. Don't worry about a thing."

Warden posed as Andreo talked and clicked away.

"I once created a wonderful story of a young prince. For it I used a young man much like yourself, a construction worker I had found. I cleaned him up, dressed him and photographed him. I said he was a Lithuanian prince of ancient lineage and sold it to a very important magazine. Everybody loved it. When I told them later what I had done they were very angry with me, of course. But it was still a nice article."

Warden caught sight of himself in a large reflector.

"Are you sure it's alright to do this?" he said. "Aren't there laws about this sort of thing?"

Andreo chuckled and put his camera down.

"In Italy, my dear Warden, there are no laws except the natural ones, which we all obey, whether we like them or whether we do not. To be beautiful... is to be loved."

He sighed.

"If I were a man I should want to ravage you. You make me raw with desire."

Warden laughed. He felt an endearing tenderness for this high priest of the sensitive plate with his flowing robes who had talked him into doing something he could never have convinced himself to do, watching him from the eye of a black box as it fixed his image forever.

* * *

The rounds of go-sees had begun again in earnest. Jimmy's face cropped up occasionally in various magazines he leafed through in waiting rooms and lobbies. It made him nostalgic for the fun they used to have. More than anything, though, he missed Valentino's joking presence greeting him with his arrival on Paolo at the end of the day.

He had all but forgotten the alter-ego photos he'd done with Andreo, looking upon them as a cosmic joke, the implications of which, the reactions they caused, he might never have to face, like a misdemeanour perpetrated on the spur of the moment and forgotten.

The last week of August Warden found himself being shipped with a select group of models to an overnight stay on the island of Ibiza, famed playground of the rich and famous. It was an elite affair with a display of expensive designer wear less for the fashion faithful than for the self-celebrated glitterati losing sight of themselves in a blind journey towards annihilation on the seaside paradise.

After the show Warden found himself spilling into a cab with five others to join in the nightlife beating like a living pulse all around. They sat in one another's laps high with the conquests they'd made. Feeling themselves so close as to be friends because they were having such desperate fun together, having hardly known each other that afternoon when they boarded the private plane.

They made their way to an all-night dance club where frenzied crowds staged their furious, forgetful lives. It was life lived outside the concept of time, declaring beauty and pleasure to be the only values worth having. Three young women demanded Warden's attention, having recognized the familiar face of the Fabiano boy, while someone else claimed to have just met a prince walking along the moonlit avenues.

At four in the morning the sprawling, ecstatic crowds were watered down with hoses, hands lifted in rapture as shirts and blouses were pulled overhead in sweaty knots of cloth. The dawn was confronted by the amazing spectacle of a horde of baboons, voices raised in orgiastic worship, dancing their way towards daylight.

Warden found himself contemplating a hand-held mirror with a dozen white streaks anointing its surface, a straw passing from one face to another of those around him. Someone suggested stealing a boat from the beach and taking a harbour cruise, but he wasn't sure if his body could deal with the simple task — which at that moment seemed monumental — of taking control of its motor impulses, and within five minutes he wasn't certain he hadn't dreamed the whole plot.

At six, he sat alone at a bar drinking mango juice and eating the roseate flesh of fresh figs from a bowl in front of him. He watched a procession of spectral creatures coming and going as if performing some ritual sacred to daylight in which their wraith-like bodies had just been made visible. He pulled himself together in time to collect his belongings and make the plane back to Milan.

16

After his initial success, Warden found himself contemplating offers outside Italy. In September, he travelled to Paris to be considered by a prospective client. They liked him so much they used him immediately in a campaign wearing jeans, a checked shirt and red bandanna set in a mythic landscape with an American flag for the sky.

Under Calvino's guidance his image took off. His features were spread across the pages of a dozen magazines, locating him squarely on the topography of fashion and associating him with a variety of products, from clothing through skincare products to cigarettes.

One advertisement made Calvino nervous about Fabiano's newest star. A shot of Warden with dishevelled hair and a whip held over the heads of several other models dressed in leather bondage gear threatened to jeopardize the wholesome image Fabiano prized in him. When his rear end found itself displaying knife-slashed jeans the following month, Calvino decided the time had come to limit the offers he took to those which moved him in a serious direction.

From not knowing how to use him, advertising directors were being told how they would be allowed to do so.

Calvino also thought it time to send him abroad to work with an affiliate agency. Italy had seen enough of him for the time being. He proposed getting Warden onto an international circuit by spring. For the upcoming season, Calvino decided he should go to England. Apart from his continuing friendship with Andreo —Valentino having all but vanished from his life — there was little he would miss. He was sent with Calvino's blessing to the Elizabeth Smart agency in London.

It was raining the day he arrived at Heathrow, as it always seems to be raining or else to have just rained, a peculiar characteristic of English weather. At Victoria Station he hailed the first in a row of sleek, glistening cabs and gave the driver the address of the agency.

Warden liked the institution immediately. The staff were organized and efficient in contrast to Maura's, though he sensed the surface coolness and businesslike nature of the agency would preclude the sort of camaraderie he'd experienced in Milan. He would also not be living in a hotel with other models. There would be little chance to indulge in an atmosphere of looks-conscious young men and women whose ambitions were geared wholly towards success in the fashion world. Here, the onus would be on him to succeed.

Smart herself was a tall, cheerful woman with gleaming eyes who'd built her organization up with her own hands in ten years. She was friendly to everyone and, like Calvino, seldom had time to spare, though she always kept an ear open to the needs and feelings of the models in her stable. She neither bullied nor cajoled her young charges. She simply gave them the best opportunities and let them do the work, making it clear they were on their own. Nor was anyone treated as special. There were no 'big, big stars' in her agency — only lesser and greater lights. Even his work with Andreo did not qualify Warden for special status. He was expected to take his place on the go-see lists with everyone else as he began making the prescribed rounds of clients.

Out in the streets London was already calling to Warden and other new faces like him. Work began coming in steadily under the patronage of the Smart agency even though he hadn't established a rapport with a particular photographer as he had with Andreo. He was ordinary once again, yet still making his mark.

His first cover shot appeared in November on an avant-garde periodical mockingly titled *Pariah*. He also appeared in some of England's most style-conscious magazines amid an explosion of indecipherable shapes and colours where he found himself constantly re-invented in the fractured mosaic of English fashion.

"Let them do anything to you but don't let them give you this dirty grunge style," Calvino admonished when he left for England. "It won't last but you'll be stuck with that look and it will damage your image."

He found himself working in a world quite different from the Italy of Versace and Ferré. The British mentality was one of a mind under siege seeking refuge in a disjointed reality influenced by the machine and the found object more than the rich Italianate love of opulence and splendour. It was a landscape distorted by a desire for novelty and a fascination with violence, undergoing a transformation wrought out of fragmentation and decomposing social values.

One day he wore an outfit created from wire mesh. It felt as uncomfortable as if he'd been wearing barbed wire. He couldn't imagine anyone wearing it for real. The following day he found himself donning some of the most expensive formal wear the city had to offer. Only this time he couldn't imagine anyone's being able to afford it. He watched the photographer race maniacally between his camera and the lights. Adjusting screws, raising and lowering reflectors, checking and rechecking the focus. All but oblivious to his model.

"I charge extra for lingerie," Warden quipped.

"Eh? What was your name again?" the man asked in a thick Scots accent.

"Marilyn."

"This layout is for a magazine called *Pariah*, Marvin. You heard of them?"

"No."

"Now, Marvin, I want you to look angry — very angry."

Warden did as he was told, gritting his teeth and grimacing. The shutter clicked away for awhile. Another wardrobe change and he returned in shirt and tie, minus the jacket.

"I want you to sit over there, Marvin. Wrap your legs over the arms of the chair and tilt your whole body towards me."

Warden complied.

"That's it."

He looked down at the clothes, half-hidden and obscured by

the strange pose in the folds of the chair. With his knees pulled up in front of him the shirt could hardly be seen.

"Will they see the clothes?" he asked.

"Sod on the clothes," the photographer scowled. "This is art, not fashion. You have to give those bastards what you want. Don't let them tell you about it, you know?"

The photographer clicked away for awhile then leaned on the camera.

"That was just great — so primitive, you know?"

* * *

After several weeks of living out of hotels Warden took a small furnished flat in Holland Park. He found himself the object of some curiosity as he moved in with his piles of luggage. A blue-haired young man stared at him from down the hall.

"Hello," Warden said.

"Hello, I'm Ivan," said the young man coming to greet him, hair sticking up like the antennae of a large insect. "Though sometimes I'm Ivy, depending on how I'm dressed," he continued, extending a bangle-covered arm.

"Pleased to meet you," Warden said.

"I haven't got on me proper skirt for a curtsey," he said, "but it's lovely to meet you, too."

"That's all right — I haven't been able to get at my clothes for days now."

Ivan stopped and looked at him. "I mistook you for a local lad," he said. "You have an accent."

"I'm Canadian."

"Imagine!" he said, without explaining what was so surprising.

Ivan helped Warden carry his belongings into the flat.

"It's a bit drab," said Ivan, looking around. "Rebekah and I can help you fix it up if you like. She's my flatmate — we're in the decorating business. We can get you deals on all kinds of things. We've got plenty of street cred. And if you like night clubs, we know all the door attendants who will let you in free."

A phone rang down the hall.

"That's me," Ivan said. "Why don't you get yourself settled in, then come and knock us up and we'll have tea in a bit?"

"Love to!" Warden said. "About half an hour?"

"Brilliant!" Ivan exclaimed.

In half an hour Warden found himself in an elegant entrance hall with a decided Victorian sensibility. Ivan showed him around, leading him into rooms containing more antiques per square inch than should have been physically possible.

"You'll find we have everything for a successful parlour," he exclaimed, as Warden followed him from room to room. "We thought we would only have to buy a flat and decorate it and move in for life to be complete."

In a drape-lined sitting room Ivan served tea on a silver service beside a plate piled high with enormous strawberry tarts. His flat-mate, Rebekah, had not returned.

"But she'll be home soon," he promised, as though her presence might be the high point to Warden's visit. "She phoned to say she was leaving ten minutes ago and she's a demon driver. She operates best at top speed."

Warden looked around, complimenting the decor and the odd collection of bric-a-brac that filled the room.

"Rebekah, again," he confided. "She's really a genius, you know," he told Warden. "She can take any old junk and make it look like something special. Her real name is Lady Rebekah Wentworth-something-or-other, but you musn't tell her I told you. She gets terribly annoyed with me for telling people she's royalty."

He went on to tell Warden a number of other secrets about the absent Rebekah, which he was also asked to swear never to repeat, including the story of a rumoured affair with Prince Andrew before his disastrous marriage, and which, Ivan informed him solemnly, had broken Rebekah's heart forever.

"She's vowed to die a spinster, collecting lovers on the side and cutting off their heads to leave on spikes in the garden." Ivan giggled. "But I don't suppose she'll really do it."

Having exhausted his supply of gossip, Ivan turned the topic to the design business. Much of their material was salvaged from neighbourhood junk shops and antique stores, he claimed. Every weekend he and Rebekah wandered through crowded second-hand stores, piling up goods along the way. He pointed out a small chandelier hanging in the next room.

"Rebekah spotted that one right off," Ivan said proudly. "She said it had potential for three hundred quid and she was right. We picked it up for five pounds, brought it home and polished every crystal. Now just look at it."

They were lounging on the sofa when the door burst open and

a young woman rushed excitedly through the doorway. Butterscotch hair tumbled from under a blue hat. She seemed tongue-tied with glee.

"Ivy, the most wonderful thing just happened! I was shopping just now in the deli up the street and there was a new girl on the cash. I ordered all these items that normally come to five pounds and when she added it up it came to just a quid. I literally threw the money at her and made good my getaway. It was lovely! I hope they haven't sent someone to follow me. It feels so good ripping someone off, doesn't it? It's better than a bargain in a junk shop!"

"Hello, Bekah," Ivan said. "I've made tea and we have company."

"Hello," Warden said.

"Hello," she said, setting her bags down and tugging at a long pair of zebra-striped gloves.

"Miss Rebekah Wentworth, I would like to introduce you to Mr. Warden Fields from Canada. Warden, meet Rebekah. Warden's our new neighbour and you'll be pleased to hear he's totally suitable for socializing."

"I am pleased to hear it," Rebekah said. "The last bunch were boors and terrible snobs. I was just thinking we needed some new blood in the entourage."

"It's true," said Ivan, turning to Warden. "We took the last girl who lived in your flat to one of the wickedest clubs in all of London, worse even than All Saints Road where the prostitutes hang out. And do you know what she did? She sat in the balcony above the dance floor for all to see, clearly bored to tears, knitting a scarf while some leather queen held out her wool for her."

Rebekah poured herself tea while Ivan munched tarts like the March Hare. Sticky red filling spilling out between fingers, crumbs clinging to lips. He proffered the plate to Warden.

"Thanks. These are wonderful," Warden said, taking another.

"They're from our local bakery," Rebekah said. "This is the best neighbourhood in all of London, I should think. It has nearly everything. For starters, it has the best strawberry tarts in the world, and that has to count for something, doesn't it, Ivy?"

"Oh, yes," Ivan agreed. "Strawberry tarts count for a good deal. Don't you agree, Warden?"

"Absolutely."

"I've offered for us to do Warden's apartment, Rebekah. Some sort of neo-colonial look, I thought. And when we get done, don't you think it would be nice to do his image over as well? Something a little more androgynous, perhaps."

"What's wrong with my image?" Warden protested jokingly. Rebekah looked him over.

"Nothing that can't be fixed," she said. "When we get done, he'll know what looks are to be used for, won't he, Ivy?"

Warden smiled at the two immodest schemers. The blue-haired young man reached over to the tray with a smile, the other hand pushing the remains of a large tart into his open mouth.

"You know," he said between bites, "I've been thinking, Bekah. It's time to redo our own place. We need to do something with the ceiling. I could do a replica in miniature of the Sistine Chapel. What do you think?"

"Capital," Rebekah answered, lifting a cup to her mouth.

They sat staring up at the ceiling as if it were there already.

17

As winter approached, the English weather began to be dominated by a thin, constant drizzle that held no promise of snow before Christmas. Warden's thoughts turned more and more to home. It seemed so long since he'd been at the friendly house on Connaught Circle or out enjoying walks in the park with his sister. The feelings remained curiously aroused and would not go away.

He received a card from his mother asking about his plans for the holidays. She had enclosed a photograph of the family taken by his father years before. It showed Warden standing with his mother and sister on the lawn in front of their house. A stone gryphon sat poised on either side of the entranceway, claw-throated and stiff-backed, guarding the staid residence through long nights in the quiet neighbourhood. It all seemed far away, as though it belonged to a previous existence. He phoned to say he'd be home in a week and spent the next few days shopping for gifts.

He landed at the airport on one of those bleakly Canadian days that resonated at the very core of his being. A wintry sunset matched the orange glow in each living-room window. Everything was suffused with a sense of stability and order. He imagined hard wind-swept faces staring from behind endless rounds of beer in front of endless rounds of *Hockey Night In Canada*. As if the entire country were held in the unreceding throes of endless winter.

It was strange to think he was back, even harder to believe he once belonged there. The lands he had visited seemed more real as they obeyed the relative laws of time and mutability compared to the absolute unchanging homeland.

The lion heads at the gate watched his re-entry into the sacred groves of the family under shadowy eaves, lace encircling the windows, withered vine stalks on the outer brick walls. The house stood before him now, welcoming, accommodating, surviving all the changes within him.

Lisa met him, arms around him in hugs as huge and greenly welcoming as the pine and holly wreathes on the front door. She ushered him in, apologizing that no one had picked him up at the airport, amid exclamations of joy on his return.

"You're back at last, Ward-Boy — I can't believe it!"

In the hallway he set down his bags and took off his overcoat. His mother and father were both there to greet him and make the scene complete. He had already eaten but Beatrice brought out food for him anyway, insisting he eat as she watched over him, as all mothers must continually attend to their children's needs even when they have been away a long time.

They wanted to hear all about Italy and England and his work. He indulged them, telling of the shows he'd been in and of the erratic Sr. Calvino, about go-sees and photographers and his trips around the Italian countryside. He described the abandoned house he discovered in the mountains of Elba and the quality of light in the late afternoon on the tiny island where Napoleon had once been held prisoner and how amazed he was that even the least educated Europeans spoke two or three languages fluently. He even mentioned Valentino's name several times to see if it elicited a spark of curiosity. He went on talking till they were satisfied they knew him again, that he hadn't changed beyond all recognition. Then finally they let him go up to bed, happy with the season and the return of the prodigal son.

He stayed a week, long enough to feel he'd never left and to fall back into routines he thought he'd outgrown. They made the requisite list of visits to relatives and ate holiday dinners as a family, together again at last.

One night after dinner, as he sat at the table with his parents, he touched on the subject of his new-found sexuality, almost as an afterthought. He had couched it in the ridiculously transparent guise of 'What if someone you knew... ', leading to an embarrassed silence on the part of his parents, who avoided each other's glance. His father cleared his throat several times as though something had lodged there. Warden could tell from their reaction that this was not an entirely new thought for them. His mother was first to speak.

"I just hope you're being careful," she said, bypassing his question altogether. "There are so many more things to worry about these days than when your father and I were young."

She got up and went into the kitchen where they heard her clattering the dishes, as though cueing her husband. Walter spent an inordinate amount of time wiping his mouth with a napkin. At last he looked directly at Warden. "Whatever you are, Warden, doesn't change who you are for us."

Warden waited for him to say more. His father seemed unable to muster anything concrete in the way of advice, possibly for the first time that Warden could remember.

"Young people seem to feel a need to experiment with things these days that your mother and I never even thought of," he said, choosing his sentences cautiously as though the wrong word might explode in his face. "There's nothing wrong with that in itself," he said. "Though I can't speak from experience."

If Warden had expected conflict, he was disappointed. It was the others who now faced the task of adjusting to accommodate the entirety of his identity, as it had just been revealed to them.

He pondered the changes he'd undergone since he last saw them. He felt no different now than then. It was simply a decision he'd made to accept what was already there, inside him. From then on it became a gradual emerging, a wresting of the contours of the figure within the sculptor's stone, bit by bit.

There was an awkward silence as his mother returned bearing a tray of dessert, armed with a vast selection of spoons. All eyes were on her as she laid out the utensils. She looked up and smiled.

"There we are," she said, and sat again, spooning out a sticky trifle.

His father avoided looking at anyone.

"I just want you to know I'm being responsible and sensible," Warden offered, to reassure them. He shrugged. "I wanted to let you in on who I really am. As a family we don't really talk much about things like this and I just wanted to tell you I'm okay." He shrugged again. "That's all."

They thanked him for his honesty, assuring him he could tell them anything whenever he wanted. Both his parents seemed relieved when the talk was over. Of course, he hadn't known what to expect. It had been a strangely passive acceptance. In fact, he thought it almost a refusal of acceptance. Whoever he might declare himself to be, they seemed to say, he could not change any prior notion of him they had held before his declaration.

The day before Christmas, Warden took Lisa shopping. Stores hummed with the buzz of holiday shoppers. The streets were filled with the bright lights of mercantilism. In a jewellery store on Bloor Street, Warden asked to be shown a strand of pearls laid out behind a counter. The clerk's face said he couldn't be bothered by the whims of youngsters and did not care to disturb his display for them. Warden insisted.

"Would Mom like these?" he asked Lisa, holding them in the light when the clerk brought them out.

"I'll take them if she doesn't. What woman wouldn't die for a set of basic black and pearls?"

The clerk sniffed when Warden asked the price. He pondered the sum, bringing out an expensively-crafted wallet. The clerk became more obliging.

"Will you be paying by Visa or Mastercard, sir?"

Warden looked over at Lisa.

"I'll pay cash," he said, pulling out a sheaf of bills.

He pocketed the necklace and they left, laughing as they went.

"What an old fart!" Lisa screamed with glee. "Did you see the look on his face when you pulled out that wad? Let's do it again!"

In a book store on Yonge Street they browsed through fashion magazines looking for pictures of Warden but all they found was a shot of Joe on a bicycle, smiling at a girl looking back over her shoulder. He told Lisa about Joe and Jimmy and others he'd worked with.

"It's hard to think of you as famous, Ward-boy. That's something only other people are, not my own brother," she said. "But I'll get over it. Let's find a bar."

"You're not old enough to go in bars," he protested.

"And you're too young to be such a prude. Let's go."

She took his arm as they walked up the street to a glitzy hangout for the city's glamour set. They deposited themselves at the bar, packages spilling onto chairs beside them. Warden looked at his sister. Hair neatly cut, fingernails trimmed and polished. She'd changed a great deal in less than a year. It was as though she'd skipped adolescence, going straight from a tomboy to a young woman.

"What did you do exciting while you were gone? We missed you. Did Mom tell you we visited Aunt Emily in Florida?"

It was all coming out in a rush. He smiled at her eagerness. She was pleased to have him all to herself away from family and friends, sharing something adult. He ordered for them both, refusing her alcohol. Playing big brother. She protested, but barely.

He watched the bar fill up around them with anxious faces in a desperate search for something. Lisa focused on him. "Did you try any drugs?" she asked conspiratorially.

"Well... yes, actually. I think it was cocaine. Somebody gave it to me after a show. I probably shouldn't be telling you this."

"I tried it once, too. I didn't like it. Ecstasy's better."

This wasn't the reaction he'd expected. Did that make him a bad influence? Not if she'd already tried it, he guessed. She toyed with her glass of soda waiting for him to speak. What else to tell her? What had been important to him at that age?

"How is school?" he asked.

"Pretentious. I just don't get the other kids. All they care about is who's going out with who... whom. I mean, I'm only sixteen. I'm not depressed because I don't have a steady boyfriend and I don't think about marriage all the time. I slept with this Tony guy a couple of times. It's no big deal. It's not a problem for me but these girls are, like, suicidal if they don't have a Friday night date. Don't you think that's a bit much?"

"You're sleeping with guys at your age? How do you get condoms?"

"Oh — take a pill. You sound like Mom."

"You told Mom you slept with somebody?"

"Relax, will you? I'm not stupid. No, I didn't tell Mom about Tony and I got the condoms from Louise. What about you? Did you meet anybody in Italy?"

He was surprised by the question. "Well... "

"Come on — out with it," she demanded.

"Well, you may find this hard to believe but I did sleep with somebody... "

"Just a somebody? Name and occupation, please."

She was mocking him. He took a breath.

"It was with another guy."

"And... ?"

"Well, that's it — I slept with another guy, Lisa."

"Yeah — and? Was it, like, good or what?"

Warden looked at his sister. It occurred to him he might be missing something. He wondered if his parents had prompted her.

"Do I know you?" he asked. "I mean, I just told you I slept with someone of the same sex and you ask me was it good?"

She looked at him with her most worldly look and shook her head.

"It's a known fact that three-quarters of the world's population are bisexual to some degree or other and the rest probably wish they were."

"I think your estimate may be a bit high, little sister."

"Big brother, you're not nearly as cool as I thought you were." She took his hand. "But I still love you. Anyway, I heard Mom and Dad talking about it yesterday. Mom's totally cool about it. It seems they've suspected for some time but now that you're a success Dad says it isn't his place to tell you what to do anymore, so you're off the hook."

She put her drink down on the counter. He watched it slide across the shiny surface.

"Let's blow this popsicle stand," she said.

"Like you're blowing my mind?"

"Eat it up."

18

For the next two months Warden travelled the continent working the fashion circuit. In February he was included in an article touting the half-dozen upcoming male models held to be worth watching.

When questioned regarding his work, he spoke intelligently about the career he'd found himself in almost by accident. He no longer thought of himself as simply a tool obeying mutely in the hands of others more knowledgable than himself, having gained some insight into the degree of power his image carried.

His face had begun to weave a mythology all its own, taking on a dimension outside the pages of the magazines he appeared in. He was stopped not infrequently by passers-by who recognized the likeness of his printed counterpart. A woman accosted him in Bond Street one day to ask if he'd appeared in magazine advertisements.

"I knew it!" she exclaimed, delighted with her talent for observation. "Actually," she confided, "you look much taller in person."

By March he was exhausted by the hectic pace of fashion shows and photography sessions. His looks, normally healthy and glowing with vigour, had taken on an unrested appearance. Both Smart and Calvino urged him to take a hiatus. He'd been going strong for nearly a year at this point.

"I know just the thing," Rebekah said one afternoon as they sat in the drawing room of the flat under a ceiling adorned with Ivan's newly-painted acanthus leaves and rosy-cheeked cherubs.

There had been a break that week in the relentless grey that constituted English winter. An early spring or at least a continuation of mild weather looked quite possible.

"Why don't you take a trip to my cottage in Whitstable? You can stay a week or two — however long you like. That way you can get out of the city altogether."

She went on before he could accept or protest.

"No, no really. It's quite small — just a stone cottage, actually, but it's right on the seashore and it's so restful and quiet this time of year. It should be just what you need."

Warden looked at the eyes begging to be taken up on the offer, as though it would in some way cement their friendship.

"Alright," Warden said. "Can I go this weekend?"

"Anytime, dear boy," Rebekah said, delighted he'd accepted. "It's only two hours by train. And the best part is you'll be all alone, which is just the medicine you need."

* * *

Inside Victoria Station, gothic shapes stood breathing sooty smoke as the loudspeakers soberly boomed out the departure times and curious-sounding names of destinations. The station echoed with conversation and the shushing of engines.

It had been raining all afternoon, small leaks in the high ceilings compounding the greyness dripping inside and out. The pigeons inside the station seemed conscious the darkness was an early, deceitful one and continued wheeling about under the dome of the roof. Warden waited in one of the many slowly moving queues for his ticket. When the clerk handed it to him he pointed off to the right.

"Platform five, lad. If you hurry you'll just be able to catch it," he said. "You'll see it when you get there."

Two trains sat idling on either side of the track. There was no sign to indicate which was his. He looked around the busy crowd for a conductor. Other passengers clambering on board seemed to know where they were going. He asked a man in a raincoat if he knew which train went to Whitstable, and then another man, but no one knew for sure. A whistle blew and the train nearest began to come alive segment by segment. He jumped onto the moving platform, backpack knocking about as he shifted and climbed the few steps.

The door closed with a bang. Inside, most of the seats were taken. Near the door, a face. Not warming or inviting but almost with an absence of expression, a witholding, except for a pair of haunted, burnt eyes. Short, coppery-brown hair shaved close over the ears. Though somehow the hardness did not mar his beauty but rather enhanced it. Warden pushed the hair from his own brow with a free hand. Train picking up speed in response to a series of staccato whistles above.

"Excuse me," Warden said. "Do you know if this train goes to Whitstable?"

The eyes looked up.

"How the fuck should I know, mate?" he said with scarcely any emphasis or interest, then turned away.

Warden watched the lean face with its taut cheekbones turn to look out the window as if across a great distance. Eyes stared straight ahead. Pale acetylene reflection of a flame in ice.

A young woman seated nearby turned.

"Yes," she said quietly, "this train stops at Whitstable."

He wasn't sure if she'd taken pity on him because of his accent or because of the rudeness of the young man sitting wedged into the corner. Ancient leather jacket like dried papyrus, black military boots bunched up on the seat across from him. He looked back with a glance that might have been a flash of guilt or acquiesence, but did not move his feet to offer Warden a seat.

That was the extent of their exchange. Warden continued down the aisle till he found an empty place. Even with his back turned he felt the presence of the other agitating, almost lifting him out of his seat. When he turned to glance at the seat by the door its occupant remained in the same position of defiance and aloofness, staring out across icy distances of his own making.

The train stopped regularly at a handful of industrial towns strung along the countryside in the dull afternoon. Warden lost himself in a magazine and did not turn again until he heard the muffled whistle as the conductor came by to announce his stop. He stood and hoisted his pack onto his shoulders, making his way to the door. The other had already gone, leaving his seat empty, the window without anyone to stare out at its passing view. Warden felt relieved but also strangely disappointed. As though he'd hoped to find something more in the harsh, unsmiling face.

He stepped off the train onto a lamp-lit platform where shapes suggesting benches and gates hovered in the surreal fog of evening. Lamps glowed like candle flames within a fringe of shadows. To his surprise he discovered there were real flames in the glowing bulbs, as though he'd stepped out of the train into a previous century.

He set out following the globes of light winding along the carefully curving streets. Homes glowed behind curtains, their windows flattened into frames, intact with the warmth of private sentiments and invisible inhabitants. He imagined old Victorian furniture and kindly neighbours living placid, peaceful lives in the fresh smell of salt air. Not far off he heard the gravelly hush of the sea as he reached the stone cottage on Island Walk.

Inside, the dwelling was a well-preserved doll's house of neatly ordered furniture. Wooden rockers, shelves for china, a wide collection of books centring around a fireplace. A narrow staircase led to the second floor with two small bedrooms and a cold-water bath. The air was damp and almost as cool as outside. The house seemed to be pressing its pale blue walls towards him as if warming its hands at a fire long cold and now relit.

He lit the fireplace. Rebekah had warned him there was no other heat, electricity having been put in just the year before. He took stock of the pantry's few provisions, some boxes of hard biscuits and preserves. In a small freezer he found two meat pies and took one out to thaw. By the time his tour of discovery was over the cottage had begun to fill with the scent of burning wood. He heated his supper in the oven and read a volume of poetry before going to bed. He heard the vacant pulsing of waves as he climbed under the soft down covers, thinking he could stay awake all night. Then he fell asleep.

He woke early. From the window he saw how close he was to the water's edge, a stone's throw from the wooden buildings and wharves wreathed in nets. He dressed and walked down to the beach, a field of fist-sized stones. Trudging over it was like walking on ball bearings. Occasionally, he saw lodged between rocks the long spiny combs of fish skeletons. Gulls wheeled overhead looking for others not yet beached. Waves dragged in and withdrew abruptly. There was no one about. The cold was eating through his sweater by the time he returned.

He lit the fire and made a breakfast of hard biscuits and jam. He would remember to buy eggs and cereal and milk when he went out. The radio played a mournful Sibelius tone-poem. It seemed to go with the dismal greyness of the landscape. At ten o'clock he went out again and bought food from a cheerful grocer. Warden imagined everyone in such an ornamental town would be friendly and was glad not to be disappointed. From the grocer's wife he got directions to a bus stop where he could catch a bus to visit Canterbury in the afternoon.

Outside, he passed the houses that had seemed so warm and inviting the night before. He half-expected to find the roadways bustling with horses and carts but real cars passed him instead. People walked by in ordinary dress, yet they were different from their counterparts in London and other cities, as if untouched by the passage of time, as though its essence had not seeped in to meet them there in the quiet backwater.

On every corner sat a small antique shop, as though the air of antiquity the town exuded were its major product and could be found on shelves like any other. At one end of the road, a pub mirrored a church set on the corner across from it like rivals in trade. As he passed them, the town's inhabitants stared in curiosity trying to place him in their mental geography. Finally, deducing him to be a stranger, they would smile and nod.

In the afternoon he caught a double-decker bus, climbing the hilly roads connecting small towns in the district, watching fields of black bracken pass by from where he sat atop the vehicle as it teetered and tottered along towards its destination. Canterbury itself was a fairy town with a funny Lilliputian people who held medieval associations for him, neither the architecture nor the countryside around doing anything to dispel their identification with other millennia. The town seemed to smile softly, musing its secret of time's leap backward into itself.

Not far off he found the gates to the great cathedral, an ancient stone structure before which the present walked in the guise of modern-day tourists. They seemed to be searching for a sign, an indication of the ages it had witnessed in its colossal architecture, like a relic of living time. It gave the feeling of life lived at immense distances. Warden touched the stone with his hand.

He entered among the brittle bones of arches and pillars vaulting like ribs on the ceiling of the church. A stone-carved scroll of the Archbishops of Canterbury listed all, beginning with Saint Augustine in 597 AD. Warden's mind found itself stretched to the limit trying to encompass such vast epochs of time. Like conceptualizing the size of the universe with a naked, solitary eye.

The cathedral was calm, unmindful of the coming and going of the speckled drift of tourists, their footsteps tapping on marble steps like raindrops on pewter. He wandered through the sleeping place of royalty and religious heads whose likenesses were carved on the tombs and walls. Statues stood with arms draped in flowing robes of stone, their smooth beards stiffened as though posing for a portrait.

He walked among great prophets seized and stupefied in their issue, an hourglass sifting through history thick with the pale moss of time. Jet streams of grey stone rose like knotted ancient roots twisting and winding their way to the ceiling echoing with the hallelujahs of marbled saints.

Warden stepped aside to avoid a rush of schoolchildren on the smooth steps. As he turned he found himself facing the haunted, incisive gaze of the young man he'd encountered on the train the day before. He felt as though he were wrestling with a spirit as he stared into the cold grey eyes that seemed to be laughing at him.

"So you found your stop, then?"

"Yes... I found it."

"No thanks to me, I suppose."

"Yes, well... I... I found it."

"You just said that — you don't have to stand there looking stupid over it."

Warden had no idea how to respond to his abruptness and rudeness in the quietness of the cathedral. Or any place else, for that matter.

"Do you like tombs?" the young man asked, indicating the vaults, his face as cryptic as the stone masks around them.

"It's interesting — all this history," Warden said.

"They're very old. Once you're gone you're a long time dead."

Warden took this for a sign of humour. Perhaps the frozen flame in his eyes betrayed an inward gentleness.

"We don't have things as old as this in my country. Except for a few rocks."

"Well, you will someday."

A smile flashed, brilliant and unexpected. As startling as a shooting star.

"Are you staying in Canterbury?"

"Not far from here. I like to come back to visit now and then. Somehow it always seems more natural in here with everyone lying down. It's prettier than graveyards, though God knows they'd be more useful making fodder for the grass and trees."

Warden found his humour as enigmatic as his behaviour. They walked together almost accidentally, as if unable to part. Warden watched him as he spoke. Emotions flickered across his face like stars, covered over immediately by a stony visage, as if there were storm clouds in his soul. Reflecting nothing, finally. They stood at the entrance, having come the full length of the cathedral. The young man held out his hand as though a decision had just been rendered in Warden's favour.

"Joshua Behrens," he said, shaking hands.

"Warden Fields."

They were outside now. Warden could smell the salt air. Joshua asked if he knew the Black Bull Tavern in Whitstable. Warden had seen it earlier as he walked through town.

"I'll be there about eight this evening if you care to join me for a drink."

It was hardly even an invitation — just a notice of where he would be should Warden happen to be there at the same time. Joshua smiled again. The sun opened and closed like an iris behind the clouds. Warden was aware of shaded feelings, a hand sheltering a candle from the wind as he regarded the knife-like features of the man beside him making the landscape around them seem vaguely silly or insignificant in some way.

19

After supper Warden walked to the beach. The sun set as he watched fishing vessels towing their cargoes homeward, weighed down in the waves as the light thinned and seagulls followed like black flags in the eddies of the restless engines.

The Black Bull was just around the corner from Island Walk. The tavern was a mock-up of a ship's quarters, with lifebuoys on the walls and portholes for windows. Rough-hewn logs supported the structure filled now with cheerful patrons. Joshua leaned against a post, glass in hand, talking to two young women. He wore a grey wool sweater and a red bandanna around his neck. His hands were clothed in black fingerless gloves. As he talked he tilted his head. His eyes locked into those of his listeners. Acknowledging and mocking at the same time.

When he saw Warden he walked over to meet him. Warden was surprised by his eagerness after the casual invitation he'd been given. Joshua introduced Warden to his companions, two villagers named Wendy and Hillary. He explained how they'd met exploring the famous cathedral, not mentioning the train incident of the previous day.

"Ohhh, it's a lovely place, isn't it?" cooed the one named Wendy.

It was lovely, they agreed.

"Are you American?" Hillary asked.

"He's from Canada," Joshua said, surprising him since Warden hadn't mentioned it. "You can hear it in his accent."

"Are you?" Wendy exclaimed in surprise. "It sounds like a lovely place."

He wondered if she meant in the same way the cathedral was a lovely place.

"I have an uncle in Canada," Joshua said. "We haven't heard from him for years — not since I was a kid."

"Why don't you try phoning him?" Hillary suggested. "Doesn't he have a phone?"

"Well, I would but he's a deaf-mute," Joshua said, grinning at Warden over their heads. "So he couldn't hear it ringing if I did phone. And even if he managed to pick it up at the right time he couldn't say anything."

He tilted back his head and laughed at his own joke.

"Oh, you!" she said in exasperation. She turned to Warden. "He's always been like this — even in school. Always the cheeky one."

The two women plied Warden with more questions. Others came over to meet him. Joshua seemed to be well known. Eventually Wendy and Hillary and the others departed, leaving Joshua and Warden alone. Warden found Joshua surprisingly easy to talk to considering his experience at their previous encounters.

"What brings someone like you to Whitstable?" Warden asked.

"What? You don't think I belong here?" Joshua said mockingly. "Actually, I grew up around here. My mother still lives outside of town."

He put down his glass and eyed Warden.

"And what's a good-looking Canadian like you doing in England?" he asked.

"Working as a fashion model."

Joshua scowled suddenly. "Fashion — it figures," he said. "With a face like that, I mean."

Warden looked at his intense expression to see if there were any humour intended in the remark. "I'm not sure if I should take that as a compliment," he said.

"Fashion's a rather objectionable pursuit, to my mind. It's self-serving and communicates nothing. It's fascist to choose the most physically perfect and try to make the rest of us adhere to a set rule of thumb."

Warden was not entirely caught off guard by the attack. "I think you've got the wrong idea," he said. "Models are chosen primarily for a size, not a look. We're creating standards, not ideals. And no one says you have to adhere to them, either. You obviously don't, judging by your appearance."

"I don't need people telling me what to do or how to dress."

"And what exactly do you do, before you cross-examine me any further?"

"I'm a pop singer," he answered casually.

"Is that why the counter-culture image?" Warden asked.

"That's not what it's all about."

"But you obviously create your own standards of fashion."

Joshua smiled wryly at having been caught out.

"You might say so."

"So that makes you a cultural rebel. And what is pop music besides cultural fashion?"

"Don't go too far, mate — I don't accept that. Some pop music may be nothing more than a fad. My music's very political. It has a different intent altogether."

"Intellectual fashion, then."

"That may be, but it's not done out of any egotistical, self-serving interests."

Joshua was grinning at Warden's counterattack, one of the few he'd ever encountered.

"I think I might just like you," he said, raising his glass with a tattered glove. "You're cheeky in your own way."

Behind them a group of rowdy patrons had broken out into

song. It grew louder. Joshua turned to look. They were slowly joined by others singing 'You'll Never Walk Alone' in drunken, comradely fashion till a good proportion of the bar's patrons had joined in.

Joshua scowled. "That's the type of nationalistic machismo that causes fights at football games. There was a good, bloody row a while back and a lot of people got killed over it. You express your enthusiasm by making a lot of noise and being overly fond of drinking. Then one day you end up in a fight and kill someone over a football match."

Warden thought for a second he might confront the crowd. The singing died to a rowdy laugh amid hearty back-slapping. Joshua's rancour faded with it. He placed his hand on Warden's forearm.

"Are you going to invite me back to your place for tea?" he said, looking into Warden's eyes. "Or do you have company?"

Warden grinned in surprise.

"I'm all alone, actually."

"Good — that makes things less complicated, doesn't it?"

"I haven't got any tea to offer you, but I bought some coffee today."

"Sounds barbaric, but I accept."

They left the bar and headed for the cottage along the darkened cobblestone streets. Joshua walked sturdily beside him.

"What if I hadn't asked you to come back?" Warden said.

"I would've come anyway."

Joshua began singing an amusing song about being small in a world where only tallness counts, voice a warm husky baritone in the foggy air. To Warden, he seemed to have an uprightness about him that had nothing to do with everyday manners and morals, or the oppressive respectability by which the masses conduct their lives. It was strength that stood alone. Joshua stopped as they passed the beach, invisible in the darkness.

"Here — let's have a quick row, shall we?"

Warden could just make out the long piers extending in front of them.

"Do you have a boat?"

Joshua smiled quickly.

"We'll annex one," he said.

Warden followed him over the rocky beach past rows of boats flanking the docks. They creaked and groaned in the darkness as though talking in their sleep.

"This one'll do," Joshua said, indicating a small skiff. "Climb aboard, mate."

Warden stepped in as Joshua slipped the knot off the landing, pushing the boat out and leaping in at the last moment. They slid out in the darkness. Warden watched Joshua's silhouette settle into the seat across from him and take hold of the oars. He swung them in an arc above his head, and the boat floated noiselessly over the surface. Warden listened to Joshua's measured breathing with each stroke taking them in a slowly widening circle. He stopped rowing and sat for a moment as if listening.

"Do you like this feeling? This nothingness? It's utterly empty — free from everything."

"It's peaceful," Warden said.

Joshua bent over the bow and brought up handfuls of freezing water dripping through his fingers.

"The ocean is immense. It's so big it's amazing. It never asks you for anything — not your name, not what you're thinking. I think it would be possible to be totally content out here forever. What do you think?"

"I'd get hungry."

Joshua laughed a deep laugh. It was the first time Warden had heard it clearly.

"You know, you're different," he said. "You're not like the rest of those pretty boys. I felt it when I saw you. I like you."

Warden didn't reply. He wanted to say something reassuring in return, felt incapable of expressing it in a way that would sound natural. Joshua's silhouette straightened suddenly.

"We'll go back now."

Now Warden felt rude, as though Joshua had offered him something genuine and he hadn't accepted. He watched Joshua's back as he took up the oars, completing the circle and returning where they'd started.

They walked up the lane to the cottage. Inside, Warden lit a fire. Once it was going, he went to the kitchen, bringing back coffee. Joshua took the cup offered. Room flushed with heat. Warden picked up a poker and pushed the logs back into the grate to reduce the flare-up.

"Why don't you stop puttering around like a servant and come and sit with me?" Joshua said.

Warden turned, poker in hand.

"Why don't you sit on this?" he said, but came over and sat and

130

stretched his legs across a chair. Joshua lifted his own legs and settled them across Warden's. Warden looked up in amusement.

"May I?" Joshua remarked ironically.

"Go right ahead — I like my friends to feel they can abuse me."

"You model types are all alike."

Warden talked about his family and his life back in Toronto. Joshua surprised him by taking an interest. He sketched in a few details of his work in Italy in the last year, and how he came to be in England. For his part, Joshua talked of living in London and a problematic younger brother who stayed with him. His mother lived alone outside Whitstable on a small estate. Their father had died when he was young. He had an older brother no one had heard from in years and a renegade sister who'd married an American and lived in Los Angeles, travelling back and forth a great deal. They were staying at his place now.

Flames hissed and threw shadows around the room. Warden could feel Joshua's gaze on him.

"So am I staying the night with you?" he asked, almost gently.

Warden turned to look at him. "That's just what I was wondering."

Joshua followed him upstairs to the bedroom where they quickly pulled off each other's shirts and sweaters, letting them fall like discarded skins, shivering in the cool air. Joshua's hands were warm and forceful.

"You're nice to look at — so lovely to touch," Joshua said.

It was the first time he'd been touched by anyone since leaving Italy. Joshua was rough, passionate as he explored Warden's body. There was a murky odour about him. Vinegary. Emanating from his hard, white flesh. Not sweet like Valentino's bronzed, flower-scented skin. Warden suspected he abstained from deodorants for some vague political reason. Washed only when he felt like it.

They came together in the dark. Dispelling moons. Displacing planets. Clinging to each other like children cramming their mouths with sweets. Lips kissed the soft down of Warden's throat, moving slowly upwards in search of his mouth as though pressing wine into a chalice. Hands caressed him, his body accommodating to the touch. Darkness vanishing and dissolving about them as though they were lit from within.

Warden felt smooth skin under his fingers, muscles recoiling in motion with them. Warm lips brushed his own, falling over the periphery of sight. Gravelly stroking of stubble across his chest.

Steadfast shapes, swollen, muscular, glistening like ripe fruit at the centre of marble navels, carved torsos.

Flesh strained and shuddered in a sudden trickle of pearls on the tongue like the weeping of surf till they lay shipwrecked, bodies creased and tangled among the sheets. In the faint light from the window their chests heaved with the joy of spent need. The languorous surfeit spilling over onto the sheets.

20

Ivan and Rebekah were sitting in the drawing room when Warden returned. Rebekah was polishing chrome studs on a long leather strap. Ivan, blue locks transformed to flaming red, was talking animatedly on the telephone.

"Hello, everyone!"

"Hello!" Ivan said covering the mouthpiece with his hand. He plumped up his hair with his free hand. "How d'you like me new 'do?"

"Stunning!" Warden said with a wink.

"You're on another cover," Rebekah informed him.

He set his bag down and went to the coffee table where his face gazed back at him from the framed ellipsis of a magazine. He picked it up, trying to recall what photography session had yielded the image, then let it drop with a splash.

"So jaded by success already?" Rebekah asked.

He smiled and shook his head.

"No — just thinking."

"Mmmm — I thought your trip would have cured you of that."

"How was it?" Ivan asked. "Did you have a nice time?"

"Wonderful — I had a great time! I wish you'd both been there with me."

"You were supposed to be resting, not having a great time," Rebekah admonished.

"Oh, it was very relaxing."

"Meet anybody interesting?" Ivan asked.

"Yes, I did, in fact."

"Oh? Do tell," Rebekah said, her fingers continuing their rubbing motion. "I smell an adventure."

"It's nothing, really. I met someone and we spent some time together. I had a very nice time."

"Nice time my eye," Rebekah snorted. "You had a fling — I can see it in your eyes. Now you're blushing, even."

Ivan placed his hand over the mouthpiece again.

"I can't even meet men in London and you find them in remote fishing villages. It's absolutely tragic!"

He removed his hand from over the phone.

"No, no — my place isn't big enough for boxing, I'm afraid," he said to the person on the other end.

"It's his new business," Rebekah whispered in answer to Warden's puzzled look. "He's joined some sort of male escort agency." She held up the object in her hand. "He's got me polishing all sorts of things I don't even know what they're used for."

"Yes, darling, I have whips and chains," Ivan said, and rolled his eyes at Warden. "But believe me, I can get much more inventive than that."

"And he gave out our number without telling me," Rebekah said crossly. "Now he wants me to answer the phone with, 'I'm your transformer' or some such thing, in case it's for him. What if my mother calls? How can I explain that to her?"

"Well, you'll just have to come over and find out then, won't you?" Ivan said, and hung up.

He gestured at Warden loosely with his hand.

"Oh, everything's so difficult these days," he said. "Thank Goddess, you're back. We've missed having a man about the house, haven't we, Beckah?"

"He's been having a fling without telling us," Rebekah said, as though disapproving of an errant child.

"Naughty boy," Ivan said, reaching over and tweaking his ear.

"I didn't say anything about having a fling and you two practically have me married off to someone you've never even seen!"

"Well, we think it's wonderful, of course," Rebekah said. She looked up from her work. "Just think — if you'd never come here at all and stayed in North America you would've ended up married to some woman you didn't love and having a past like Tom Sawyer."

They both looked at her quizzically as she went on polishing.

"Anyway, while I was away I met a very interesting guy," Warden offered.

"In Whitstable?" Rebekah exclaimed. "I find that hard to believe."

"We met on the train from London on the way there, actually."

"Mmmm... ," said Ivan. "That's always fun between whistle stops. Difficult timing it, but definitely fun."

"What's he look like?" Rebekah pressed.

"Tall, good-looking. A little on the tough side."

"Tough! No wonder you're never interested in all those polite young men I introduce you to whenever we go out."

"His hair's cut very short, shaved over the ears, and he has flat, grey eyes that look right through you."

"Bah — and you're not having a fling!" she exclaimed. "I can see the signs. What else do you know about him. What's he do for a living? Is it an economically feasible match?"

"He's a singer, actually. He's got a band called Wheel of Fire. Have you heard of them?"

Warden looked at the two faces staring at him.

"You had a fling with Joshua Behrens?" Rebekah said, incredulous.

"Yes — that's his name. Then you've heard of him."

"My dearest darling, anybody who knows anything knows who Joshua Behrens is. He's London's biggest underground star. It's like asking who the Queen is. If the band would only record they'd be world famous. He's practically a cult hero."

"What's he really like?" Ivan asked, coyly. "Is he as bad as they say?"

"Well, he was a bit 'cheeky' as you Brits would say. He's also very political," Warden said. "He fights for social causes. The band did a lot of work during the anti-apartheid movement."

"Back in the good old days when there were real causes to fight for," Ivan scoffed. "Now all you hear is 'Poll Tax, Poll Tax, Poll Tax'."

"Anyway, he's very nice. I liked him."

"'Nice!'" Rebekah snorted. "I don't think that's a word I'd use to describe that one."

"He's so raw," Ivan said, trilling the word so they all laughed. "If I weren't such a lady I'd ask how he is in bed, you lucky tart, you," he said, tapping Warden's arm.

"Very well-mannered and every inch a gentleman, I'm sure," Rebekah interjected.

* * *

The following evening Warden rang Joshua's number. He listened to the voice that answered, oddly formal and polite in an unexpected way. It suggested a strong, secure world that made him want to enter into it, as though he were standing on a doorstep looking in.

"I'm free this evening. Why don't you come round?" the voice said.

"How do I get there?"

Joshua's house turned out to be in a long row of townhouses. The rain was coming down in convulsive sheets when Warden arrived, making the street lamps shiver like a chalky silver flame.

"My humble abode," Joshua said, closing the door behind him as Warden brushed himself off.

The house was warm inside. Warden followed him down a hall whose walls were cracked and in need of painting. They entered a room where three people sat in tableau looking bored or distracted. The walls were decorated, or not so much decorated as occupied, by strange objects framed and hung up in blazons of colour. A radio emitted an abrasive grid of sound to which no one seemed to be listening.

The others in the room had the air of people engaged in a running argument so habitual it hardly involved passion or the need to listen so much as continual restatement. Blue cigarette smoke hung in meditative layers above their heads. Outside the rain fell without cessation as a necessary counterpart to the lifelessness of the sitters within.

"This is my family," Joshua said in a way which included everyone as if there were no need to individualize or differentiate their massed inertia.

The sitters stirred as though waking from sleep. A tanned, well-dressed woman smiled at Warden, the most fully awake of them all.

"Hello," she said in a smoky voice. "I'm Josh's sister, Tanya." He shook her extended hand. "This is my husband, Bill."

An over-dressed, uncomfortable-looking man turned to Warden, hesitating slightly before offering a hand.

"Good to meet you," he said with an American accent.

"That's Troy over there in a coma," Tanya said, pointing out the final figure in the room.

Warden looked to the far end of the couch where a young man sat in shadow. His dark hair was cut in a lopsided bob, the ragged edges looking as though they'd been severed with a razor. Even in

135

the dark he appeared wan and pale. He held a thin hand up to his forehead, the long, bony fingers obscuring his eyes as though to ward off scrutiny. A ridiculously large ring glittered on one finger.

"Is she still outside?" Joshua said.

"Yes."

It was Troy who answered, surprisingly, as he'd been silent until then. Warden wondered if they were trying to get an escaped cat in from the rain.

"Tiffany, honey, come inside," Joshua said.

He walked over to where a curtain breathed slowly in and out of the room. Warden was startled to see a little girl of four or five staring in at the gathering, a pout of determination on her elfin face as she stood just out of reach of the downpour.

"No, I won't come in."

"Come inside, Tiffany dear — we don't want you to be struck and killed by lightning," Tanya called out brightly.

The pout rippled with rebellion.

"If I die it will be alright because I'll be much happier in another life."

"Tiffany!" Joshua spoke sternly to her. "Come inside now, please."

She stepped in and stood passively in front of him. He crouched down, opening his arms to hug her.

"That's better. Here's someone I'd like you to meet now," he said. "This is Warden."

"Hello, Tiffany," Warden said.

"Are you another uncle?" she asked petulantly.

Joshua picked her up and swung her onto his shoulders.

"I think it's bedtime," Tanya said. "Are you ready for bed yet?"

"I don't want to go," she said, still pouting, clinging to Joshua.

"What if old Josh puts you to bed?" he asked in a gentle voice. He reached up and tickled her till she laughed.

"There now — that's better."

She laughed again. He put her down and took her hand. The pout returned.

"I'll tell you what," he said. "If you come up to bed with me now, I'll take you somewhere special before you go back to America — just the two of us, and we'll really enjoy ourselves."

She pressed her head against his leg.

"I don't want to. If I'm not enjoying myself I'll just sniff some white powder like Aunt Tanya," she said.

A scowl crossed Joshua's face and Tanya looked embarrassed. Joshua took her slowly up the stairs.

"You'll see. We'll visit the swans in the park. Say goodnight to everybody and you'll see them in the morning."

He picked her up again. Her head hung down on his chest, a mask of despair, as she said goodnight and they went upstairs together.

"Bill and I are going out for something to eat, Troy. Do you want to come along with us? We can talk some more," Tanya said, listlessly stubbing out her cigarette.

"Why don't you eat here?" Troy replied.

"There's nothing to eat," she said.

"Sure there is — there's plenty to eat."

"Like what?"

"Well, there's chips and burgers... or there's burgers and chips," he said sarcastically.

Tanya stood up and Bill stirred again. They wandered down the hall, Bill following Tanya.

"We'll be back by eleven o'clock," she said as they went out.

"Suit yourself."

Joshua returned as the front door shut.

"Where'd they go?"

"Off to fill their gullets," Troy replied, coming to life now that they'd gone, as if their presence had been responsible for his immobility. "All they ever do is eat. It must be an American pastime."

Joshua sat next to Warden and pulled a cigarette from a pack.

"When are they leaving?" Troy asked. "They're starting to drive me crazy."

"It's alright, they'll only be here another day or two before they head back."

"They're having problems again. I heard him calling her names in the middle of the night."

"What sort of names?"

"Oh, I don't know — the usual sort."

"Well, don't worry about them. They can't make you go with them against your will and they'll stop soon trying to convince you."

He turned to Warden.

"Would you like some tea?"

"Sure."

"Troy?"

"You know I don't drink tea. How many times do I have to tell you?"

"What did you say?" Joshua asked mockingly.

Troy ignored him. He struggled to open the pocket of his shirt. He slipped something out from between his fingers and put it on his tongue.

"What do you have to take those pills for? I can't get through to you when you're like that."

"I get anxiety attacks. You're giving me one now. And they help me find peace of mind since I can't have any privacy in this fucking hole."

"Do you know what privacy is?" Joshua said. "It's just being alone wherever you are, no matter what's going on around you."

"Well, that's really nice to know," Troy responded. "The next time I'm having an attack I'll stop and think about that one for awhile."

"Look, I'm not saying that drugs don't or can't help. I just don't think habitual use of them is any substitute for peace of mind, or talent, or inspiration or even a shortcut to any of them."

"Jawohl, mein Kommandant, which means, 'Thanks for the advice, Shithead'."

Joshua went to the kitchen and came back with a pot of tea and two cups. Troy watched Warden as he drank. Warden saw him clearly now, pale, delicate features and eyes ringed with emptiness like light locked behind silent halls.

"I've seen you before," Troy said. "You're the Fabiano Boy."

Warden was surprised, not so much at being recognized but that someone like Troy had noticed — and remembered — his face in the layout of a magazine.

"What's this? You're somebody famous, are you?" Joshua said, refilling his cup.

"There's one ad where you had a mask above your head and a sword in your hand. I used to call you the Lone Ranger, like that American hero."

Warden smiled at the description of himself.

"Real heroes don't come from the pages of magazines," he said.

"You have to be ready for anything to happen," Troy replied cryptically, retreating behind his hands again.

Warden watched the boy with the alien features and dark eyes, as if he'd come from a distant star, flickering with a small flame constricted somewhere inside him. He stood shakily. His shadow trembled on the wall behind the couch as if it were unattached to him. Not sure what shape it should assume. It was only then Warden saw how slight he was, his thin figure looking as though it would snap in half like a wafer.

"I'm going out," he announced.

"Are you going to Tabu?" Joshua asked.

"I'm sick of Tabu," he complained. "They're just a bunch of tired old wankers there. All those girls have copied my new hairstyle. I'm sick of it all."

He put on his coat and went out. Joshua shrugged at Warden as if to say there was nothing to be done.

"Welcome to my world," he said. "Troy's problematic, as Tanya is fond of pointing out. She thinks he's in the wrong atmosphere here. They want him to go to America with them. But he won't go. He's a very talented lad. This is his work on the walls. It shows incredible imagination for a seventeen-year-old, don't you think?"

Warden looked around at the objects on the walls. They lingered on the edge of the bizarre. It wasn't painting so much as makeshift collage fixating on the fragmented relics of a modern lifestyle.

The work was populated by creatures — half-human, half-animal — pursued by inner fears and agonies. In one piece, a headless chicken carried a bowl of blood while at its heels a shrieking dog disembowelled itself. Fried-egg shapes leaked out between trees in abrupt concentrations of colour and texture. The pictures were set in frames covered in splashes of paint, lacking all subtlety of application. Joshua touched Warden's shoulder.

"So you are human after all," he said, his mouth set in a grimace that could have been a sneer or an expression of pleasure.

"So far as I know. What made you think otherwise?"

"I thought you might be someone I just dreamed up over the weekend, like the Fabiano Boy."

"That makes two of us then. I hear you're pretty well known yourself."

Joshua laughed.

"For too many things, I'm afraid."

"And here I thought you were just another nice guy," Warden said.

Joshua laughed again.

"No. I may be more and I may be much less, but I'm not just another nice guy."

"And Tiffany... is she your daughter?"

Joshua's face betrayed a momentary look of surprise. It vanished just as quickly.

"Yes, she's mine. She lives with Tanya and Tom. I don't care for the way they bring her up but, as you can see, I have only myself to blame."

"Why?"

"Because I can't raise her. Do I look like a proper parent?"

He stubbed out his cigarette, exhaling the last drag with finality.

"Her mother's an addict," he said. "If Tanya hadn't taken her they would've placed her with a foster home. I have enough with Troy on my hands here. It's all I can do to keep him in school. He wants to be independent but I have to make him see knowledge is important in this world. It's the one thing you can't buy," he said, as though its inaccessibility from commerce were in itself a virtue.

He leaned forward and brushed Warden's lips with a kiss.

"I haven't had a chance to touch you yet. Are you staying the night?"

"I'd like to..."

"Good. Right this way."

In Joshua's room Warden could make out a floor littered with discarded books, clothes and other barely discernible objects. A blue glow like pale fire came from a neon tube hung on the wall in the tangled letters of the word VACANCY.

"I didn't have time to do any decorating before you came," Joshua said, pushing aside sheets and books. "I hope you're not fussy."

"I can handle it."

Joshua pulled him down to the bed, limbs and lips tangling in an embrace.

"We won't be needing this," he said, reaching up to a string above them. He pulled it and the neon sign went out. "You fill up the space well."

"I thought it referred to a state of mind," Warden joked, his hand on Joshua's chest.

"I could get used to this," Joshua murmured.

"What shall we do about it?"

"Let's fall in love and live happily ever after."

"Alright."

21

A week later, Warden was taken to the warehouse where Joshua and his band practised. When he spoke about it, Joshua had made it sound like something between a fall-out shelter and a shrine to radical politics where a small, devoted band of followers lived apart from the mainstream.

From outside it resembled a derelict fort with boarded-up windows and a padlocked door. An overgrown path led to a back entrance with the words NO FEAR ZONE painted in bright red lettering. They made their way into a cavernous space ruled over by giant industrial sculptures and a life-size swordfish replica hanging from the ceiling. The dimly lit walls were obscured by drawings like palaeolithic cave scrawls, depicting bizarre beings and strange acts.

Figures moved about like a colony of nocturnal molluscs, camouflaged and shut out from the light. It was a landscape of spiritous shapes in a cold, flickering light, someone's abortive attempt at founding a new society on barely habitable shores, groping their way tentatively in the darkness. Invested with an immobility born of despair and alienation, they had raised a flag over the bones of the old social order as if to make of the real world a fiction, though it remained unaware of its proclaimed death by the citizens of this secret, reconstituted world. He was seeing in close-up the core of a profound alienation.

A young boy of about thirteen greeted them carrying a rat perched on his shoulder. He wore paramilitary garb with the words 'Affluence Stinks' scrawled across the front of his T-shirt and a cross shaved into the hair over his left ear.

"Hello, Tommy. How's Virus today?" Joshua said.

"He's alright. Had a bit of a scare, though. A big, red tabby almost caught him yesterday."

Joshua rubbed the boy's head affectionately. He walked on as though he'd passed inspection. Others greeted Joshua as if he were a politician making the rounds of his constituency. They came to a doorway and entered a low-ceilinged room housing a fridge and gas stove and a cupboard area stocked with cans and bottles. He struck a match and lit the stove, placing a battered kettle on the metal burner.

"I hope you don't mind roughing it a bit," he said. "This is home to some of the band. It's where we practise. It's also home to a number of others."

"How many people live here?"

"Hard to say — we don't do a census," he said with a wry smile. "From thirty to sixty at any given time. It depends largely on the season and the economy."

"Rebekah and Ivan have taken me to a lot of really different places since I've been here, but this is really... different," Warden added with a comical shrug.

"Pussycats, darling," Joshua said, straddling a chair across from him. "There's a whole world here your trendy little friends have never seen. You couldn't understand it, not being born here. Not unless you grew up in the English class structure and saw how people live their whole lives trying to fulfil someone else's expectations."

He got up again, lighting a cigarette at the stove, walking animatedly around the room. He attempted to explain why those who lived at the space, known as Sanctuary, had chosen to withdraw from society rather than suffer its ills or try changing the system from within. He himself, he claimed, was still willing to try to change things and to that end Wheel of Fire had been formed.

"What do you stand for?" Warden asked, feeling naïve in the face of so much political theorizing.

Joshua stopped pacing and looked at him. "Ourselves... and liberty... the freedom to be who we are without having to fight to survive in this system of greed and corruption. Just because we're born into this world doesn't mean we have to accept things we feel are fundamentally wrong."

It was in this underground arena that Wheel of Fire had been spawned from the shared ideas of a handful of social delinquents struggling towards a new vision, a way out of the moribund and cynical twentieth century. Here they gathered and dreamed of a new reign, a new frontier, burning the old letter of the law. They belonged neither to the right nor the left, Joshua insisted. Together they had come to mistrust the mechanistic promises of socialism, yet despised the selfish ideals of capitalism. It was a retreat born of despair and frustration from the failure of all political promises.

"Life is obscene. I often feel there's no hope for society and unless it changes it will eventually destroy itself. Sometimes I think doing anything at all to change things is just prolonging it. You either float along with the scum on the surface or you go underground — they leave you no choice. It's the only way to be when you're powerless."

Warden watched the sudden coming and going of emotion on his face, remembering the harshness of Joshua's words on the train and the surprising gentleness of his touch the next evening. His face bore the solemnity of a child contemplating a world of wonders while in his eyes lurked a subterranean angel dreaming of destruction.

The kettle whistle blew. Joshua flicked his cigarette onto the cement floor. There was an underlying intensity with which he did everything — even smoking was a rebellion, not a pleasure, not even a pose or an attitude for him. It was a strike at society's hierarchies which he instinctively defied even in repose.

"Are you always so serious?" Warden asked, as Joshua placed a cup on the table in front of him.

"I think I pretty well am, actually. There's not really a lot I find amusing in this world." He looked directly at Warden. "Though you make me feel like a teenager again. I found everyone so antiseptic and fawning till I met you," he said, taking Warden's face in his hands.

*　*　*

When they woke, it was early afternoon. Light seeped through the cracks in the ceiling. Warden ran his fingers over Joshua's chest. Joshua moaned, half-asleep, and reached a hand out towards him.

"What time is it?"

"Past noon. I had an appointment this morning... I guess I missed it."

"Important?"

"Mmmm... sort of."

"Well, then, don't worry. They'll make you another one."

"Do you always sleep in this late?"

"Sometimes. Usually later."

Warden sat up to pull on his shorts. Joshua rolled over and put an arm around his waist.

"Where are you going? Did I say you could leave?"

He felt lips brush softly against his back.

"I don't remember asking you. Besides, I thought you were still asleep."

"What? After I've let you molest me and get me all aroused?"

143

Joshua lifted the sheets to reveal an ample erection. "Don't think you'll get off that easily."

"You'll have to adjust," Warden said, slipping from his grasp.

He pulled aside a corner of the blanket on the window. The sky was clear with tall clouds in the distance. Joshua raised his arms like a crab scuttling away from the light. A dusting of chest hair showed in the crook of an arm where it bent to cover his face.

"Coward," Warden said, slipping on a T-shirt. "We've missed it anyway. The day, I mean."

"Nothing to miss," said Joshua. "Nothing of consequence ever happens in the daytime."

"Except your sleep, I suppose."

They left Sanctuary to walk through a park. A man in tattered clothes stood by the gate with his hat extended. Four gangly youths with shaved heads and dirty clothes had gathered, watching him. He waited nervously.

"Do you want money?" the tallest youth asked. "Is that why you've got your hat out like that?"

"Yes," he answered warily.

"So do I. I want money," said the boy in a deceptively polite voice. "I want your hat, too."

Another boy in a brown and green shirt struck a wooden match and flicked it towards the man's hat. It grazed his sleeve and fell smoking to the sidewalk. A second match bounced off his chest while a third landed inside the upturned hat.

"I want his cane," said another boy, joking with his friends.

More matches flew at the man, striking him and falling to the ground. He stood stiffly, barely moving. The first youth reached out and took a coin from the hat and flipped it into the air.

"What's this, lads — are you stealing from the blind now?" Joshua asked.

They laughed gruffly.

"Ahh — we're just having a little fun, Josh," said the tallest boy. "No law against that, is there?"

"Don't steal from the poor, lads. That's what the government's for. You need to be like Robin Hood — steal from the rich and give it back to poor sods like this one."

He took the coin from the boy's hand and let it fall back into the hat. Warden watched them scatter and disappear into the park, skipping stones and balancing on fences like any other twelve-year-olds.

144

"They respect you," Warden remarked when they'd gone.

"Why shouldn't they? We're all family here," Joshua replied. "This is my neighbourhood and I've been around for about a million years."

Warden wondered how he saw himself. As soldier or saviour? As innocence corrupted or holding out arms to embrace a shattered world? He could be furious with the world's injustices one moment, then human and kind, loving its weaknesses and imperfections the next. He seemed to want to make a heaven out of earth, unable to leave behind the wounded of the world, taking them all into his hands one at a time.

* * *

Warden travelled all spring as Calvino sent him a steady flow of work. Each time he returned to Maura's they treated him on his arrival the way he'd seen them do with the big star of the summer before. He was never long in one place and easily lost track of where his image would turn up next.

On one magazine cover, a lock of hair curled charmingly over his forehead made Rebekah proclaim him a movie star. Elizabeth Smart herself placed it as the opening shot in his new portfolio which she sent abroad. Although he had ceased to be amazed where his face would pop up next, Rebekah continued to exclaim over each appearance, buying several copies of anything in which he appeared. He was amused as she palmed the glowing pages of the magazines, her face alight with pleasure.

"For God's sake, Rebekah, you practically live with the man. What do you need all those pictures of him for?" Ivan chided.

"I've never known anyone so beautiful before," Rebekah gushed one day when they were alone. "I think I shall always love him."

Because of the unpredictability of his schedule, Warden found himself pulled into Joshua's lifestyle as his own slowly turned around. Frequently they slept overnight at Sanctuary. Lying in one another's arms they seemed to be listening to a noise in close-up, a fever burning in the very marrow of their bones as though their hearts were on fire. The greased, polished machines of their bodies barely appeased the hunger that fed on itself, leaving them both trembling afterwards.

Living at night and sleeping in till afternoon, Warden often found himself going out just before midnight. Three times in one month he showed up at photo shoots looking so haggard they had to be rescheduled. His booker sent him to a tanning salon to get some colour in his pale face. When he missed a flight to Italy one day because he failed to wake up, a whole day's shooting had to be rearranged. Calvino was furious.

"What do you mean you overslept? I would rather you tell me you were in an accident. I am very angry with you for this!"

He apologized and caught a later flight so he'd be there that evening and have time to rest for the next day. It was the 'bad' behaviour of the lazy models who were too successful that both Jimmy and Calvino warned him about when he started working. He promised himself he would do better.

22

If Joshua Behrens and Wheel of Fire were unknown it was simply because they refused to record their music or promote themselves other than through public performances. Among the youthful crowd that considered itself in the know, they were among its worst kept secrets.

Had the group chosen a commercial route to success they could have walked quickly into the heart of the music world. Their aim, however, was not artistic progress but rather political affiliation against what they perceived as the forces of power and corruption, including such hallowed institutions as the recording industry. Instead, they aligned themselves with the practitioners of cult following, quickly becoming the new messiahs of underground culture.

Warden first saw them perform at an anti-drug protest. The event seemed in actuality to be not so much a rally against but rather in praise of drug use in all but name. Heroin was making its comeback as the drug of choice for a new generation of dispossessed youth. The auditorium was filled with the nervous energy of junky hands and bodies when they arrived, an ethereal band of magi drawn onward by a dull, deceitful star.

The venue had once been a theatre of aristocratic bearings. Now covered in day-glo spray paint, it had buried its past beneath the lurid colours, giving up the ghosts and melodies of music-hall nostalgia. Its interior was gutted and the seats removed to turn it into a dance floor. Along its walls a forest of scaffolding supported light and sound systems. Bodies clung to the gridwork, barnacles buoyed high above the sea of moving shapes on the floor below.

On-stage a band dressed in Santa outfits thrashed frantically. The song's nearly incomprehensible lyrics matched the violence of the music while dancers slammed heedlessly into one another. The singer cried out, 'Dance! Dance! Dance the Armageddon!', urging the participants on in their nihilistic fury. Warden watched with fascination as bodies on the floor collided with one another again and again.

"It's what they used to call slam-dancing," Joshua said in answer to Warden's curious looks.

Someone let loose a bag of feathers, sending thick handfuls floating upward in the blue and red lights playing over the crowd. A body fell — or jumped, rather, for it seemed a self-willed act — from the scaffolding and landed on the crowd below, knocking down several dancers and disorienting others with the force of its fall. The dancing continued without pause as did the shedding of physical inhibitions at an even greater rate. Another body belly-flopped into the crowd from the hightowers as the band wound up its frenzy of masturbatory violence.

"What are they doing?" Warden asked in disbelief.

"It's a kind of ritual," Joshua answered. "They take one or two out a night in ambulances. The others are luckier."

Acts of total cathartic destruction seemed the intent as things were shattered and shredded all around. A couple copulated on the floor beside the stage. The music ground on and feathers floated upwards. Everything seemed a pretence for posturing or destruction. As though either could come with unwitting ease. Someone attempting to scramble on-stage was smacked over the head with a guitar by one of the Santa-suited musicians, sprawling backwards into the crowd.

"I hope he's alright," Warden said.

"He'll be alright when he wakes up in the morning. Sid Vicious used to do that sort of thing here and it's been the same ever since," Joshua answered, as though it were merely a matter of history.

Warden sensed a dominion of pieces over the whole as a wanton eclecticism became the order of the day. Love and sex and violence mingling casually in a snarl of sensation. A dark netherworld existing solely by reason of its own desire, creating its own rules of order. They were as frivolous, Warden thought, as the hedonist fashion crowds bent on their forms of pleasure.

This was a culture erected on the belief that there was no longer any culture, and everyone wanted to partake of the spoils. Its message was not a denial of the past so much as a total renunciation of the future, as though anything beyond today were not merely insupportable, but almost unthinkable. An all-consuming present was the only conceivable reality. The new vulgarity had come to demand its reign and for the moment the world was lit by a new light burning with sickening excess.

"Welcome to the abyss of unmeaning," Joshua said as they picked their way through the crowd.

The band on stage had finished its set, tearing their Santa suits to shreds at the end of the song, already having annihilated everything else around them while feathers whirled in the air. The crowd continued dancing like elements in chaos even after the noise from the instruments stopped.

Joshua left him to go backstage. Warden watched as the band made its way on. Joshua came out last wearing the tattered Chanel No. 5 T-shirt which had become his trademark at performances, a symbol for the anti-fashion crowds who demanded their icons of status as much as any other. Lights flashed on and Warden felt himself momentarily blinded.

Joshua stepped into the light, taking refuge in its momentary radiance. A bass note pulsed as he reached toward the microphone. Percussive sounds joined the bass, giving direction to its formless urges. Feathers continued to fall from above.

"You know who we are," Joshua's deep voice boomed over their heads.

There was scattered cheering as though to say the crowd did know who was addressing them.

"I'd like to say we're glad to be here as part of this protest today in urging everyone to take the issue of drug abuse seriously. And we do... hope you're taking it seriously."

A guitar joined in, creating a smooth surface as he broke into song, his presence magically aloof like an intoxicated god prancing before them. His voice contained a boyish wistfulness, a solitary note of hope and joy weighed down by despair, the sound of rain burning. It seemed to lift the darkness overhead, releasing them from the dismal truths of a world whose redemption lay in self-destructive impulses. His shadow fell over them, hands raised in absolution through the rays of light as he stood contemplating the world caught in his gleaming fist.

The band played three songs and then, their set over, slipped out as the applause roared after them. Stage hands rushed out to make arrangements for the next act before chaos again took hold of the audience.

After the performance, Warden brought Joshua to meet Rebekah and Ivan at a nightclub in Soho. Rebekah arrived in a tuxedo, hair slicked back from her forehead. Ivan wore a strapless gown with a fur stole, greeting them with extravagant waves and kisses from across the room. The crowd turned to look.

"Ivan, you're gorgeous!" Warden gushed.

"D'you like it?" he asked, twirling to display the costume. "I've been working on it for weeks."

"Versace would kill to say it was one of his creations."

Ivan raised a gloved hand to his brow as though overwhelmed by the compliment.

"Darling," he said, turning to Rebekah. "We'll have to keep this one around. He's good for a girl's ego."

Joshua quietly surveyed the outrageous couple as Warden introduced them. He had worried about bringing them together, remembering Joshua's tendency to bridle at anything he didn't approve of. The frivolity of those he considered privileged was always a pet peeve.

"Charmed," said Ivan, stretching out a gloved hand. "It's not every day one gets to meet musical royalty."

Joshua took the hand proffered as though unsure whether to shake or kiss it, but Ivan pulled it from his grasp before he could decide.

"That's enough for now — you can come back for seconds later if you want more."

"Most people find once is more than enough," Rebekah interjected.

"Darling, you're just jealous because I'm more beautiful than you for once."

Ivan and Rebekah settled in across the table.

"You make a lovely couple," Warden joked.

"And so do you two," Rebekah said.

"I expect you'll be getting married any day now," Ivan said with a sigh.

"Ivy — you're brilliant!" Rebekah exclaimed. "What a wonderful idea!"

"What did I say?" Ivan asked.

"A celebrity wedding, Ivy! Just think of it! 'Famed gay pop singer marries top male model!'" she stated with all the vehemence of a newspaper headline.

She turned excitedly to Warden and Joshua. "You must! And it'll have to be some place really special like St. Paul's with a real ceremony and full regalia. And it'll definitely have to be a drag wedding," she declared, the idea growing as she went along. "We'll put Ivy in charge of all the costumes."

"My sense of taste and styling is second to none," Ivan concurred.

"But only close friends will come in drag. The guests will have to dress normally and content themselves with being ordinary," she stated. "We need to show the world that not every gay man's a wimp and every dyke a lady truck driver. What do you think? It's brilliant, isn't it?"

Warden tensed, waiting for Joshua's response, expecting at the very least a curt reply to her question, but he just laughed and put his arm around Warden's shoulder.

"Alright," he said. "St. Paul's it is. You're in charge, then. And I'm telling you now, I look hideous in lilac."

23

Wheel of Fire's original mandate had been based on an agreement by the band's members not to pursue popularity or commercial success. Except for what was needed to support themselves they turned over their earnings to maintain Sanctuary as a rehearsal space and haven for others. Once they found themselves in vogue, however, the question of recording was brought up again and again as they were frequently approached by representatives of recording companies.

Joshua was in favour of the enterprise. He was supported in this by three other members. Only Jah, the group's drummer, was opposed, seeing it as a betrayal of their vow to remain a vital political force undiminished by commercial concerns. He chastised the others for wanting to transgress their ideals, warning them they would find their aims compromised and fallen.

"It's a way of spreading our beliefs and finding a wider audience than we could reach strictly by performing," argued Kareem, the group's bassist.

Jah shook his head soberly, his multicoloured dreadlocks moving in concurrence with his dissent.

"That's not the point," he broke in sharply. "We've agreed that private property is public theft. If we make a recording we are creating a product to be marketed. We're turning our ideas and our music into an object for consumption. And it won't stop there — these record companies are already talking about our image as if it's something to manipulate to make their product more marketable. I say it's a total sham," he declared.

Apart from Jah, the other members were willing at least to consider the offers. Eventually a compromise was reached, with a recording made by an independent label to be sold only in smaller record shops with a reputation for fairness. Larger chains and department stores were circumvented entirely.

So practised at the art of obscurity were they, they didn't even put names or photographs on the cover of their one project, making not the slightest concession to commerce or popularity. This did not deter the hordes of fans who knew of the collection long before its release proper, however. Nor did it prevent them from making pirated copies of their own.

The recording was made without editing or sound-enhancing technology of any kind. They were one-take performances with all the flaws enshrined — feedback squeals, wrong notes, erratic rhythms — lionized like flaws in the face of life itself, the creators proud that none of their skills had been engineered or manufactured in recording the powerful raw energy of their sound.

With the circumspect release of the recording, Wheel of Fire became the darlings of the musical press as well as the legions of underground fans who had long been aware of their existence. The media quickly took up the cry, hailing them as a brave new presence on the musical scene, until the band parodied the press itself as sycophantic followers of musical fashion in a song called 'Media Whores'.

Joshua had several run-ins with journalists who were perplexed by the idealism of his beliefs in contrast to the sudden surges of temper with which he expressed them. He began to be portrayed as a young man full of anger for everything, including himself. The other band members were characterized as both heroes and clowns, while the crowds attending performances grew with every barrage against them.

That summer the band was occupied between playing engagements and negotiations for filming a video. The song 'Don't You Think I Know' portrayed a spurned lover following his beloved through her conquest of hip society like a modern-day Orpheus' descent into the underworld with his cynical observations of all she has become in the process, cataloguing the regrets of his unrequited love along the way.

At Joshua's urging, Warden was cast as the neglected lover in pursuit of his beloved. Warden asked Joshua why he wanted him in the video rather than himself.

"Because you're prettier than me, that's why," he said.

The song proved to be a surprise dance-floor hit with its blend of rock and ska taking over the volume dials of the hippest dance stations. A pop-scene tabloid writing up the video described it as 'banal, paste-up punk', declaring Warden the sole point of interest, describing his face as one 'that unfolded slowly, petal by petal, like a rose in bloom'.

In the clubs they were greeted with the aura of celebrities, dancing on the floor while their images played in giant form on the luminous screens above. They watched as Warden's face came to life along with the sound of Joshua's penetrating voice. On any given night an emcee might stop the show to point out their presence to the audience.

Nights were bursting with possibilities. They had achieved the illusory suspension of movement, the holding of time in one's hands, as they drew all the glitter and brilliance in around them, retreating from the restless shores of the everyday that devoured life.

The music beat on as video screens threw light on the dance floors and the partying went on as though no one worked at 7 am that day or the next day or any day ever. Time was marked by the frenzied comings and goings of the party crowd colliding on their way home with workers rushing to repeat all their yesterdays over and over again, wearing blank looks on their faces as though they'd lost something precious and couldn't remember what it was in the harsh glare of morning, grateful at least for the numbness routine afforded them.

Warden was never sure exactly where he fit into Joshua's life, straddled as he was between hip society and the fashion mainstream, an anomaly in either case. The latter he knew to be a mere veneer stretched so thin it could scarcely be called a facade, rather just the illusion of a facade, which changed its face at every moment.

Joshua's world claimed depth and meaning while offering poses of rebellion and cynicism as its consumer products, glorifying the tragic and pathetic. He was not fooled by the demand for freedoms it had not earned nor the right to ignorance and apathy it readily claimed for its own.

Still, he could not just step out of either world into one entirely of his own making. Both had, to some degree, claimed him for their own. He was as much the Fabiano Boy to the first group as he was the lover in Wheel of Fire's video to the second. The question remained to what degree he could still claim to be himself.

* * *

The band's growing prominence in London's underground gave way to an interest in the personalities behind the scenes. The watchful eyes of the media flickered over the exotic figures dwelling among them. Sanctuary had become home to any number of wanderers and refugees from the narrow pathways of society. From within its walls emerged characters whose dress and appearance were worthy of the indiscreet stares of passers-by and neighbours who could not quite fathom the alternate society harboured in their own humble borough.

One day Warden was introduced to Maurice, a hulking black man with the gentlest eyes he'd ever seen. Maurice was a refugee from a guerrilla movement that had been instrumental in helping to dismantle apartheid in South Africa. Two years earlier his wife and children had been killed in a raid on their village in retaliation for his involvement. He fled the country knowing it wouldn't be long till he was caught and killed as well.

Maurice enthralled Warden with stories of sabotage aimed at the government. He was well-known for his ability to dynamite power installations, causing massive blackouts, without human casualty. His efforts disrupted the country, bringing chaos to the regime. Public support grew with each successful attempt. Money appeared stuffed in envelopes at the group's headquarters as Maurice became a folk hero among the population.

Warden became used to sitting in on the fervent meetings convened to discuss possible ways to aid people like Maurice in reclaiming their lives. It astonished him to think how his own life had changed. The long, grey vistas of his staid Canadian existence seemed light years behind him now, finding himself plunked down in a hotbed of rebellion, contemplating first-hand issues he'd known only as ideas in books and newspapers before leaving home.

Maurice suddenly disappeared from Sanctuary one day, leaving no trace he'd ever been there. When Warden asked where he'd gone, Joshua merely replied that he was 'too hot' for them to harbour any longer. A week passed. One night the police raided the warehouse, using a drug search as an excuse to tear the place apart with axes and physical force. Little was found of interest. Two runaways were seized and everyone was questioned.

"Where were you earlier this evening?" a surly bobby demanded of Joshua, taking down his name.

"At choir practice," he replied sarcastically.

"Don't give me any smart business!"

"Don't you believe me?" Joshua asked.

He began to sing the opening phrase of 'Ave Maria' to the amusement of those listening.

"Shut your bloody yap!" the officer yelled, cuffing him so his lip bled. "I know who you are, you piece of AIDS-bait."

Warden lunged forward to come between them, but Kareem held him back by the arms.

"Don't get into it, mate," he warned quietly. "You'll only make it worse for all of us."

The event was recorded with great diligence by the press who smelled a larger issue behind that of general rebelliousness and the notorious lifestyles of outrageous pop stars. The attention already focused on them continued to grow.

* * *

Throughout the summer Warden flew back and forth between England and Italy. Fabiano continued to use him to promote the coming year's fashions after receiving strong reactions to his ads. Once again the photographer was Andreo. When he returned to Milan at the end of June the new billboards were up. Response to the campaign was overwhelming. Warden was asked to attend a publicity event with some of the corporation heads who had requested to meet their star.

"What'll I say?" he asked Andreo that afternoon, unconvinced he should go, though Calvino urged him to stay the extra two days and accept the offer.

"Just say something so honest they'll think you're being witty,"

Andreo replied. "Corporation heads are very stupid."

He phoned Joshua in the afternoon. The voice that answered was groggy and thick with sleep.

"I just wanted to hear your voice. You sound so far away."

"I miss you, little fashion prince. When are you coming home?"

"Tuesday, I think. There's a publicity event I'm supposed to attend tomorrow night."

"Well, make it soon. I miss you."

"Alright — I miss you, too."

* * *

In London a typical weekend went by with the impact of a mushroom cloud. Invitations appeared as if by manifestation of pure will. New clubs and venues were continually coming into existence for the sake of those who could not bear to be in the same place as they had been a year before, as though new surroundings indicated some external sign of progress.

At the height of it, clubs seemed to open and close with the quickness of a fan, causing a brief flutter of air currents before lapsing into memory. Sometimes it seemed as though weekends never really began or ended but simply merged into one another around an unspecified mid-point of any given week merely for the distinction of calling one successive and the other regressive.

A new club, Radiation, vied with the established venues for the privilege of turning away patrons from its constricted interior one hot summer night. It had been designed to resemble a nuclear reactor with a glowing green dance floor. The florescent interior represented a world framed by its own nuclear anxiety. Ivan came dressed as a well-known member of the royal family, but the guise was more of a deterrent than an insurance to his admission.

"Let me through," he screamed. "I'm a close relation of the Queen's and I can have you shot."

No one paid much attention to the screaming drag queen griping about a lack of appreciation for creativity. Both Warden and Rebekah would also have been turned away, perhaps having neither menacing nor creative enough appearances to satisfy the brooding miscreant at the door, himself a victim of some private holocaust of muscle and bone. The doorman seemed dimly aware of Joshua's identity, however, and finally let them enter.

The interior was ablaze in a haze of light as they wandered

among creatures both sacred and odd. They danced and drank what seemed like a tremendous amount and no one paid any attention to the hour. The lights on the ceiling shone like a holocaust moon and after awhile it had simply become time to move on. Rebekah appeared suddenly, taking him by the arm as they flowed out into the glittering night moving like a spectacular mist breathed over them by the city's secret life.

They arrived somewhere and entered a building where they travelled up many long flights of stairs to the top floor where everyone seemed to be dressed in drag of some sort — anything to evade the truth of what it was they were or might be — vanishing behind clothes, make-up and hats as easily as behind attitudes and poses.

Figures smoking numerous cigarettes went by, trailing endless furs with flocks of jewellery like some sort of glamorous kitsch in a dazzling new aesthetic. Pillbox hats with veils seemed to be all the rage. There was one floating down every staircase or passing by at arm's length, just out of reach.

The hostess, a woman — or maybe a man, no one seemed quite sure — wore a gold satin gown with enormous shoulders as though Joan Crawford had been resurrected for the evening. Her hands were covered in immense glittering rings. She appeared before them like a twentieth-century Marie Antoinette, all coquetry and charm, with her curious collection of guests. She waved to Joshua, then spied Warden for the first time and made a great fuss, shrieking and holding onto him.

"At last I get to meet the young man in your life," she exclaimed, surveying him and spinning him around. "He's altogether lovely!" she cried, fussing over Warden a moment before turning abruptly. "Well, darlings, enjoy yourselves — there's a whole world of madness in here," she declared as she went off to greet the newest arrival.

Rebekah soon found someone she knew and Ivan floated off in hopes of meeting other royalty. They disappeared from around him complaining of asthma or harassment or anything at all as strange hair styles and outrageous fashions moved through the crowd. After awhile even Joshua disappeared. Warden remembered meeting a woman who told him her son had been in a coma for over a month. Just the day before he had been thrashing about, she said. Finally, just as she thought he might die, he regained consciousness that afternoon.

"But I just had to come out tonight anyway," she told him, as though asking his pardon for enjoying herself. "You understand, I know."

He smiled and nodded as people winked by like elemental properties reacting to currents of change. At one point he found himself in a bathroom the size of most living rooms, its walls and ceiling painted entirely black. A life-sized mannequin with blood-red fingernails proffered hand towels. Warden stood over the toilet, concentrating his aim to hit the bowl. Something stirred to his right. He looked over to see a man lying fully clothed in the bathtub, legs extended over the lip.

"Why don't you come and piss on me?" the man said. He held out an empty glass. "Do you give free samples?"

The door opened and Joshua peered in.

"Everything alright?" he asked.

Warden smiled drunkenly. The man in the bathtub looked Joshua up and down.

"How 'bout the two of you together, then?" he said.

"Let's go," Joshua said quietly to Warden, then stepped over and turned on the shower. The last thing Warden recalled was seeing the man in the tub don a pair of dark glasses under the stream of water.

The next day Ivan recounted the end of the party. At four in the morning a crowd arrived, climbing the stairs in a long queue led by a well-known London drag-queen. In they marched, lifting their feet in tandem like a troop of soldiers, picking things up and breaking them as they went along. Spilling perfume in toilets, tearing down curtains, smashing vases. The hostess, he recalled, managed to restrain her temper until she discovered someone had eaten all her orchids and spat them out on the carpet.

At six, the police were finally called in by an exasperated neighbour while the remaining guests threw knickers and brassieres at them from the windows above. Meanwhile, Ivan had wandered out onto the balcony, leaning over until he found himself face to face with 'a mad old cow' living in the adjacent flat. She stretched a gloved arm across the divide and introduced herself as la Contessa di Castleville. She was 76 years old, dressed all in black and kept thirteen cats. Ivan promptly joined her in his own royalty drag and sat amusing her until nearly eight o'clock. As he left, he addressed her by her royal title. She hastened to invite him back, saying, "You must call me Agnes, dear — just you and nobody else."

24

Within a year and a half of embarking on his career Warden had been photographed on more than a hundred separate occasions, appearing on the covers of five magazines. One Italian periodical, reviewing the decade's fresh crop of models, dubbed his "the face that turned on a nation", referring specifically to the Fabiano ad with the trumpet for which Andreo had won an advertising industry award.

At a newsstand one day a face caught his eye as he flipped through a magazine. Broad cheekbones, sparkling eyes, mysterious smile. The face bore an ingenuous charm, as though the model had not been posing but rather sitting casually across a table in a café sipping coffee and happened to look up just as the shutter was snapped.

"Qui est cette fille... ?" read the caption beneath. From what he could make out, the intrigue of the model, who had photographed with only one photographer, was that she was entirely unknown, had no agency and had never appeared in public. The photographer was Andreo. The face was his own.

Warden flushed with embarrassment. He paid for the magazine and brought it home. In the flat he compared his image to the one in the magazine. His reflection in the mirror revealed how much he had changed in less than a year. He was altering rapidly, turning from a boy whose fluid androgynous features could pass for a young woman's into the solid angularity of a man. His face would never again pass for anything but what it was. Its structure, its architecture, had changed irrevocably.

Rebekah knocked and opened the door, calling out. He tried to hide the magazine but she grabbed it from him.

"Oh, ho!" she said knowingly. "Getting vain, are we? Or just worried you can't live up to your image? Don't worry, you're not losing it."

She smiled and looked at the photo she held in her hands.

"Oh, my!" she said, looking back at Warden.

Warden was ready to admit the truth and have a good laugh with her over it.

"A secret love? Who is this woman? She's incredible!"

He smiled as it dawned on him that Rebekah suspected nothing. It was not till several months later that she would learn how he had been talked into performing the trompe l'oeil with his image.

"Nobody suspects a thing," Andreo told him over the phone the very next day. "They loved the photographs so much that I had to release them, bello. They wanted to use you both for next year's campaign. I had to talk them out of it. 'Who is she?' they kept asking. 'What agency is she working for?' etcetera, etcetera. Boring me with their questions. I told them she doesn't have one and I've never seen her since — which is the truth, is it not? As far as the agencies are concerned, they all want her and yet she doesn't exist. That's the best one yet, don't you think?"

Warden could hear Andreo chuckling to himself over his own joke.

*　　*　　*

At the beginning of July Wheel of Fire headlined at an anti-racist benefit. Twenty thousand showed up at the outdoor arena to give support to the event spanning an entire afternoon and evening, with six groups performing in total. Wheel of Fire was scheduled second last. The crowd was tired and restless, having sat through more than six hours of speakers and performers by the time the emcee came out to announce their appearance.

"We've got to show the world that we won't put up with it any longer, that there is a political conscience and it has a voice!" his voice boomed into the evening sky. "And for that reason, it is my great pleasure this evening to introduce to you a group that has become synonymous with its support for social causes and its ability to speak for those who have no voice of their own!"

There was polite response to his words but the applause grew steadily as the band made its way onto the makeshift stage surrounded by a sea of faces. At Joshua's appearance the crowd took on the sound of one mouth cheering. Lights snapped on like thunder as fingers shaped a pulsating rhythm. Warden watched Joshua exhorting, singing, his body straining with the effort. Voice soft one moment then furious the next, thrilling them with its urgent inflections.

A ring of young boys sat in front of the stage, heads keeping time to the music, wearing hard stares and Chanel T-shirts and red bandannas just like the figure cavorting on-stage. Their eyes were intent on Joshua, mouth pulled back in a perpetual sneer, crooning and snarling out the words to the songs.

They'd saved their hit number for last and the crowd was on its feet dancing to the waves of sound. The song ended suddenly as a hand mike flew into the air. Lights blinked out like quickly discarded crystal. The band slipped away in the darkness to the solid cheering of the crowd.

Backstage they were met by a small band of journalists. The group's members shuffled past, declining to comment. Joshua had consented to speak on behalf of the benefit, yet the majority of questions were directed at him. When pressed about the band's future he merely acknowledged they were considering an extensive tour. A woman with a shrill voice who seemed to have no idea whom she was addressing asked Joshua to what he attributed the band's "popularity and phenomenally successful career".

"I didn't know we had one," he said with a wry grin as the other reporters laughed. "But whatever success we've had has come through following our own mandate instead of seeking to satisfy public desire."

"How do you see the role of the artist in society?" an earnest-looking young man asked as microphones extended towards Joshua's face.

"First of all, I don't think artists can detach themselves from the social or political issues of the times in which they live. The purpose of Wheel of Fire and other groups like ours is to stimulate action and provoke change. Given a consistent show of conscience like the one exhibited here tonight, I think we're doing just that."

"You've got a new look, Josh," someone yelled.

Joshua grinned and ran a hand through his hair which had grown longer since Warden met him.

"Yeah — sleek and vicious. That's me. But don't worry, I'm still the same simple boy I used to be."

A few of the reporters laughed, sensing a new, easy-going manner.

"You'll be in *Teen Tales* before you know it," someone else said.

"That'll be the day," he retorted.

"How is your model friend affecting you?" a voice asked.

Joshua turned to scrutinize the enquirer. He recognized the mustachioed face and critical gaze of a journalist from *Headset*, a trendy weekly publication that purported to cover news and culture with a social conscience. He'd been among the first to be down on the band when the press attacked them.

"All my friends affect me," Joshua retorted, his voice cool and noncommittal.

"That's very touching," the reporter replied.

Warden watched Joshua's face strain and tighten. The woman journalist inadvertently defused the situation.

"What would you say is the difference between London and New York?" she asked, as though she'd cribbed her questions from a *Rolling Stone* guide to rock interviews.

"About five hours," Joshua quipped. "I thought everyone knew that."

More laughter. The activist reporter persisted.

"What about charges that Wheel of Fire has sold out?"

"What about them?"

"*Fuschia Schock* and *Fetish* magazines both reported you as the face to watch this year. You've just made your first recording and now you're even making videos. For a band with such a strong stance against publicity that adds up to a lot of coverage."

"I'm this year's face, am I? And last year you wrote that I was the arsehole to watch for. I was last year's this and next year's that. You'll have served up the whole of my anatomy before you're through."

Nervous laughter.

"Isn't it all just a wind-up, this evasion of publicity thing?" suggested another reporter. "You're just making yourselves more intriguing. What you're really after is popularity, isn't it?"

Joshua turned to face him.

"Perhaps that's how it looks from where you are, but I don't see it that way at all. You see, we put up with people like you because you help to get our ideas across. That's precisely the point of benefit concerts like today's. But don't mistake that for wanting popularity. I don't want your acceptance."

"Acceptance clears, Joshua," someone suggested.

"So does money," added the mustachioed journalist, smirking at his own wit.

Joshua's eyes glinted.

"How much have you given to AIDS research lately?" he spat out.

Microphones were held tensely outwards, like hostile forces made nervous by their proximity to the enemy.

"You see," he went on, "we're all just stepping stones in the ultimate revolution of life. Neither you nor I are the end result of any of it. If you don't like that, you'd better ask for a transfer off the planet."

The interview over, he brushed past them through the narrow corridors of hastily planned walls and floors, stepping over wire coils and electronic equipment. Warden followed. Outside they were greeted by hordes of fans, mostly teenaged boys. Joshua hastily signed a handful of autographs then slipped through the gates with Warden behind him. Neither one spoke till they were back at Sanctuary making tea on the gas stove under the harsh electric bulb. Joshua sat at the table smoking angrily.

"They really loved you, all those people tonight," Warden finally ventured.

"Because they jump up and down and scream and try to look like me? They don't even know who I am."

Warden shrugged, placing the teapot on the table.

"Imitation is admiration — it's flattery."

"Imitation is your business, isn't it?" Joshua retorted.

The words cut through him. Joshua spoke angrily as though he saw in Warden's comment all he despised, the lies and treachery emanating from every nook of discreet society, its academies of sin and the perjury of conformity against which he was constantly waging a private war, obsessed by the glaring red eye of his demons.

"You've got to stop thinking so methodically, Ward. Imitation is just a cheap attempt to own something that's not yours. It's just more consumerism."

Joshua stared across the table at him, his face inaccessible, refusing to let anything penetrate beyond his own principles and beliefs, which were inviolable. Joshua held up a hand.

"What have I got here?" he asked.

"A hand."

"What else?"

"Five fingers."

"Right — those are your five senses," he stated. "And if I cut them off what have I got?"

"A stump?" Warden tried to joke.

"Freedom. Rid yourself of the prison of the senses," he said, curling his hand into a fist. "Then you can fight. Don't you understand yet? That's all there is. If you don't see that, you know nothing."

He seemed to want to eliminate every hold the world had over him. To Joshua, the known face of fact was reducible to a solitary

162

state of mind, separating and resolving all the contradictions of flesh in an effortless annihilation of everything outside himself.

"Why can't you be happy with what you have, without worrying about why it's there or trying to pick it apart, if only for one day? You live in a world of absolutes. The rest of us aren't strong enough to do that."

Joshua looked at Warden as though suddenly realizing he was not alone. His face softened. He put a hand around the back of Warden's neck and smiled in that reassuring way he had of turning worlds around in a single glance.

"I don't think I was ever really happy until I met you," he said. "But you don't know what I'm like inside. You can't know. You're too pure."

It sounded almost like censure, or a warning, rather than praise, a land whose beauty was too rugged to be enjoyed by a passing tourist ignorant of its dangers.

"I know who you are," Warden stated. "I couldn't love you if I didn't."

The cool gaze met him from across the table. It seemed in that moment they moved forward an infinitesimal amount, bridging their incongruous backgrounds till the differences had begun to seem less significant.

"Anyway, I guess what's important is that you know yourself, how far you'd allow yourself to go. That's what really counts in the end."

Joshua offered his hand across the table. Warden gripped it, reassured, like coming home to find the house lights already on, gleaming in the distance.

"You know I'd do anything for you," he said.

*   *   *

Less than a week later, Warden arrived at Sanctuary to find the band sitting around the performing area. Jah straddled a dilapidated couch across from Joshua, his feet slung over the edge. The others waited, attention focused on the two original members of the band.

"It's all become a sell-out, Josh." It was Jah speaking. "We promised ourselves we wouldn't go the way of all commercial bands and that's exactly what we've done."

Warden sat quietly to one side and listened.

"What do you want, then?" Joshua said.

He paused. "I want out. I've had an offer to veejay for a club in Brixton. I can't take it anymore. We're turning into pop idols. We've let them take our image and put it in a wrapper for people to buy like some cheap product. It's exactly what we've been against from the very beginning."

Joshua looked to the remaining members. "What about the rest of you?"

"We're with you, Josh," Kareem said, not looking at Jah. The others nodded their consent.

"Alright," he said. "Looks like we're still on as a band, then." He looked back over to Jah. "What about Sanctuary, Jah? Don't you believe in that anymore either?"

"I'll be leaving soon." Jah hesitated. "You're just going to end up becoming a part of everything we've stood against."

"I'll take that chance," he replied.

Jah stood to leave, glaring at Warden as he went. Joshua turned and saw him sitting there.

"Know any good drummers?" he quipped.

He seemed to be containing his feelings in front of the others. Later, sitting alone, Warden sensed the anger he felt over Jah's defection and his parting comments.

"He says we're becoming too popular! What's the point in having something to say if you don't let anyone hear it?"

He ran his hand irritably through his hair. He was angrier that someone should suggest he'd based his actions on ego or pride than that his oldest friend and associate should be leaving.

"Can't he see that we're just at the point where it's all beginning to add up to something?"

His self-searching made him question his own motives, but gave no answers to the contradictions lying under his skin like points of vulnerability, while his principles stiffened with each assault. The anger flared up and died again quickly, subverted to quiet cynicism.

"You know, my whole life I've never done what I was told," he said. "When I was a little boy my mother warned me never to look directly at the eclipse of the sun, so of course I just had to," he said. "Do you know why I did that?"

"No — why?"

"I was hoping you could tell me. Maybe it was so I could have a cute little dog and learn to read braille."

25

On Sundays Rebekah and Ivan hosted an open house for artists in their flat. Warden invited Joshua and his brother, Troy, who brought a portfolio of his work. Among these was a collage of various photographs of Warden cut from magazines. In the middle of the piece Warden sat under the bough of a tree sheltering him from a malevolent sky. His head was split open with a bottle of coke and a canister of Chanel cologne pouring into it. In the background a series of imaginary animals boarded an ark in a long procession. Troy had titled it 'The Mortality of Heroes'.

Rebekah pronounced it 'brilliant' and took to Troy immediately. She offered to introduce him to several important art collectors who could include him in their galleries. She also asked for one of his pieces to hang in their flat as the work of an up-and-coming young artist about town. Troy was thrilled by the attention, becoming quite animated around her.

The room had filled with guests deliberating over wine and hors d'oeuvres passed around on silver trays by immaculate waiters. Joshua sat on the floor by the fireplace away from the others. Cradling a cup of tea in his hands, he unsettled the room with his tindery gaze. He had a genius for altering the metaphysical weight of his presence, to darken or lighten it at will and make it act on his surroundings and those near him.

Joshua was not swayed by Rebekah's glamour or her social connections, as evidenced by the well-heeled crowd around them. His reputation as artist and cult figure, however, had an effect on her. When she asked curiously about Wheel of Fire and Sanctuary, he answered with surly disinterest. Troy interrupted them.

"You mean that squat with all those oddballs and their social politics? Boring. Just give me the money and I'll run with it as far as I can get, thanks kindly."

"Hear! Hear!" cried Rebekah, jubilant at having found someone who shared her cynical sense of humour. "Three cheers for the grossest forms of avarice!"

Her voice rose and fell excitedly as she chattered. For the first time since meeting her Warden wished she would be quiet. The accusations Joshua had turned aside from the previous week, that he was becoming part of all he once despised, weighed heavily on him. There in the flat he was surrounded by a reminder of all he reviled in the glitter and pretence of a superficial world.

He sat, snapping small twigs between his fingers, ensnaring their questioning glances while his eyes stalked the room like a panther. In his shabby, almost tattered clothes, he looked out of place in the elegant quarters. He suffered the gathering resentfully, a deceptive calm on his features belying the potential eruptions beneath the surface. His mouth tightened at the frivolity around him.

"Why did you bring me here?"

"Don't worry — we won't stay long," Warden told him. "I'll just say hello to everyone and then we can sneak out."

Troy, Rebekah and Ivan clustered around an art critic who praised Troy's work in a cultivated accent as though he were a newly discovered prodigy. He discussed his creation in light of the emergence of a new trend he termed 'naïve creativity', praising and comparing it favourably with artistry of a more formal design.

A woman standing nearby asked if he considered suffering to be all-important to the artist's vision. He laughed, not unkindly, at the notion that it was the personal purgatory of the artist that makes the inner self ripe for artistic pronouncements.

"While it's true suffering can build character," he conceded, "so, too, does success in a most extraordinary way. And of the two I can tell you which I would prefer to suffer from."

The group broke up in polite laughter. Warden looked at the paunchy little man fingering his glass of wine deftly in one hand and pointing at the crowd with his neatly-trimmed beard. He went on to name a number of artists who had increased their output of notable works in accordance with their fame and success. Joshua remained by the fire, a look of smouldering offense in his eyes at the witticisms being unspooled with great ostentation around the room.

Rebekah, discerning his mood but not the cause, attempted to lighten the situation by announcing her plans to host a wedding for Joshua and Warden. She began gleefully describing her proposal for the event. Joshua looked up at her contemptuously.

"My life is not a social event — stop trying to host it," he snapped.

Heads lifted, half turned towards the scene, and then resumed their merry buzzing. The critic continued.

"Thus I would urge you to affiliate yourself with a commercial institution," he told Troy. "They'll put your talents to good use and make a rich man out of you in no time. Witness van Gogh," he said. "Had someone promoted his work he would have been a wealthy man while he was alive, and probably lived a lot longer. Instead, having sold only one painting in his lifetime and been reviled as a madman, he is now seen to be the most influential artist of the twentieth century with, perhaps, the sole exception of Picasso."

Joshua's eyes glittered weirdly in the room's crystalline lights. He stood and turned towards the critic.

"He probably would have painted a lot of shit for the rest of his life and lived to regret it. The price of art is simply the gauge of someone's desire to appropriate. And desire is easy to manipulate, as any good hooker or drug peddler will tell you. It has nothing to do with the value of art and less with the worth of any artist, living or dead."

"You may be right," the critic said in his clipped phrasing. "But, ultimately, what it comes down to is who has the money and what that person is interested in purchasing. That is what most idealists — and I assume you to be one — fail to recognize. We live in a material world. And art is merely a commodity."

Eyes in the crowd moved back to Joshua, as though watching the movements of opposing players across a game field.

"Given the opportunity, artists can contribute to the social consciousness of their time. Many artists influence the choices made by the next generation by pointing out the mistakes of the present one."

"Ah, sadly I must disagree with you. For if art seeks such aims, then it is no longer art but politics or, rather, propaganda. In any case, I'm not here to debate the worth of such causes, meritorious as they may be. I'm here merely to purchase — which, you will be quick to point out, being the intelligent man you've shown yourself to be, in days past was called 'plunder and pillage' and which now invests itself with the politer, more politic term of 'commerce'."

He returned his attention to Troy.

"Which is why, I repeat, you must work in the commercial realm. There's always room for a good artist in the corporate stables."

"Hear! Hear!" Joshua cried, raising his cup to the room. "To sheep everywhere!"

He emptied it and set it down on the table. No one moved.

"You may not agree with what I say but you could at least be a gentleman about it," said the art expert, beginning to show a crack in his surface cool.

"You mean we should lie to one another and call it good manners?"

The others listened in embarrassed silence. Troy watched with a mixture of apprehension and anger at having his success spoiled by political philosophies he cared nothing for.

"There's no need to be abusive, Joshua," Rebekah broke in to chide him.

He turned to her.

"Excuse me, did you bleat?"

People moved away, turning to stare from a distance.

"You're all so polite and witty here," Joshua went on. "How does it feel to know you're the best that society has to offer?" He singled out Rebekah again. "You with your Miss Dalrymple smile and your pretty manners — who do you think you're fooling with your upper-class attitudes? You'd tart it up for anybody with money or reputation. Lady, indeed."

Ivan lifted a glass to his lips, his delicate fingers crowned with a lacy sleeve.

"Now, now, dearie — don't be vulgar. We still have to respect you in the morning, if only for the missus' sake," he said.

"And you... " He turned to Ivan. "I never know whether to treat you as a man or a woman. Where are your tits?"

Ivan bridled.

"I'm not in drag."

"Not in drag? Oh, thorry — me neither. It must be a hormone deficiency. Period. That's it — it must be your period."

He turned to face the room.

"You're all just a product of your class."

"And what should we be products of?" Rebekah snapped.

"How about your brains?"

Joshua turned and left. The drinking and chattering resumed as people breathed sighs of relief that the hurricane would not come their way. They quickly recovered their lost attitudes and poses, like the last of a great era burdened with a social responsibility they had never wanted.

Rebekah reached for Warden's hand.

"It's alright, go after him — I'll make apologies for you," she said, smiling sadly. "People understand what artists are like."

"I don't think Joshua would want to be apologized for."

Joshua was at Sanctuary, smoking and sitting on the performing space when Warden arrived. He crouched down before him, putting his hand on Joshua's knee where a rip in the denim left a patch of skin bare to the touch.

"You didn't wait for me," he said quietly.

Joshua sat looking away as though he hadn't heard. Suddenly exhaled a harsh cloud of smoke. He brought a glowing butt up to his mouth before flicking it onto the concrete floor.

"We don't have to do everything together," he said.

"No, of course we don't... " Warden began to say.

Joshua cut him off.

"Stop patronizing me! You sound like those bloody arses back there. 'Yes, please.' 'No, thanks kindly.' They make me sick with their feigned politeness, as if their stiff little formalities and witty comments make them superior."

"Yes, you made that quite clear."

"Jah was right — I am getting sucked right into it, becoming a part of it all."

"What does Jah know? He sells phoney philosophy the way some people sell cheap watches. What's wrong with you anyway? All I ever get anymore is your bullshit anger directed at me because I happen to be closest in line."

Eyes averted. Smouldering as if they would ignite the floor. After a moment, he spoke again.

"Do you remember Maurice, the black chap who was here before that big bust-up?"

"Yes. Of course."

"He's gotten in touch with me. I've got to go underground for awhile."

Warden stared uncomprehendingly for a moment as he took in what he was saying. Feeling like a fool for not having seen it already. He crouched before Joshua, aware for the first time of cracks that had appeared — he didn't know when — disparate ideals, worlds separating them like a sea of dissatisfactions. He shook his head softly.

"What... you want to go away? You never told me this... " he said softly. "To do what?"

"There's a political group Maurice has got connected with. They work against oppressive regimes in different countries. It's something I should have been doing already."

"And what about me — were you going to ask me to go with you?"

"It's too dangerous, this work we have planned. You're not

meant to be a target for bullets."

"And what makes you so privileged?"

Joshua's eyes carried in them the cold light of reason of the person he'd encountered on the train a year before. Whatever else had been there had vanished, like a flame fallen into a pool of melted wax of its own making, drowning in its desires and extinguishing itself.

"Where do you think we're going together, Ward? Look at us. We have different ideals and goals. We just compromise one another trying to fit into each other's lives."

"Is that what you think? Is that all I mean to you? What about love, Josh? Or is that just something you experience between you and twenty thousand people at an anti-racism protest? Are you even capable of loving just one person? Is that why you can't raise your own daughter?"

Joshua glared, face defiant with the burning agitation of misappropriated justice for every wrong that had ever happened, that ever could happen. Yet the look was limp instead of rigid. The defiance was more an absent-minded protest holding itself in place, a pose he'd perfected and didn't know how to give up.

"You just don't get it, do you?"

"What's to get? I love you. I try so hard to be someone you can love, to be what you want. I really make an effort to fit into your world."

"That's just it, isn't it? You can't be something you're not. You can't just put it on like new clothes. It's all just another pose, another trot down the catwalk for you."

"That's not fair!"

Joshua turned his head, dismissing him with a wave of his hand.

"Don't you love me?" Warden demanded, a challenge more than a question. "Did you ever love me?"

Joshua turned back to him.

"Love is a selfish emotion, Ward. It wants to own — to possess. You can't possess another human being."

A thought running through his head. *He's throwing me away.* Warden grabbed him by the shirt and pulled him violently around.

"I am talking about us, goddamn it! I don't want your fucking philosophy!"

Joshua did not move to release his grip.

"What good does love do? Can it stop suffering? Does it feed the hungry or help with injustice? How can we hide our heads in the sand and call it love? Do you think you can solve people's problems with love?"

Warden stared for a second, then his face contorted. He curled his hand into a fist and smashed it into the face that had enraged him.

"There's your five fucking senses, you asshole!" he screamed. Tears like surprised children peering out from his eyes. "Say something, you jerk! Hit me back!"

Carried by the force of his anger, he lashed out again, harder. Joshua staggered slightly, putting up his arms to ward off further blows. He rubbed his cheek where he had been hit, as though contemplating a strange thought. Not looking at Warden.

"You think you're so goddamn noble and above it all, don't you? You're just another egotistical asshole preaching that we're all better off dead while you steal all the joy and pleasure in the world instead of letting others enjoy it."

Joshua turned to look at him. "Give it up, Warden. We can't spend our lives propping one another up with emotional crutches."

"My God! You actually believe this crap... !" Warden began.

He looked as if he would say more but the moment passed — or else there was nothing to say — and he went outside and sat on the steps along the path. After a moment he heard the door open. He turned to see Joshua walking towards him. Face calm, like a saint. Free from all desire as if barely aware of his own passing without need or want in a universe of pain and suffering.

Their mouths met in a violent kiss. Warden pulled back to see Joshua looking down at him from a cool distance. Something in his appearance spoke of a brief marriage of anger and love, as if this moment of betrayal had been contained in him from the beginning. As if somehow it had all been planned to happen just like this, at this very moment, and it could not have been otherwise. A thief raiding his heart.

"You were right, Ward. You're a much better person than I am. You're nobler — purer. Perhaps one day I'll catch up," he said, as if it were a light he had borrowed, returning it now with casual attention, no longer terrified of the dark.

"I thought you were a true individual, Joshua, but you're just a sheep of another colour."

"I never said I was anything but what I am."

Warden looked up. His heart held, as though waiting for the first drop of rain while all around him the wind stirred in the darkness. Strange to look on the face he loved most to find it had changed into something he could no longer recognize. Where there had once been two Joshuas, one loving and kind, with a willingness to trust and hope, and another who spoke only with learned emotion, now, filling the space inhabited by its predecessors there was a new spirit consumed by a despairing belief in the ultimate cipher of its own existence, penetrating everything like winter's cold.

"Don't you see this is all there is, Ward? We have to do what we feel is right in whatever way we can."

"What about your music? Aren't you doing there what you most want to be doing?"

It was a desperate stab in the dark. Warden knew it would not sway him.

"We're just preaching to the converted now. What good does that do? And how long does it take to show results?" He held up his fist. "This is all there is — right here, right now."

Warden looked up as though to find a hole he'd fallen from ages ago, to return through it and seal it behind him so no one would ever have to fall through again. He wondered how he could fit back there, looking up at the sky, ceiling without end.

"Are you alright?" Joshua asked.

"Yes — I'm sorry I hit you."

"Friends, then?"

"Friends," he said nodding, trying to smile, wondering what he should miss first in all the darkness and emptiness surrounding him. Feeling like the unicorn that it would perhaps be better to miss this trip than to go it alone.

He looked at Joshua's face intent on annihilating the Tree of Knowledge of Good and Evil all by himself. As he sat there a sound caught his ear like a low note pulled on a cello and dying slowly, receding, till he recognized it as the drone of an engine passing on a distant street. He thought of the houses spreading out around them, into the city and beyond, the darkness behind the windows, the silence in each room. Above, branches glowed black in the moonlight while banks of clouds like anonymous armies carrying banners passed by like scarves in the silk hands of time.

Part IV:
All the Fallen Sons

26

At the end of August an offer came to work on Ibiza again. Warden accepted, looking forward to leaving London for a respite from the familiar things which bore the face of all he was missing.

He had effected a complete separation from Joshua, or rather, Joshua had disappeared from view. He no longer received news about him from friends or heard announcements of the band's performances, if they still existed. Even the radio seemed to be sparing him the pain of hearing their music, at least in the daytime. He'd gotten his life back on an even keel, avoiding the night-time hangouts and endless parties of the week-long weekends, once more tending to his career and spending quiet hours at home.

The show on Ibiza went quickly, with a single run-through in the afternoon. The other models showed him the polite deference reserved for colleagues known to them by reputation only. After rehearsal he went off to eat, sitting alone in a café under the late summer sun. He felt removed from it all.

In the evening, after the show, he mingled with the crowds on the boardwalk. Couples strolled by in half-shadows while the moon hovered like a hollow wafer on the horizon. The sky looked alien to him, as though he'd never seen those particular stars before. While he'd been caught up in the memory of something else they'd changed, and were still changing, as though unable to settle into a new order.

At an open café a band plied the night air with a fugitive beat. The music stretched like taffy as people swayed, laughing and dancing, restless with the illusion life seemed to be offering. The sounds splintered, fragmenting the old and the familiar as if to find some spontaneity within, though old the moment they were born. Along the beach, clubs rained arabesques of light and sound against the black nimbus of sky. Screams of delight spilled into the warm air.

None of it seemed to hold.

What was it for, all the movement and fury, he wondered? To overload the head. To blind the heart. To grasp at something as far off as the stars in their mute simplicity, unmoved, untouched by the baboon wail rebounding from nameless shores. He understood it at last, the baboon's dance, that irresistible urge to twist and shout the night away in a frenzied contortion like a group howl at the moon designed to keep the light at bay.

The beach glowed like a restless sliver of sand as he walked along. The wind trailed behind in flickering shadows, the whole universe an empty cul-de-sac that took on the shape of nothingness. Above, the stars wheeled by in magisterial perfection, a band of voiceless vagabonds drunk on their aimless wanderings, like dice playing at being a loveless god. He felt a passing, mute and slow. Stars dropping into a bottomless canyon, as if forever fallen from grace.

* * *

In September, Warden flew to Milan to meet with the representatives of a German cologne company. They were conducting a search for a face to personify their newly created men's fragrance, offering an exclusive six-figure contract to the right model. To Warden, both his career and Italy seemed too distant to merit attention, let alone interest.

He arrived in the city in the early afternoon. Light streamed from the sky. He made his way to the Albergo Sirtori, carrying his bags up the stairs. It was uncharacteristically quiet, unlike when he'd first stayed there.

Irena appeared on the steps behind him. Warden set down his bags and smiled.

"Ciao, Irena."

Her face flushed with momentary pleasure when she saw him, then settled into something less welcoming. "Ciao, Warden," she said hesitantly, pushing a wisp of hair behind her ear.

"I'm only here for a few days. I was hoping you could put me up," he said, sensing the uncertainty in her voice. "But if you're full I'll go somewhere else."

She made a gesture with her hands that was half-apologetic, half-something else.

"It's not that," she said.

She told him she had not allowed models to stay at the albergo in more than six months. In the last year, she'd had money stolen and several of the rooms had been broken into by someone using keys taken from the desk. She'd threatened to take the whole modelling contingent and report them to the passport agency, jeopardizing their livelihood in Italy. At present, a high-school band was staying there.

"It's alright," he said, picking up his bags.

She looked as if she couldn't make up her mind, then relented, lifting her arms in welcome. She would take him in, she said. He had always behaved well before. She put him in a single room on the top floor next to the rooftop patio.

At his old agency he was greeted with effusiveness by Calvino and the others. The lobby was filled with curious faces, none of whom he recognized, a whole new crop replacing the models he'd worked with the summer before.

The meeting with the cologne company representatives was being held in the agency so both Calvino and Maura could attend. Calvino reminded him it was an important meeting. It would be the biggest thing he'd been offered so far. There was only one other model they were considering, a young man based with a rival Paris agency. He and Warden had started together and done as well in the same period of time.

After a few minutes Calvino called Warden into the conference room. He introduced Warden to the executives, then took his seat beside Maura who sat smiling harshly in a corner. Warden shook hands with the four men who wore nearly identical brown suits, suggesting that their identities depended somehow on being in close proximity to one another. He listened as they described their product and the proposed campaign and what they were looking for by way of an image. What appealed to them most about his, they said, was the refreshing wholesomeness which had, thanks to proper rest, returned to his features, none the worse for the wear and tear of his life in the past year.

He sat distractedly while the interviewers went through his portfolio, asking questions that had little to do with anything, he thought. He felt impatient with their finicky attention. Calvino began to look annoyed. Maura's face betrayed something like fear. When at last they were finished he thanked them and left the room. Calvino rushed out to call him back but he had already gone.

Warden called Valentino that evening, hoping to meet with him. A trail of letters between them had died out the previous spring. Valentino's mother answered, saying her son was in his second year of training. She remembered him, she said, and would pass his greeting along.

In the trattoria all the familiar faces were gone, though he received a nod from the old padre behind the bar, shirt still unpressed. The International Table, its traditions long since forgotten, had been taken over by tourists with expensive cameras mopping their sweating brows.

Warden walked slowly back to the albergo. Sun lit up the courtyard, the soft rays falling in a hush. The school band was out performing and the place was empty. Even Irena's children were not around to disturb the quiet.

He went to bed early, waking occasionally through the night, feeling caught at the edge of an abyss. He sat up, struggling for realization of what was troubling him. Consciousness, returning from the ends of the universe, answered unequivocally. It was Joshua's absence affecting him with the quiet ineluctability of waves rolling up on an empty beach.

The next day he arrived at Andreo's studio carrying an armload of white lilies. The photographer came out immediately, crushing both Warden and the lilies in an ecstatic hug. He released him and took the proffered flowers in their tissue like an enveloping halo, holding them in his arms like a baby.

"So lovely," he said. "Such exquisite flowers to eat up all my oxygen."

And then his laugh, like colours dissolving in the air.

"Va bene. How are you, my boy? You look more beautiful than when I last saw you. How do you do it? You must reveal to me your secret and we will make millions together. Even my photographs do not have such lasting power."

In the studio, Andreo showed him a series of advertisements he'd been working on for Jean-Paul Gaultier. "I like to work with this man because his imagination is as crazy as mine. There is nothing I can do to shock him," he said with a smile.

He brushed a lock of shaggy hair from his face, standing over a tabletop covered in the requisite piles of photographs and papers.

"And now," he said, when he had put away the proofs and taken Warden by the hand, "you must tell me what it is making your bright eyes so dull and unhappy this day."

Warden told him of his life in London over the previous months, and of his eventual parting with Joshua. Andreo sat and listened with compassion. When he spoke, it was neither deferential nor patronizing, but as one who accepted and understood everything.

"But that is very sad," he said. "Who knows why God gives us someone for our very own with one hand and then takes them away with another?"

To Warden, it had been a shock to find himself thus betrayed, like a boy who expected always to be a child waking one morning to discover dark silky hairs growing in the secret places of his body.

"I felt like we were heading along in the right direction, but somehow we missed the turn-off. And now it's too late to go back."

"Ah! You're feeling sorry for yourself because things did not work out as you wanted. You must beware of falling in love with the dream, bello. I warned you that what I create with you — all those pretty pictures, those beautiful clothes and people — must be left inside the pages of books and magazines. Did you think whenever you wanted you could go back to it like you fly off to Paris or London and find that it will always be exactly as it was when you left? Those things can blind you if you let them. It is another existence we pass through for a minute and then we must let it go when we are through."

"Then what good is it?"

Andreo smiled.

"Like anything worth having, it is worthwhile only as it gives itself to you. You must let things be as they will. Dreams have a way of becoming a terribly commonplace reality when they come true."

Andreo motioned for Warden to sit. He took a seat beside him.

"Now I will tell you a secret: when I first started taking pictures for the famous fashion designers I was delighted and felt myself to be in heaven. It was a privilege to photograph all those brave, handsome knights and lovely maidens in their new creations. They were beautiful, the clothes were beautiful, my photographs were beautiful. I was so happy!"

He looked over to see if his audience of one were enjoying the performance.

"Then, one day, I started listening to some of these people and the words coming from their mouths. Madonna mia! I had made a dreadful mistake. They were all beautiful on the outside but inside they were very silly, like children. Only they were not children! I felt I had fooled myself and everyone around me, just like these designers who make up their silly creations and tell the world that everyone must wear them to be beautiful and important this year. That is why now, when I take my pictures, I pretend I am walking through a beanfield listening to a lot of beautiful, stupid vegetables. And when I stand still and take my pictures, I pretend I am a scarecrow and if I am in a bad mood I will wave my arms around and shout to startle the beans and keep the crows away."

Warden was laughing.

"Do you think the truth must always be so beautiful, Warden? In this world where everywhere we must look on the appearance of injustice and suffering? The truth may set us free, but it will hurt us first. Perhaps that is what your friend Joshua was trying to tell you."

"He believed in one thing, I believe in another. He wants to help people by taking direct action because he doesn't believe in anything beyond the here and now. For Joshua that's all there is. For some reason I have more patience — or apathy, he would call it."

Andreo laughed kindly and put his hand on Warden's shoulder.

"A philosophy that condemns the material world yet admits only of our physical existence is the most material one of all, it seems to me. It is hard to believe in anything beyond what we can see and feel. Things stay, love goes. This much we know. It is very difficult to see beyond that. For myself, there are many things I would like to believe in: charity, kindness, generosity. But when I look into the faces around me I see only emptiness mirrored back."

Andreo shrugged, releasing his grip on Warden's shoulder. He stood and walked over to his desk.

"I am not boring you, am I?"

"No — go on."

"Tell me — if love were a colour, what would it be? Red like a beating heart? Or purple with passion? What do you think?"

"I think love would be colourless," Warden said after a moment.

Andreo smiled. "You are probably right," he said. He pulled a large portfolio from his desk drawer and held it out to Warden. Its pages were filled with photographs of children, some poorly dressed, others somewhat better-off. In one, an adolescent boy supported himself on a pair of crutches, his left leg ending in a stump wrapped in rags.

"Here you see the exquisite flower of politics," Andreo said. "These are the children of war — political wars, economic wars. There are many kinds of struggle in this world, many places needing healing hands and hearts."

Warden took the book into his hands, touching the cool plastic covers protecting the photographs. Page after page revealed dozens of similar images. The through-line, the connecting principle of each, was the brilliant smile Andreo had coaxed out of each child, despite their conditions.

"When humankind has pity on all things, only then will we be a noble race," Andreo said, turning a page before his eyes.

Warden felt his breath catch, a quick fluttering as though a small bird had become trapped inside his ribs. He stared at the barely recognizable features of a child's face disfigured by fire. The boy grasped a tiny, orange kitten tightly to his chest. His features radiated not the obvious pain and sorrow of his condition but an instantly recognizable human joy and beauty beyond the suffering and disfiguration.

"What makes me dwell on the fact a child has died or is in pain? Why not just forget about it and go on with my business? Do you think I imagine I can change such terrible things or stop the suffering by taking my pictures? What can I do?"

Warden looked up at him. He shook his head dumbly.

"So what good is it, you must be thinking, that one silly man takes his pictures and remembers such things when others forget? I tell you. It is like television. Even when it is raining outside I can turn it on and find the sun shining elsewhere. It helps me remember we can create a world better than the miserable one we have here. These photographs let me know something exists beyond the sorrow and the suffering."

He closed the book.

"Somehow we must believe in miracles," Andreo went on. "In my plain way I am trying to show people the vacant inaccessibility of our lives, how we leave ourselves unopened to one another. We must be simple and caring — there is nothing else."

Andreo reached out to take one of Warden's hands in his own. "You are a very privileged person, Warden, because you have been allowed to bring beauty into this world. Your image is written on the face of it."

He looked over to his camera.

"And I have been allowed to capture it, and for that I shall always be grateful."

27

While waiting for the cologne company's decision, Warden made plans to return home. He felt as though he'd suddenly awakened to the realities of a full-fledged winter coming on. Grief and mourning intact, he was ready to face his family.

The east coast of Canada opened like a wound, bleak and empty in the dawn. Banks of fog hung over grey water, peeled back here and there to reveal small, icy crags on the Newfoundland coast. It offered little more to viewers from above than it had to the Vikings a millennium earlier, leaving scant traces to attest to their hard-won presence on the barren rock. They floated by like a feather in mid-air, trespassing above the unchanging landscape.

Lisa met him, walking breezily towards him through the airport lounge, cigarette in hand. She hugged him fondly, then lifted one of his bags as they headed out to the car.

"Welcome back to Trauma, big brother," she joked. "You've come home to a cauldron of burned nerves and poisoned minds, my own mostly. Mom hardly talks to me and Dad swears I'm not his daughter anymore. School has just about done me in. By the way, I got my license yesterday, so you're taking your life in your hands."

Sunlight lit up the car interior as they joined a long line of traffic jostling into the city, snaking under and over the concrete bypasses. Along the highway, trees burned into the sky with a speckled drift of colours attesting to the advancing autumn. He could have been starting back at university in his final year. Except for everything that had happened.

"It's only my first month and already I'm miserable. I study all night and spend most of the day sleeping. I rarely see anyone except when Mom brings a tray of food to my room. Usually she just leaves it outside the door."

"No doubt Dad's been giving you the When-you're-through-it-will-all-have-been-worth-it speech," Warden chuckled.

"I have that one memorized by heart. The competition to get

into university was vicious. I don't know why. I've never seen so many rats clawing to be let inside a cage before. But now that I'm in, I just may stay. I've already decided whatever it is out there they call life I want no part of. I haven't read a paper in weeks. When I do I just flip to the TV guide to catch all the re-runs of *Let's Make A Deal*. Better than life itself. And much easier."

She stabbed out her cigarette and looked over at him.

"And how are you, Ward-Boy? How's your friend the pop singer?"

"It's over," he said matter-of-factly.

"Oh-oh. I knew something was wrong. You hadn't written in awhile. I'm sorry to hear it, if sympathy will help. I've got a monopoly on it these days"

"I'm alright."

"Well, I hope so. You're going to have a lot of smiling to do while you're here. I need some help getting back into Mom and Dad's good graces again."

In his room the linen seemed freshly changed, though the bed probably hadn't been slept in since he was last home. His mother came out from the kitchen wiping her hands on an apron. Lunch was ready and the three of them sat down to eat together.

After Warden's nomadic lifestyle of the past eighteen months, home life felt reassuringly mundane. He once again belonged there with all that was settled and solid. His mother seemed happy and even surprised him by expressing an interest when he suggested an outing later in the week. When his father returned from work they caught up on one another's lives, eating supper and watching the news together. Warden found himself thinking that for once he was doing what he wanted to do, instead of what was expected of him.

After two days, he phoned Milan to find out if there had been any word from the cologne people. He heard Calvino's wine-coloured voice on the line as it rose and fell in soft undulations.

"They don't know whether they want you or not, darling. They think you're becoming over-exposed."

"What did you tell them?"

"I told them that your price was going up soon."

When Warden hung up there was a vacancy of feeling where he should have felt a surge of regret. He realized he didn't care, as though there were no place left inside him to accommodate any more feeling.

He went for a walk downtown. The Toronto skyline had grown

but the streets were empty. Nothing seemed familiar in the tall buildings as he passed through the business district. Lights gleamed in the falling dusk with the impermeability of money.

When he returned, his mother was upstairs in her room. Lisa had gone out with friends. He talked with his father awhile, both of them stabbing at various subjects with little success till the buzzer on the kitchen stove sounded. They ate supper as though in a series of gestures of diminishing significance engaged in solely to protract the time. After washing the dishes Warden tried to read, but his attention faltered. He thought of phoning Ivan and Rebekah, though he knew it would be the middle of the night there and realized he had nothing to say that couldn't wait another day. Or even until he got back.

When his father went to bed Warden curled up on the couch and picked up his book again. He woke to find the book closed on the floor beside him. His forehead throbbed. Flickering shades of red and purple covered the wall going up the stairs.

The light emerged from beneath his mother's door along with the sound of soft voices. He knocked and entered. A TV cast ghostly rays around the room. His mother was asleep. She looked ageless beneath the covers as he stood there, guarding her from he knew not what, watching the face of the first woman he'd ever loved in the light of late-night re-runs, distant worlds inhabiting places in time as far off as other galaxies.

Around the room faces stared down at him, the spectres of a gleaming shadowland gallery. Great-aunts and -uncles. Forgotten family gatherings. Children long since grown and raising children of their own. Warden studied a wedding photograph of his parents, his mother in a white dress, long hair trailing over her shoulders, his father in a stiff black tuxedo. They were watching him back, those lovers about to become his parents. Had they foreseen this moment years hence when they would be perceived thus by their son? They posed as if they were there still, looking down at him from their place on the wall. He wasn't sure when he realized she was really watching. She began talking about an advertisement she'd seen him in recently.

"I thought you had eye make-up on," she said gently.

He was embarrassed.

"Yes — I did, I think," he said.

"We'll have to trade make-up secrets someday, honey," she said and they both laughed.

He was struck with a sudden urge to consume her, to crush her in a grip that would last forever or annihilate them both, keeping her with him long after she had gone, like a photograph, only to release her when he chose. He realized there was so much missing between them, all the things that had happened to him. Too much ever to catch up on. He wanted to tell her about Joshua and his music, how his eyes looked at night and the sound of his voice, the rough comfort of his arms and all the things he'd wanted to do to help others in the world.

"Mom... "

He began and stopped, looking down at her.

"What, dear?"

"Nothing — everything."

"That's a lot — could you say it a little slower, do you think?"

"Well, I just wanted to tell you things... about me."

He faltered.

"Like what?" she said, her voice as soft and startling as a first snow.

"Well, I had a friend... and... I guess I just wanted to tell you about him."

She reached out a hand towards him.

"Was he a good friend?"

"I think he was the best friend I've ever had — except for you."

And suddenly he was crushing her in his arms in a single motion that carried him across the space between himself and her bed and he couldn't be sure which pain he was feeling, whether for having missed her or for losing Joshua. And then he was telling her all the things he wanted to tell her about Joshua, and Rebekah, and Ivan's multicoloured hair, as she caressed his head and wiped his tears.

"Where is he now?" she wanted to know.

"I don't know — still in London somewhere, I guess."

"You must have loved him very much."

Her voice was like a child's, full of belief in Christmas and miracles. She spoke with the lucidity and clarity of those who see over great distances at a single glance.

"Love is the most elusive thing of all," she said. "When we find it we often make the mistake of trying to hold on too tightly. But you will find it can span any distance, any time — the fuller the heart gets the lighter it becomes."

They lay together unspeaking for awhile.

"Will you be going back soon?" she asked.

"I hadn't really thought about it — I could probably stay for awhile," he said.

"You mustn't stay too long," she said. "You have your career to think of now."

He started to protest but knew she was right and there was no sense in the pretence of an argument.

"Do you remember when you were a little boy how you would sit with your face pressed right up against the TV screen? I would bring you your dinner and put it on the floor beside you not to disturb you."

He laughed at the memory.

"You were my golden child," she said. "You made the world beautiful for me. You asked so many questions I knew I could never answer. You wanted to know everything right away."

They talked awhile, then silence came in to regain possession of the room. Sometime later he awoke with a start. Had she cried out? He heard his heart beating like a ghostly drum. The fuzzed-over TV screen, signed off for the night, had retreated to a vacant landscape of petrified dreams. He got up and turned it off. His mother slept.

A glow crept into the room from the far side of the valley. The sunlight was beginning to light her silhouette as she lay there like a bird, wings tucked in under the blanket. So frail. Around her eyes the skin had relaxed, revealing the lines of age creeping into her face like little lies thieving around the edges.

Warden went downstairs and out into the garden. The air carried the cool, restless edge of autumn. Sun lit up the tops of trees. Heart-shaped leaves filled like empty sails in the half-light. Branches straining upward as though fearful of being left behind. He felt suddenly as if the entirety of space were too small to contain his feelings.

Across the valley the dawn light was being matched by a glow in the windows of houses up and down its sides. Everything in its place, as if arranged by a pair of perfect hands. It was exactly as he remembered it. Tiny prisms of light split the air. Early morning commuters passed along the streets on both sides of the valley. He allowed himself a sigh that broke the stillness.

The sun moved higher, lighting its way up the valley floor, while all around antennaed rooftops slept. He felt cut off, separated from the sleeping distances spread before him. It was the beginning of a fine September morning.

For a moment it all seemed to hold, executing a magical truancy in time, the stars dimming their wicks for a brief instant. He felt caught in a flux, a slow-motion stream that takes eons to make itself known. He was surprised by the appearance of all that had once been so familiar. It seemed to say it had done without him, no longer needing him. The rooftops, the garden, the valley — none of it had changed. And he, being changed, was no longer a part of it. He left the next day.

28

When Warden returned to England the oncoming season was less in evidence than it had been at home. Rebekah and Ivan were pleased to have him back, and told him so. They spent most evenings at home and made plans to do things together.

One Saturday night returning from a restaurant, Rebekah was driving. Ivan had fallen asleep in the back seat. It was raining lightly. She was speeding and had run a red light when they were stopped by a police car. She rolled down the window. The police officer looked at the pretty young woman smiling sweetly up at him.

"In a hurry to get somewhere, miss?"

"I'm sorry, officer. Was I speeding?"

"You were travelling almost twice the speed limit."

He mentioned the light she had run and the fact that it was raining, making conditions more dangerous. She looked remiss.

"I'll let you off with a warning this time," he told her. "But be more careful, please."

"Yes, I will, officer. Thank you."

Once around the corner she stepped on the accelerator. They sped forward in the rainy streets.

"Ha!" she exclaimed. "Works every time. Never pay for anything ever!" she cried gleefully, speed and delight, deception and pleasure, inextricably interlinked in her mind.

Warden began pursuing work in earnest again. His booker at the Smart agency was pleased with his newly reformed attitude, confiding that had he not been such a good breadwinner they would have sacked him long ago for his erratic behaviour. He set about making up the damage he'd done to his reputation. He was becoming re-acquainted with a life he barely remembered, finding peace and contentment and waking in the early hours. Mornings he spent in the garden behind the flat, the sky outlined by an optimistic pink light, dry and luminous, that began each day.

He enjoyed most when it rained, walking through streets that smelled of forests and mists. He felt a renewed interest in his physical well-being, cycles of growth and change strengthening from within. In the garden behind the flat, cool light like fallen shards of sky.

As the season progressed the clouds glowed with expectancy, belying the oncoming winter. He went out walking one afternoon and returned, light-hearted and exultant, more than just an echo of his former self.

As he entered the flat, his telephone was pulsing in short, flat tones. He picked up the receiver. At the sound of the other voice he felt the gaping canyons opening below him. It was Joshua, inquiring how he'd been, asking to see him. The voices in his head protested as the sound of his heart amplified a hundredfold.

*　*　*

Warden stood under the arches behind the small church. The sky was grey and dismal. He stamped his feet and rubbed his hands together to keep warm as he waited.

Joshua came striding towards him across the churchyard like a soldier. It took all of two seconds for the full weight of feeling to come tumbling down again. Emotions he thought long since packed away, memories stored and forgotten, were revived the instant he looked into those timeless eyes that seemed to be offering comfort for all his troubles in their absence.

Joshua's voice was soothing, speaking to him in friendly, intimate terms. Warden remembered the first time he'd heard it, its ragged edges at war with the world. He listened to it now for whatever truths it concealed.

They talked for fifteen minutes, catching up on each other's lives. Warden told him of his trip home after the failed cologne campaign. Joshua had been abroad, too, travelling to a number of European cities, drumming up support for his political interests. He'd just returned from Germany, he said, where he'd been training in guerrilla tactics with an underground support group.

Wheel of Fire had disbanded, reforming recently into several splinter groups, one of which had retained the group's name in hopes of picking up the career he had abandoned. Their first single was just making its onslaught on the pop charts.

"Do you miss it?" Warden asked.

Joshua laughed, running his hands through his hair.

"All that seems a lifetime ago," he said.

Warden was aware of light filtering through the rainclouds above the trees as they spoke.

Joshua grinned boyishly at him. "But I miss you," he said. "You were right when you told me that once you love someone you never stop loving them."

"I — I think of you a lot," was all Warden could reply.

He wanted to say that Joshua's face was all he saw in every face. In every landscape. That there could be no other face for him. His heart beat as if there were only one more thing left to say. As if it were already funnelling towards them like a vision through the trees. He looked into the grey vistas of Joshua's eyes, the clear, open space before thoughts come in, registering all his reawakened feelings like a barometer of hope.

"What will you do now?" Warden asked.

Joshua shifted his stance. His grin faltered for a moment. "I'm leaving again. To continue my work with the group."

The vistas in his eyes rolled on into other landscapes, as if moved by a great efficiency of purpose. Warden realized he'd never been there at all. There was an awful sound of distance in his voice when he spoke again.

"South Africa was just a start. There are terrible things happening in other countries. Rwanda might be next. Zaire is going to reach a boiling point in the next few years if something isn't done. It's difficult for us to fight back," he explained. "In some countries people aren't even allowed to organize publicly or protest for freedom of speech."

Warden envisioned him on the front lines. Bandaging the wounds of fallen heroes. Putting flags back into their hands with rallying cries. He wanted to accuse Joshua of becoming a cliché. But that was just being cynical, he knew.

"If there is even a suggestion of resistance or a simple request for disinvestment by multinational companies, it can be interpreted as criminal activity," Joshua went on. "You'd be surprised by what's going on right under our noses. In some cases, the authorities can do whatever they choose to stop us."

The feverish ecstasy of martyrdom glowed in his eyes. A dark angel riding on his shoulders. Paper heroes, fallen idols. Warden wondered why he was telling him this.

"In some places where we've staged protests the police have opened fire on crowds. Many of the political leaders are in jail facing the death penalty for their beliefs. They can detain you for as long as they want. But don't worry," he said, placing a hand on Warden's shoulder, "I won't be doing any gun carrying. I'll be an organizer from this end of things — sort of a fund-raiser for a political party except we're outlawed by the government. That's why I wanted to see you, in fact. I need to ask a favour."

"What do you want from me?" Warden asked, feeling Joshua's eyes on him.

Joshua pulled an envelope from his jacket. It contained documents of some sort. He held it out.

"They're bonds," he said. "You can negotiate them for us."

Warden reached out for the envelope as though touching fire. It contained ten paper bonds. Ten blue-green slips made out for £1,000 each.

"I can't do it without their making a credit check on me," Joshua said. "But you could do it, Ward. With your clean-cut, good looks they'd never suspect you for a second."

Warden hesitated, looking into Joshua's eyes as though reading their depths. He felt something coagulating inside, like a phlegm that restricted his breathing. He coughed and felt it dislodge slightly. An absurd idea presented itself. Maybe love is a chest cold, he thought. A chest cold loosening bit by painful bit.

"What would I have to do?"

Joshua outlined the simple actions that would allow him to deposit the bonds into a foreign account which someone else in another country far away could access.

"I even have a name for you to use," he explained, as though it were a game they were playing with his identity. "It can't be traced back to you."

Warden hesitated.

"Take your time to think about it."

"If I think about it, I won't be able to do it."

"I could tell you where we got the bonds... " Joshua began.

"I don't want to know," Warden interjected.

"And it's not without risk. I can't promise you that."

"What if I don't do it?"

"I'm out of here tomorrow." He hesitated. "I'd chance it myself if I thought I could get away with it."

He felt the wind blowing his hair, lifting it like fallen leaves. He remembered Joshua's telling him to know how far he would go. What he was capable of doing. 'Anything for you', he'd said. His will seemed petrified, inhabited by something turning him with a force impossible to resist. He nodded slowly. Joshua outlined what to do, which questions to be prepared to answer. He handed Warden a passport with his face and someone else's name on it.

Warden looked at the document in his hands, then back up at Joshua. For a moment Joshua, too, seemed to be someone else. His deep-set eyes and close-cropped head suggesting a child acting out the role of militaristic saint. Saint Joshua. Warden put the envelope and passport into his pocket.

"Here's one for Robin Hood," he joked, making light of the moment.

He turned and walked across the square, down the street. A sound like a clock ticking in his head that might have been his heart.

* * *

Warden entered the sleepy-looking bank and joined the queue. Its lobby had been designed to suggest the need for quiet, rational discussion by visitors to its interior. Black-and-white tiles beneath his feet like squares on a chess board, one move leading inexorably to the next. Joshua had said it would be an easy-going, relaxed branch. No one would pay much attention to him. How could they miss the bonfire blazing at the centre of his hands?

The line fanned out and headed towards either of two wickets. Customers whispered unheard vows to faces at the open windows like a private confessional for sins of commerce. The features of those around him suggested something just below the surface. As though aware of things he couldn't fathom.

One by one the line slipped away in front of him. He felt consumed by an urge to turn and walk quietly away. To quell his inner terror and retreat through the open door at his back and across the quick distance outside. But his hands belonged to someone else now. A madman threatening to reach up and strangle him should he turn back or flinch.

The queue shortened until he was at its head. Someone stepped away from the counter and a woman motioned him onward, smiling as if she knew him. He went to the wicket and spread out the contents of the envelope, explaining in an absurdly casual voice what it was he wanted her to do. 'This is my body — eat of it,' said the voice in his head.

There was something odd in the arch of the woman's eyebrows. The way her eyes avoided his as she gathered up the slender pieces of paper in her hands. There was a strange catch to her voice as she excused herself, smile still in place with something moving so fast behind it he couldn't be sure what it was as she turned and went to the desk behind her. There she conferred in dark whispers with another clerk, older, officious-looking, who also seemed not to be looking at him directly.

The light seemed too strong. The room narrow and restrictive. He'd forgotten how to breathe. His heart beat murderous and slow, lost now inside him. He looked away from the clerks conspiring his destruction to glance at a clock as if he might have somewhere to go. He was sure they were taking advantage of the moment to look at him openly, before all the others. People seemed to move away from him, as though alerted to the possibility he might be dangerous.

At that moment, Warden could not have said whether he fully understood what he was doing. Perhaps, he thought later, he really did not know. Did not completely understand what he'd undertaken to do for others. For love. He felt something like the vestigial remains of a wing torn from a spot just below his shoulder blades. For that reason, it had been a relatively simple act to walk into a bank and attempt a financial transaction on behalf of another party.

Later, in the courtroom, in a voice that rose and fell with histrionic conviction, his lawyer would argue Warden hadn't known, hadn't fully understood the extent of his actions. Claiming he was duped by the do-gooder intentions of others and painting a portrait of those people — smarter, stronger, rapacious — who held a very real power over him through an innocent desire to help. But in the light of what followed, he could never really be sure if that were true.

He had an urge, just once, as he stood at the wicket, to look over his shoulder out the window and across the street. To know whether the face he might see would be one of almost holy beauty or extraordinary ugliness. Or just unbearably ordinary. But he did not do it, did not turn, as the uniformed man with the faded grey face came up and stood very close and led him — submissive, naked, blind — to an office in the back of the bank.

29

The trial that fall was a small sensation taking on, as trials do, a sense of dimension proportionate to the lives of those cast in its lead roles. It lasted less than two weeks, during which a number of witnesses took the stand, including the teller who'd accepted the stolen bonds, as well as several character witnesses testifying on Warden's behalf. Elizabeth Smart was there as his employer and a reputable English businesswoman. Calvino's was a conspicuous absence. Warden's parents, having travelled so far to be there, had to content themselves with sitting and watching the proceedings from the gallery.

From the start, the public came to marvel over the trappings of glamour placed on display. Issues of money, celebrityhood and revolution drew long queues of curiosity seekers. Here was one who had lived the high life, his face imbued with a strange familiarity as they recalled seeing him on their TV or in daily newspapers and magazines. In apprehending the crime and its perpetrator, they were trying to understand the difference between his life and their own, pressing their faces up against the dirty shop windows of another world.

When Warden was brought before the court for a reading of the charges there was a hush, followed by a soft stirring as neighbour leaned to neighbour venturing opinions as to the likely outcome of the trial. The restless sway was admonished by the tap of a gavel and the proceedings were set in motion.

The bank teller was first to testify. She glanced at Warden anxiously from time to time, as though she feared he might attempt to silence her testimony with a private arsenal tucked inside his jacket that had escaped the notice of the courtroom guards. Apart from identifying him as the man who had handed her the bonds, she had little to say other than that she'd thought him exceptionally well-dressed for the neighbourhood.

Warden's lawyer built a case around his client's infatuation with the seductive ideals of clever revolutionaries who had preyed on his naïveté. He hoped to encourage the sympathy of the jury by portraying him as a young man whose judgement had not before that time erred in any way and who had acted impulsively, without fully comprehending the forces unleashed by his actions.

In response, the prosecutor tried to make out that the court was dealing with not one simple irresponsible action but, rather, with a wilful insubordination on the part of a privileged young man. Warden's desire for notoriety, he claimed, had led him to commit a crime that would more befit a Robin Hood in the Middle Ages before the implementation of modern forms of social justice. He portrayed Warden's social milieu as one of idle playmates and jetsetters seeking adventure, saying it should come as no surprise that charges like the one he was facing would eventually befall someone living such a life. Warden had ignored his social advantages, he claimed, and hid behind his good looks just as he was now playing at being good to elicit the sympathy of his jurors to escape what he had coming.

In the end it made little difference — his reputation was spotless. His past was clean, according to all who testified on his behalf. References to his scholastic and athletic achievements were brought up like a list of accreditation for his life. He was seen as a solid youth who had had a momentary lapse of judgement, having fallen into bad company and been seduced by the socialistic aims of helping the underprivileged and fighting against oppression and injustice.

Before the week was out, the tabloids had given the trial an open debate. The *Daily Mirror* depicted him with the sheen of a martyr struggling to Golgotha. The *Sun* raised the ghost of his celebrityhood, seeing his social activism as a red herring thrown into the parade-ground of the trial. Both papers carried drawings of the courtroom where the drama was being played out alongside photographs from his career. Public fascination grew with reports of the trial along with an unabashed sympathy over the plight of one so handsome and renowned.

His lawyer was largely successful in separating his idealism from the anti-social actions perpetrated thereby. The public was looking for a hero. All that was needed was a good-looking young face with a spotless reputation to bring out cries of 'our lad' and 'brave boy' from the voices of morning paper vendors.

Again, with their nose for sensation, the press latched onto this angle and began declaring him a modern-day Robin Hood. One paper went so far as to take an on-the-street reader poll, finding fully eighty percent of those polled in sympathy with his aims, although opinion was divided sharply as to the means of carrying them out.

In the middle of the trial, Lisa phoned. Warden could hear her voice over the wire, consoling, a small comfort to him now so far away. She asked how the trial was going and offered words of support. They had little else to say and soon brought the call to an end.

* * *

He would remember later the faces of those who sat in judgement upon him, their boredom and their amusement, the occasional flash of interest at the unfolding of his life before their eyes. And mostly their bewilderment to think that the same thing could happen to them but for the long grey vista of dullness that separated their lives from his. They huddled like a gathering of lantern holders searching the darkness, trying to read the scrawls etched on the walls of his life. Gleaning truth from the nuances of his past.

Rebekah was called on as one of several character witnesses. She dressed regally, embodying a sense of aristocratic propriety he'd never seen in her before. Besides mentioning her background and social prominence, the lawyer took it upon himself to remind the court that her worst transgression was a small list of traffic offences which, as he pointed out, were common enough to nearly everyone who had ever driven the streets of London.

Warden's lawyer asked about her relationship with his client — the circumstances under which she had come to know him as well as her opinion of him as a person who might be capable of stealing for his own gain.

"Not possible," she declared. "He would never hesitate to give you the shirt off his back or anything else you might ask of him, even if it might lead to his own detriment, as seems to have been the situation here."

When asked why she thought he might have committed the act he was accused of, she replied simply, "Sheer enthusiasm — he wanted to help others not as well off as himself."

She attempted to tell the court tales of social atrocities she herself had heard, of violence and segregation and inadequate care centres for orphans in foreign countries. She spoke as though she were making bold sketches on bright paper for the entire courtroom, her voice ringing with a whole history of inflections. His lawyer finally cut her off, thanking her for her opinions. She seemed to Warden more remarkable than ever.

After that day's session, a reporter eager to get a statement asked

Warden as he was led from the courtroom what thoughts he had of his home.

"I miss it... " he began, feeling a wave of emotion hit him. His eyes searched the crowd for his parents. "It's very big and open. There's a lot of space back home. I wasn't used to the crowds when I first came here."

He remembered his first awkward attempts at describing it to Valentino. He had fooled himself about his country's true nature, underestimating its worth. Whatever else it might have been, it was lost to him now.

"And what do you think of England now that we've dubbed you our twentieth-century Robin Hood, Mr. Fields?"

"It's a very amusing nation," he said, as the crowd around him chuckled. He felt as though he were giving a bad performance in a ridiculous melodrama. "That's all I have to say."

"Good luck to you," the reporter called out as he was led away.

Warden's behaviour had been exemplary through the whole trial. Apart from his recent social life the prosecution had found little that was in any way damaging or reprehensible. Even the tabloids were losing interest in his story. The laundry had been washed and the dirt that came out was trivial compared with the events of the real world.

The next day Rebekah was unexpectedly called to the stand again by the prosecutor. She responded politely as seemingly irrelevant material was covered once more. The prosecutor asked her to recall for him her remark that enthusiasm might have led Warden to the consequences of which they were now deciding the outcome. He asked if she thought such enthusiasms might not be obsessive and had she ever had any obsessions herself.

Yes, she had, in fact — an obsession with shining shoes. "At one point," she declared, "I owned seventy-two shoe brushes," covering her flippancy with a coy smile.

"And no doubt many pairs of exceptionally clean shoes," he replied with an icy smile. He pondered his next question. "Miss Wentworth, how close would you say you were to the defendant?"

"Very close."

"Intimate?"

"Not that close."

There were titters in the gallery and among the jurors.

"I believe you said at one point that the defendant, Mr. Fields, would gladly give you the shirt off his back. Do you remember saying this?"

"Yes."

"Then would you say you were close enough to share one another's clothes?"

"Well, if I had to but I doubt that there's very much in each other's wardrobes that we might want... " she began, but he cut her off again.

"Have you ever traded clothes with the defendant?"

"Of course not," she said.

"Then what would you think if a young man like Mr. Fields were suddenly to start wearing women's clothes, for instance? Would you still call him 'enthusiastic' or would that fall under the category of 'obsessive behaviour'?"

Rebekah suddenly looked very frightened.

"Why — I don't... know."

Warden's lawyer broke in to stop the questioning as being groundless. The prosecutor spoke privately to the judge who overruled the objection. He then asked Rebekah if she knew what a transvestite was. She looked briefly out to the courtroom and saw Warden cover his face with his hand.

"Yes," she answered.

"And what would you think, miss," he went on, "of a young man who dresses up in women's clothing?"

"I would think it amusing," she snapped, "as I have a sense of humour."

Warden's lawyer leaned over and whispered to him. Without taking his eyes off Rebekah, Warden whispered back. The prosecutor produced a set of photographs and showed them to Rebekah.

"Would you kindly tell the court what these are, miss?" he requested.

"They're advertisements... for Fabiano Jeans."

"And the young man in these photographs is the defendant, Mr. Fields, is it not?"

"Yes."

"Have you seen these photographs before today, miss?"

"Yes."

"And do you know who the other person in these advertisements might be — this person here, right beside Mr. Fields?"

He pointed to the other figure in the photos. Rebekah did not answer immediately.

"Miss?"

Rebekah looked out across the courtroom.

"Yes, I know," she answered, tight-lipped.

"Thank you, miss," he said. "That will be all for now."

She stepped down from the stand, passing by Warden. Her gaze held him like an invisible magnet. Her lips were drawn, her cheeks strained, as though she were already in pain for what he was about to face.

The court listened raptly as the devastating evidence in the photographs was revealed. Warden heard the scandalized reaction over the revelation he knew would haunt him for some time. In the crowd, he saw his mother's face folding like a crushed flower, his father's a cold, white moon reflecting back everything that came towards it.

By the time the prosecution was finished, Warden's reputation as an innocent defender of public interest had been irreparably tarnished. Tabloids that were once on his side now screamed out the sensational disclosures. Headlines were emblazoned on street corners the next day as the court proceedings began. 'Robin Hood or Maid Marion?' demanded one. 'Transvestite Trial Causes Public Outcry!' proclaimed another, while under his photograph the caption read 'World's most beautiful woman is one of Europe's leading male models'.

They dragged up stories of a perverse lifestyle he had been engaged in at the say-so of 'witnesses' swearing to events that never happened, damning him with inaccuracy and lies. He stood accused now for the same looks which once had lifted him above the mire. Once again the gallery was full. Spectators were evicted for pushing and shoving. Several times the judge admonished her courtroom to silence as they watched from overhead, excited by the revelations his pictures had stirred up, while Warden's lawyer tried to salvage the case he had watched fall to pieces around him.

The Fabiano company immediately pulled the offending ads featuring their once-favoured model, issuing a retraction by company heads denying any knowledge of the actions of either the photographer or model involved in the advertising campaign. All subsequent ads were cancelled effective immediately. Ironically, sales for the clothing company had never been better.

Warden talked to Andreo by phone that evening. The photographer's voice trembled, overwhelmed by the event and sorry he'd ever taken the pictures. Too late to deny the consequences, blaming himself for what had happened. Warden was moved, reminding

Andreo he was not on trial for the photographs but for a senseless action which he had clearly admitted his mistake in doing. Warden could feel him holding out his heart for the agony he was enduring.

"I smell the world in it — small, mean and empty," he said. "I have created a terrible destruction that has hurt an innocent. In Italy such things would never happen. Who would have thought something I could do would bring such unhappiness? Put on your best face and brave the world. Goodbye, goodbye."

*　　*　　*

In her summary prior to his sentencing, the judge stressed a need for exercising responsibility in one's actions and warned of the dangers that might result by taking the law into one's own hands. What would happen to society, she asked, if every individual did such a thing?

Ivan leaned to Rebekah who sat silently awaiting the verdict, whispering it would be a far sight better if those who took the law into their own hands were half as responsible as authorities were irresponsible to the world.

The judge continued, advocating an individual and collective care in the exercise of power, citing a Buddhist proverb which stated that in order to make it a better world, it is first necessary to better fill the place in which we find ourselves.

"We must not lose the scale of things," she instructed, "the notion that smallness counts and that every effort is not wasted if directed towards a positive end."

They waited as she spoke, impatience barely restrained, hoping to glean some hint of his penalty from the morass of words as she strove to isolate the faults she wished to rid society of. At last the entire court seemed to breathe a sigh of relief when she sentenced Warden to a twelve-month term.

The public and jurors dispersed, some congratulating Warden and the lawyer who had effected such a miracle, while others left, satisfied by the turn of events which had captured their attention for a short while. His mother barely restrained her urge to cry. Rebekah kissed him and squeezed his hands over and over again.

30

He awoke to the sound of memory. Warden looked around the small grey room with its neatly functional shelves, tidy beds and fresh linen, as though its inhabitants were guests at a seaside resort. The cell was dim. Its contours emerged in a dull sliver of light falling through the window on the far wall. From outside came a sound like doves' wings beating mutely against stone. He pushed himself into a sitting position and rubbed his eyes, sleep receding like a departing tide. A bell tolled seven times.

He stood and peered out the window across a courtyard where the dark of oncoming night crept up the edge of the sky. The sound continued, wave-like, its narcotic rhythms slowly condensing into human voices. It was rest hour. The inmates had returned to their cells and were conversing across the courtyard through the windows high above.

Presently the sounds distinguished themselves into words, individual strands of conversation weaving in and out of a web of voices, greeting, gossiping, warning of informers among their rank. It was a nightly ritual. The swapping of information like a trade in precious commodities. It passed like a sad river of sound while the light slowly faded, the voices coming less and less frequently as darkness fell over the prison walls.

Alderly Heath was a penitentiary inhabited primarily by young offenders. It was cut off from the rest of the city, hidden by a field and trees set around it as though it had risen naturally out of the landscape. The first impression Warden had was one of high brick walls with rounded metal contours running along their length, like the great domed arches of a mosque transported all the way through time and space from ancient Constantinople. Impossible to scale its massive heights, inside or out.

The guard escorting him ignored the whistles and jeers from the rows of faces staring out of the cells they passed. His own cell was empty when he arrived. One cell-mate had recently been hospitalized for hepatitis, he was informed. The other had been put into confinement overnight for an infraction at meal time.

The guard pointed to a bed and secured the door behind him. He was alone in his new home. He looked around. There was little that afforded any clues as to what he could expect when the others returned. A wooden crucifix and a framed photograph of a plump, grey-haired woman with a worried expression hung on the wall over one bed. The other wall was bare. He lay on the cot, hard against his back. He put his hands behind his head, stared at his feet at the far end of the bed where they stuck up like a distant border. His eyes closed. The rhythm of sleep took over his breathing.

* * *

Right after breakfast, Warden joined a gang of some twenty-odd fellow prisoners doing maintenance work, tending the grounds and other light duties. They were next separated into groups of five and six till lunchtime, continuing their labour. At noon they were herded into a large open room with long rows of tables and benches where they ate, arguing and joking like schoolboys. The oldest prisoners appeared to be in their early thirties, others looked as though they hadn't yet begun to shave. In their grey sartorial uniformity, they could easily have been mistaken for a squadron of soldiers or sailors.

Warden looked for a friendly face. No one would return his gaze under the watchful eyes of the guards, though he knew they were aware of him from the hour of his arrival.

After lunch he was taken to the prison infirmary and assigned a helpmate named Steve who showed him his stock-taking duties while saying as little as possible. At four o'clock he was returned to his cell. The door closed with a clack of lockers falling into place. On the edge of one of the beds sat a young man with his arm in a sling, his face held in profile. Strong-boned cheeks and full lips silently refused to turn and acknowledge his arrival. Warden took a step forward.

"Hi," he said. "My name's Warden."

"That's good," said the young man who did not move.

"What's your name?"

"None of your damned business," the boy snapped.

Warden walked over to his own bed and sat on the edge.

"That's fine. I'm not planning on staying here forever. I'll just mind my own business till I get out and you can do the same."

He lay back and cupped his hands behind his head.

"They told me I'd been stuck with a fucking wog," the other said.

"Sorry — I'll tell room service there's been a mistake and they can change our rooms in the morning."

"Don't get cocky with me, mate. I got this scrapping with another bloke with a big mouth," he said, indicating his sling. The bristling tone contained an unconcealed pride in the words. "You'll want to watch yourself with me. I've got lots of friends in here and as far as they're concerned the only good wog is a dead wog."

"Before we spend the next few months in total silence, can you at least tell me what a wog is?" Warden asked.

The other boy turned and looked at him directly for the first time. Despite his sturdy build, he appeared to be no more than nineteen or twenty. His face carried a surly look of disgust.

"What's a wog? A wog is a bloody foreigner! It means a worker on government service, is what it means. It's all them bloody Arabs and other foreigners who come over here to drain our economy. That's exactly what a wog is."

"You're right — I'm a wog."

Warden lay on his bed reading a paper, turning the pages slowly. The other boy lit a cigarette, expelling smoke in huge, scornful exhalations without moving. Neither spoke for the rest of the evening.

In the morning a grey pieta of light poured in the window. Warden lay quietly till he heard the other boy get out of bed to urinate in a bucket. Warden ignored him as he dressed. The boy picked up the pot and took it out to empty when the guards came along.

During work detail the other prisoners were no more talkative than they'd been the day before. They worked until lunch and broke for the meal. In the lunch area Warden saw his helpmate Steve from the infirmary. He managed to sit across the table from him. Steve answered his questions but seemed anxious not to appear interested in Warden. Warden asked why no one would talk to him. The other boy stiffened. He looked down at his plate where he stirred the yellow ooze of broken yolks with a fork.

"I don't know, mate," he said. "Maybe it's because you're not from here."

He seemed unwilling to continue the conversation. Warden left him to eat his meal which he hurriedly finished before getting up from the bench. Later in the infirmary Warden tried to talk to him again. Steve seemed more relaxed than at lunch as Warden helped him carry in supplies, checking off order lists, stocking the cupboards. He remarked that it seemed strange they were allowed to do stock control on drug shipments. Steve laughed, saying there was nothing they were handling that was worth stealing for use or trade value.

"Needles, now. They have a habit of disappearing sometimes," he said with a wink.

They continued to stack boxes on the shelves.

"What you were asking me about earlier," Steve began. "What you said about nobody talking to you? It's because they don't know you. They think you might be a nark."

"What's a nark?"

"An informer. Don't take it personally, mate — they're just protecting themselves, you know?"

"Well, how do I prove I'm not?" Warden asked, gathering a load of boxes into his arms.

"You can't do anything, really. You have to let them decide for themselves if they like you or not. If you stay out of the way you'll be alright. One thing you need to know is the guards won't help if you get out of favour with the wrong people in here. They won't try to save you."

"Save me from what?"

"Whatever."

"Who are the wrong people?"

"The guys on top — they run things here behind the scenes. You'll figure it out pretty quick if you keep your eyes open."

"And who are you in this social institution?"

Steve looked cautiously around.

"Me? I'm nobody. I just keep my nose clean, is all. I'm only in for another month anyway. Then I'm gone."

"So how do I keep my nose clean?"

"Fear is good," he answered, then smiled just a little.

Warden smiled back.

"What do you do in real life, Steve?"

"What? D'you mean outside?" He laughed. "I'm a mechanic. I hot-wired an automobile once — that's why I'm in here. What are you in for?"

"Making a donation to a political party."

His eyes grew incredulous.

"Is that illegal now?"

"It was somebody else's money."

Steve stared at him a moment then laughed and slapped him on the back, almost making him drop the boxes he had piled up to his chest.

"You're alright. If you want any more advice on getting along in here, just ask me. I'll tell you anything you need to know."

"I'm having trouble with my roommate — cellmate, I guess I mean. I can't get him to talk."

"You're in with Tom Skelton, aren't you?"

"I don't even know that — he won't talk to me."

"That sounds like Tom. He's a queer one, alright. You're lucky you didn't come a week earlier or you'd've ended up with Wayne the Knife. He's a bad sort. I hear he caught hepatitis and had to be taken out of the prison."

"That must be the guy they shipped out the day before I got there. The guard said he didn't know when he'd be back."

"Keep your fingers crossed he won't," Steve said. "Did you try offering Tom a cigarette?"

"No — I don't smoke."

"Well, you'd better start. Cigarettes are lucre in here. You can barter for just about anything with them."

"What will I need?"

"You'll find something you want eventually."

"How do I get them?"

"You have to have them sent in from outside. Whenever someone comes to visit ask them to bring you a pack of fags. I'm serious, it'll help."

He hesitated, then looked at Warden.

"Here."

He took two slightly crumpled cigarettes from his shirt pocket.

"I won't be needing these much longer — have a smoke with your lad tonight and things'll go much better. I guarantee it."

"Thanks."

"Don't mention it."

In the cell that evening the other boy lay on his bed staring at the ceiling. He did not look over as Warden entered and sat on his own bed. He took one of the two cigarettes from his shirt pocket and struck a match. He lit it and blew out the match, looking over.

"Like a cigarette?" he said.

The other boy looked suspiciously at him for a moment.

"Alright."

He sat up. Warden handed him the cigarette, lighting it for him. He lay back on his elbow regarding Warden for another moment.

"Where'd you get these, then?" he said. "I didn't think you

smoked."

"I'm full of surprises," Warden said. "So your name's Tom?"

"That's right," the boy said, grinning for a second, before his usual sullen glare took over his features again. "How'd you find that out?" he said.

"Same way you found out I was a wog — I asked."

If Warden had hoped for a conversation he was disappointed. Tom gave him curt answers to his queries, showing no curiosity in return towards the other man sharing his cell.

"What do you do outside, Tom?"

"I'm a bricklayer."

"And how long are you in for?" Warden asked. "Or is that too personal a thing to ask of your cellmate?"

"I could be out of here instantly if I chose," he said. "If I said the word I'd be out like that." A snap of the fingers. He spoke with utter confidence as if he truly believed it and expected Warden to believe it as well. "It's all who you know," he said.

"So why don't you say the word?"

"I say fuck 'em — I don't kiss anybody's arse in here," the boy answered. Butting his cigarette on the floor and swinging his legs onto the bed to indicate the conversation was over.

31

Warden fell into the rhythm of the daily prison routine. Waking early each morning. Making his bed. Showering and changing before being taken out to join the others. Later, there was lunch and then afternoons spent in the infirmary.

He soon learned the prison hierarchies. These based on the size and strength of the inmates, as well as severity of sentence. Murder was considered an impressive crime, deserving of respect. His own placed him close to the bottom of the list. There were also the groups of blacks and Asians who hung out together in the task forces and at lunch. Apportioning themselves according to race, as though in defiance of the scattering motions of entropy and random distribution over the clinking of 150 sets of cutlery.

In a place where power was the determining factor, each face was significant. No one could afford to ignore another presence on the scene, be he bit part or major player. Lives were lived more intensely within the walls that contained them, as if the outside world had been distilled into a confined space.

As for suffering, most of Warden's had occurred during the trial. The regret. The shame he felt for his family. Once in prison there was loneliness, of course. That was a constant. Not that he lacked for company, but the enforced companionship of other convicts did little to fill his inner needs. Nor did he expect sympathy or even understanding. From what he could see, he was far better off than most of the others for whom prison was only a variant on the quality of lives they had lived before and were just as likely to live after their sentences were up.

Tom became more talkative as the days drew on. His topics of conversation usually involved weapons and forms of violence of one sort or another. He also had a penchant for singing in a rough, boyish tenor which he grew more comfortable doing as he got to know Warden better. He admitted going to the prison chapel on Sundays just to sing. In the cell he was fond of singing 'Danny Boy', a tune his father had taught him.

Whenever Warden asked about his life outside prison, Tom was vague. It became apparent he'd never had much of a family life. Warden recognized the hidden seams of guilt and grief in his voice when mentioning a hard-working mother and the father who had died while he was in prison. He'd been forced to attend his funeral in handcuffs.

Although he'd expected to hate every moment of it, within a month Warden had come to find a reassuring peace in his cell. When he mentioned it to Tom, to his surprise the other agreed.

"It's alright, I guess. You get your needs met regular and it's quiet," he said. "It's nice to know someone's not going to just walk in on you in the middle of the night."

Warden kept Tom amused with tales of foreign countries and lifestyles, fascination and curiosity mingling in his open face. For his part, Tom let Warden in on secrets of prison life that had been hidden from him. When he noticed the crude tattoo of a bulldog on his left shoulder, Tom told him it had been devised by their absent cellmate, Wayne the Knife. He lifted the edge of his mattress, extracted a jagged sliver of metal from inside the material, four inches long. He brandished it with playful pride.

"We'd really catch it if they ever found us with this," he exclaimed.

He described to Warden how Wayne had heated the edge of the blade, sketching the shape on his shoulder. He then filled it in with ink from the tip of a ballpoint pen. Warden shuddered at the thought.

"How did it feel?" he asked.

"It was a fucking spiritual experience!"

"Is it permanent?"

"If I wanted to I could rub up against the concrete until it bled a couple times. Then, once I had a good, thick scab, I'd just pull it off quick as I can."

He laughed at the look on Warden's face.

"That'd get rid of it," he said. "But I don't want to get rid of it."

* * *

The first time Rebekah came to visit she arrived dressed in a blue velvet coat and cape with a broad-brimmed hat that made a minor sensation on her entrance. They were separated by a window in a room where twenty or more prisoners sat conversing with visitors. Voices dropped to an urgent whisper as though trying to cram everything they had to say into the appointed time.

"You look well," she said as she sat, a bustle of coats and dresses. "I'm glad of that, at least."

"Thanks. And you look wonderful. Is this standard visiting garb?"

She smiled and shook her head.

"I thought I might need it to bully someone or else charm them, but apparently not. They let me right in. Before I forget, I left a carton of cigarettes for you at the front desk. You didn't say what brand so I bought you something American. I hope that's alright. Is it that bad in here you've had to take up smoking?"

"No — it's currency," he grinned. "Anytime I want a favour I take out a cigarette. I'm told it works. I have yet to ask for anything."

"I'll bring you more next time I come. I thought a carton would last forever for a beginner," she said.

Her face faltered. She looked down at her hands on the shallow ledge in front of her.

"I'm — Ivan and I — we're sorry how things went at the trial."

"Don't, Rebekah. There's no need to be sorry. I think I got off fairly easily, to tell you the truth. It's going by fast, too. I'll be out in no time. Then we'll rip up the town again just for fun."

"I never asked what made you do what you did. I... think I can understand."

"Then maybe sometime you'll tell me," Warden said, with a slight smile.

She glanced at the oversize clock on the wall behind him.

"Now that I'm here I can hardly think what to talk about," she said.

"Tell me what you've been doing."

"Oh, the usual. You know how it is. Ivy found a new club nobody else has heard of. It's quite fabulous, really, and it was a new twist for us entirely — we had to pay to get in. Can you imagine? Nothing I could say would convince the doorman to let us in for free. The thrill will wear off quickly, I suppose."

Warden laughed.

"How's life inside — or dare one ask?"

"Not as bad as I thought it would be. I keep pretty much to myself. It gets a bit lonely at times. I just do my work and then go back to my cell. I have a cellmate about my own age. I call him Cruel Tom because of the sneer he wears constantly. He likes to talk about knives and karate and violence. It's his defence, I think. He sits around all day smoking and singing 'Danny Boy'. I couldn't ask for better company, could I?"

At the appointed time a guard arrived to escort him back to his cell. Rebekah's face broke into a complexity of guilt and misery. She smiled and touched her fingers to her lips, pressing the kiss against the glass in front of his face.

That evening Tom was in a playful mood, singing and telling jokes. He jumped up on his bed and wedged himself into a corner between the shelves and the window frame, hanging on by sheer force of determination.

"Look, Ward," he called out.

Warden lifted his eyes from his newspaper to watch.

"Gravity's wasted on me," he said. "I'm Spiderman."

"You're a bloody goon, is what you are."

He jumped down and sat beside Warden, elbows planted on his knees. He took a cigarette butt from his sock and put it in his mouth, cupping the flame from the match as though to protect it from a non-existent wind.

Warden gazed at the back of his freckled neck emerging from the white ring of a shirt collar. Smooth skin, short bristles of hair. Things warm and human in the spiritless grey surroundings. A guard came by just then and opened the viewing slot on the door. He looked in to satisfy himself everything was in order, then shut it again.

"He won't be back for another hour," Tom said absently.

He leaned over and stretched across Warden's bed, lying full out on his stomach.

"Hey, give a guy some room to read," Warden growled as pages fell to the floor in a flurry of leaves.

Tom mumbled something into the blankets.

"What did you say?"

"I said, 'Why do you always read so much?'" he repeated, lifting his face from the mattress. "My back aches," he added. "Why don't you give me a rubdown?"

Warden reached out, gently touching the skin of his neck, quickly moving both hands to his shoulders. The sleek strength of his back. Hands weightless as they caressed the muscles, soft cotton shirt twisting and tangling under the motion of fingers. It was the most intimate contact he'd had with another human being since his arrest.

"I heard something funny about you today," Tom said as Warden kneaded his back.

"What's that?"

Tom laughed in a sceptical manner as though to say he could be persuaded either way of the truth of what he was about to reveal.

"I heard at your trial they showed pictures of you dressed up in ladies' clothes," he said. "Isn't that funny?"

He twisted his neck up and around to look at Warden. Waiting for a reaction. Cub-like ears sticking out sharply from his face.

"Is it true?"

"Yeah."

There was a pause. Warden's hands did not stop their work.

"Why'd you do it? For money?"

"It was a joke," Warden said. "Only it backfired. It was for a magazine."

"Did you like it? Dressing up as a lady, I mean?"

"Not particularly."

"But you didn't mind it?"

"I wouldn't do it again, if that's what you mean."

"Oh."

Warden continued massaging his back and shoulders. "Does it feel any better?" he asked after awhile.

"What?"

"Your back — does it feel any better?"

"I think it'd feel better if I took my T-shirt off," he said, sitting up to pull the garment over his head. He lay back again, exposing a broad chest. Honey-coloured skin of torso, a tangle of dark hair gathered at the pucker of nipples like tiny palms around oases of flesh. The front of his trousers swelled with the strain of an erection he made no effort to disguise.

"Do you want my winkle?" he asked with childlike coyness.

Tom's chest heaved lightly. Warden did not allow himself to think about what was happening.

"Wait," Tom said in a sudden whisper.

He sat up and tore a page from the newspaper, crumpling it. He went to the door and stuffed it into the peephole.

"Just in case," he said, with the self-assurance of one who is wise in certain matters beyond the norm of experience. "Right," he said, returning to the bed where he stretched out full along its hard length. "Go ahead, do what you want. But just remember — I'm dead."

* * *

In the morning Tom lay in bed after the wake-up call. He watched Warden dress.

"Aren't you getting up this morning?"

"Shortly," he said, stretching langorously. "Roll me a fag, would you, mate?"

Warden went to the shelf where Tom kept his few personal belongings. Lucky rabbit's foot, tobacco pouch, pocket comb. He quickly manipulated the moist, brown tufts on the paper into the semblance of a cigarette. He handed it to Tom who inspected it and put it in the corner his mouth.

"Have you got a light?"

Warden leaned over and lit it for him.

"You'd better hurry," Warden said.

Tom spat a piece of tobacco from his tongue. They could hear the other prisoners moving about in the hallway on their way to the latrines.

"I'll be up in a minute. Can you empty the piss pot for me?"

Warden was amused by his charade of leisure, as though he had all the time in the world with nothing to do. When the guard came to let him out to empty the pot he pointed at Tom.

"What's wrong with him?"

"He's not feeling well. He'll be up in a minute."

"He'd better be," the guard growled. "No laying about in here. You know the rules. You'd better be up by the time he gets back unless you're reporting sick," the guard scowled as he let Warden out of the cell.

When Warden returned he could hear Tom singing.

"I'm ready now," he declared, as Warden set the fresh pot down.

Warden went to the window, looking out at the groups of men crossing the courtyard.

"Who told you about those photographs of me you mentioned last night?"

"No one," Tom answered suspiciously, as though he'd been caught lying about something.

"Someone must have told you," Warden said, watching him.

"I just heard."

"What do people in here think about such things?"

"Don't worry about that," Tom said. "I'll protect you for as long as you're in here with me, mate."

In the infirmary with Steve that afternoon Warden brought up the topic of sexual habits of prisoners. He felt safe in asking, knowing Steve, who seemed to have few friends inside, was leaving soon anyway. Steve was remarkably candid. He told Warden that sex in prison was not uncommon, but acknowledgment of it was discreet. A small, vocal group of inmates were agitating for condoms to be distributed due to the prevailing fear of AIDS.

"Some of the men think we should all be tested and the ones who test positive placed in separate cells."

Warden thought about that curious information the rest of the afternoon.

The next day Warden was informed he had another visitor. Ivan sat waiting for him at the window. He had dressed in as masculine a manner as possible, a wisp of violet hair peaking out from under the brim of a solemn grey fedora.

"Rebekah warned me I should be careful not to smile too much and upset you but you don't look so terribly unhappy to me," he pronounced cheerily.

"I'm glad to see you," Warden said.

"How are you really?"

"As you see — bound and gagged hand and foot and starving to death. They whip me every evening at sundown and leave me stripped naked in the snow before dragging me off to my pile of straw in the dungeon."

"Sounds delightful — how do I join?" he joked. "I'm glad you're keeping up your sense of humour. I'd hate to see you lose that on top of all that's happened." He looked around to see who might be listening. "I wish I had the bravery to do what you've done. I think it's really quite admirable," he confided.

"I just wish I'd had the sense not to get caught."

Ivan laughed.

"I shouldn't be such a smart-ass about it, though," Warden said. "It really was a stupid thing. I can't imagine what made me do it now."

"I think it's called love," Ivan answered for him. "I hear he's left the country, in case you're interested." Voice suddenly serious. "I gather he felt he had better things to do than rot in prison with the likes of you."

"Yes, I'm sure he would," Warden said, looking down at his hands.

"I'm just angry it's you and not him in here," Ivan said.

"No," Warden said, looking up. "I knew what I was doing."

"I know," Ivan said, meeting Warden's eyes through the glass. "Not many people would give up the one they love for a cause they may never benefit from. Though that's hardly any consolation, I'm afraid. Anyway, I am sorry."

"Don't feel sorry for me," Warden said. "It's not as bad as it looks. Though I know I can't make you believe that. But I'll be feeling sorry for you in a few months' time."

"Why is that?"

"Because the food in here is so bad that when I get out I'm going straight to your flat to eat you out of a month's supply of strawberry tarts."

"You'll be most welcome," Ivan said. "In fact, if you let me know when you're coming, I'll even make a new frock to wear for your homecoming."

32

One day Tom's older sister came to visit, bringing him a deck of cards. That evening, Tom talked at length about his family, the first time he'd done so. He recounted how, as kids, he and his four brothers and sister played hand after hand of Old Maid with their grandmother. The old woman, whose picture hung on the wall over Tom's bed, would lose purposely so they could win. All the children had loved playing with her.

They passed the evenings playing card games. Tom smoking his rollies, scrutinizing his cards through squinted eyes. Rambling on about anything that came to mind. Next to the prison guards, whom he regarded as Judases betraying their own kind, the subject of foreigners was his biggest gripe. He went on at length, slapping cards down between them as his anger quickened.

The true Brit, he argued, had blue eyes and white skin. Warden's green eyes seemed to grant him partial immunity in this all-or-nothing kind of categorization. When Warden pointed out that Tom's own ancestry was self-admittedly one-eighth Greek, Tom replied that his father's family had all been in England for more three generations. That, he claimed, was just as good as having solid citizenship.

"What happens when Big Mick's family has been here that long?" Warden asked, referring to a black inmate three doors down of whom Tom was somewhat in awe. "Will his grandchildren automatically be born with blue eyes and white skin?"

"Don't be daft," Tom replied impatiently. "There's no mucking about with fate in these things. Mick's alright even if he's... " he stammered.

"Black?"

"It's just all these damned foreigners coming here and taking over our land and our working wages that I hate."

He switched subjects easily, passing from that to describing a porch he'd built for his grandmother so she could have 'something to sit on and watch the neighbours', as he put it. He explained with infinite precision how he'd erected it board by board, nail by nail, as though he'd memorized it in detail. He exhaled slowly, watching the smoke drift around the ceiling and walls.

"Feel my biceps," he said, bunching the muscle in his upper arm.

Warden obliged, squeezing with both hands.

"Have you ever felt anything so hard?" he asked.

Every evening they played cards and almost every evening the same massage and sexual play occurred. Tom made it clear he was in control of the situation, his desire the determining factor in what happened between them.

"Say you want it," Tom ordered him one night.

"I want it."

"Alright, then, mate. Here's what you get."

It would start tentatively, hesitantly. As though Tom scorned to make the first move lest he be accused of desiring the act that followed. It soon took on the feel of something uncontrolled, a violence barely contained himself as he unleashed his pent-up hunger. Afterwards, there would be the retreat from the physical act, and Tom's smoking of a single cigarette, as though to conclude their unspoken arrangement.

Warden wasn't sure when they slipped over the boundary between what was safe and what was not. But he did nothing to stop it. He knew he was playing with mortality. Looking for his Achilles' heel. A way out. He'd forsaken the world, retiring to a secret netherworld of desire. As disconnected from life as though he'd already died. Over the last two years he had surrendered to many vices, this just one more. Tom seemed to have no such worries. From the beginning, he had the acquirer's self-confident belief in ownership, perpetrating his actions with all the false bravado of the sexually ambivalent.

Each morning, Tom delayed rising from bed so Warden ended up emptying the night pot when the guard came around. He began asking Warden to roll his day's supply of cigarettes. Warden indulged the requests with amusement. Tom confided one day that he would never ask another prisoner to do these favours for him. He alone had earned that privilege.

From Steve, he learned Tom had been bragging to the other prisoners that Warden was his servant. Calling him his 'boy' behind his back. Warden was merely amused by the childish boasts he'd been cleaning their piss pot and rolling his cigarettes. Tom became condescending, taking every opportunity to ask Warden for a cigarette in front of the other prisoners to show he'd been designated to carry them. To confound him, Warden began to offer the precious commodity to anyone present. Tom ignored this, as though it had escaped his notice.

At breakfast each morning, the prisoners ate an unappetizing meal to the sound of scraping utensils and plates. Tom had taken to heaping his plate on top of Warden's as they filed out of the roomful of tables into an anteroom where all dishes were dutifully returned. Utensils were carefully counted and checked off to reduce the risk of weapons floating around the prison. Once, a single piece of cutlery had disappeared and they had locked the entire facility, turning the place inside out till it was found.

One day Warden reversed the action. Having finished his meal first, he put his empty plate on top of his cellmate's to the other's surprise. Tom sullenly carried out both plates with a look of belligerence, followed by the hooting and snickering of the other men at the table. Later in the evening, Tom hung petulantly in the corners of the cell, casting scornful looks at Warden when he spoke. Finally, he managed to spit out what was angering him.

"You made me look like a fool in front of everyone at breakfast this morning," he said, his lip curling with anger.

"How's that?"

"You put your plate on mine so I had to carry it out in front of everybody!"

"What's wrong with that? I carry yours out for you all the time."

"That's right, mate — you carry mine! I don't carry your fucking plate!"

Warden snorted.

"You mean I should carry yours out but you don't have to carry mine?"

"That's right."

Tom continued his sulk privately for the rest of the evening. There was no card playing that night. The next day Warden was held up late taking in a shipment at the infirmary. He was served lunch in the ward with two other workers. It was Steve's last day there. Warden wished him luck as they parted.

"You, too," Steve said. "Be careful with that nutcase of yours. There's no telling what he's capable of."

When Warden returned to the cell Tom was singing, apparently having forgotten the incident concerning the plate.

They played cards again that evening. Warden won hand after hand, marking the score on the back of an empty cigarette wrapper. His tally was nearly double that of Tom's, though his mind was barely on the game. Tom's face betrayed increasing frustration each time Warden won. Finally he slapped his cards down onto the bed between them.

"Right," he said. "No sex! I'm not sleeping with you tonight unless you let me win."

Warden tried to soothe him but even with forced carelessness he still won the next round. Tom's face trembled with anger as he looked up from the defiant hand which had failed him. His eyes were glazed with anger.

"I told you... " he began, malice spitting from his lips.

"What do you expect me to do? You dealt the cards."

"I'm not sleeping with you tonight!"

"Suit yourself — I didn't ask you to."

Tom glared at Warden.

"Anyway, I fancy someone else now, so it doesn't matter."

He waited for a reaction, but Warden merely picked up his paper and opened it as he lay back on his bed.

"Did you hear what I just said?"

"You said you fancied another guy. What of it?"

"I fucked him at lunch today."

"That's nice. Did you take him out for a drink afterwards?"

Tom's fist shot out and grabbed Warden's hair, pulling him across the bed till they both fell onto the floor, knocking the empty piss pot clanging across the concrete. A cry went up in the corridor as other prisoners caught wind of the fight, banging and clanking along in their own cells to add to the confusion as the guards rushed from cell to cell to discover which one contained the real commotion.

Warden pulled himself apart from Tom, whose face burned with rage and tears. Rage stemming from more than just a lost card game. He'd finally glimpsed the betrayal in all their intimacy, understood the acts shared between them were distractions taken, not given. Desperate acts formed from a vulnerable need. In anger, he saw that he meant nothing to Warden, had never been wanted for himself beyond a chance joining in a make-believe world inside the bars of their cage.

By the time the guards arrived, Warden had pushed things back into place, smoothing his hair and straightening his clothing. The sounds in the hallway dropped to a sigh. Wind whispering through an empty gutter.

"I should've killed you the first night you came here," Tom spat out before they were taken from the cell.

The next day Warden put in a request for transfer to another cell block. He sat in a wooden chair in the chambers of the prison official who read through his record of conduct. The man clucked sympathetically but admonished him for risking his good record, warning him not to do it again.

"Alright, I'll do it this time. But you stay out of trouble, young man," he said. "You'll be out of here soon enough."

In the afternoon, the guards escorted him to his new cell. They dropped his belongings on the bed and left. That evening, when the nightly doves' cry ascended the walls outside the courtyard, he heard Tom's voice first and foremost, calling him a cheat and a liar. Howling out his betrayal while Warden lay on the cot and cried.

33

In the courtyard, the air had taken on the dull, earthy smells of spring. Warden lay listening to the drumming of the rain. He'd spent nearly four months in prison. His parole in another two months seemed secure. In the daytime he avoided the other inmates as much as possible, requesting tasks that allowed him to keep to himself outside of meals. It also helped him avoid the small skirmishes in the drug trade that went on under the noses of the guards.

He sensed himself changing by degrees. Transforming slowly, like a chemical reaction beneath the skin. Bones, blood, hormones. Crystallizing below the surface. Rising from the depths of his being. A terrifying creature misbegotten of darkness. He'd once been so eager to experience life. Now it was a scarcely believable nightmare.

He lay alone in his cell for hours, staring at the walls and ceiling, as though he had folded himself inward. He could imagine himself any size, shape or strength he wanted, disengaging himself from all that he had been. Not wanting to touch or be touched by anyone. The entire world reduced to the dimensions of his prison cell. A secret eye winked and he had disappeared.

At night, he tried to reconstruct Joshua's face in the air. Eyes clear and cold, with light emanating from the stars of some long-dead galaxy. Angry mouth. Thin lips attesting to a parsimony of spirit. It was a face he thought he'd known and could trust. As Tom had trusted his. He realized he'd simply created a picture out of his own want. The way a dream is the vision of an alternate life upon awakening, or loneliness a sketch of the idea of love, a negative plate from another world. Like any face, it was unknown and ultimately unknowable.

Not long before his discharge, Warden was held up one morning on work detail. He arrived for lunch later than usual, sitting in with the second group of prisoners, his former group. When he entered with his tray, Tom was seated in a far corner with another inmate. It was the first time they'd seen one another face-to-face since their fight. Tom pointed Warden out to his eating partner. This person, he learned later, was Wayne the Knife, returned from rehabilitation. Though he knew from Tom that Wayne was only nineteen, his burned-out, wasted appearance suggested that of a forty-year-old-alcoholic.

Throughout the meal, he sensed their attention on him. When he looked over he caught Tom staring at him as though not knowing he could be seen in return, like someone looking into a two-way mirror. When he realized Warden was watching, he made a clumsy attempt to pretend he'd been looking elsewhere. Warden made a mental note to avoid the pair at all cost.

* * *

When he wasn't in the infirmary counting supplies, Warden spent his afternoons in the library, slicing and cataloguing pages from the daily papers, filing them away. On finishing these tasks he went to the shower room, let in by the guard on duty.

It was the end of the work day and he could take his time waiting for supper hour. He stripped off his uniform and hung it carefully on a hook above the benches in the change area. Feet slapping on the wet tiles. Pulsating streams tonguing his body to an accompanying hiss. He scrubbed his arms and chest with a thick bar of lye soap.

Water splashed over his face. He barely noticed the figure slip into the stall beside him. For a moment, nothing. He came out from under the water gasping. Opened his eyes to a flash. The face of Tom's table mate leering at him. There was a streak of blood across the other boy's chest. For a split second Warden wondered what had happened.

Part of his brain alerted him to the danger, sending his right hand rushing to his cheek. His hand came away covered in blood. Another jab in his side. The floor beneath them turned bright red as a swishing current directed its movement towards a drain. Circling. He remembered thinking it was not an unreasonable sight, given the sequence of events in the last five seconds. Mind piecing it all together. He sighed and shook his head, as though that were the reaction expected.

"That'll teach you to respect your mates," he heard Wayne's high, almost girlish voice say.

"Jesus," he said softly, a second before the guard came stumbling towards them. Scared yelling for help.

* * *

His parents were there on his release, supportive as he knew they always would be. He made it clear he was not about to return to Canada immediately. They protested, but respected his decision. Borne as much of guilt and shame over his past behaviour as a simple desire not to go backwards now that he was free. They stayed two weeks then went back, reluctantly, leaing him to the world he had chosen.

Warden moved into a quiet house Rebekah had secured for him near his old flat. Once in, he seemed to lose the will to do anything more. He could make no decision about what might come next. The future was neither near nor far-off. It just didn't exist. Like the city outside his door. He lacked the appetite for throwing himself into any activity, barely having energy to nurture himself.

In the bathroom mirror he traced a pale, thin ridge from his right ear to a spot below his eye. Crossing his cheekbone like an elevation line. The other smaller, deeper. A crater on the moon. Barely missing a lung.

He scarcely recognized the person looking back. Face angular, dull. He'd been stripped of his identity, given up his body. His image ceased to correspond to memory. At first it had all seemed unkind, undeserved. Now, he thought, maybe it had been a kind of liberation.

It was summer, all things renewing themselves with a fervour and faith in their abundance. Rebekah had found him the sunniest, most cheerful place she could. She came by often in the afternoon, alone or sometimes with Ivan. They sat in the front room with its homey bay windows, often not leaving until the sun had set.

Some days he seemed somewhat optimistic, almost cheerful; others he was listless, detached, as though he had given up. Ivan's talk of wild clubs and dinner parties did little to amuse him when he was in these states. Rebekah would try to get him to talk or suggest a walk.

"But, of course, I can't make you do anything you don't want to," she chided, hoping to goad him into action. "I've seen old men in wheelchairs with more enthusiasm."

The light had begun to settle above the tree line for the evening. Warden stared past her out the window, appearing not to be listening.

"Really, you can be most exasperating, Warden! The least you could do is answer me. Some days you're like a large house with a lot of empty rooms in which I could stumble about for hours looking for someone to be home."

He smiled feebly.

"There — a response! That's all I wanted!" She touched his arm. "I'll leave you alone now. You've no doubt had too much of me for one day."

"I'm just feeling sorry for myself."

She clasped his hands with her own.

"I understand how you feel. But you can't stay like this forever. You've got to get on with things. Life won't wait."

She pulled on her gloves. Warden made a movement to rise.

"No — I know where your door is. Stay there and rest."

Her smile turned on him sadly as she went out. He listened for footsteps on the stairs, the latching of a door. The sounds died. He felt something precious leaking through the seams of his life. Time took on a shadow of preening, empty with passing as it searched for something to hold onto. A desperate fluidity that cannot touch or be touched. He wanted to cry, but couldn't.

That night Warden dreamed about his mother. He was on Isole d'Elba again. As she walked down the mountainside toward him it seemed he had not seen her in many years. Her hair was long, as it had been in her wedding pictures, but she walked with the use of a stick. Body gnarled and withered like the rock itself. She did not hurry as she came towards him. When they met she did not smile or embrace him.

"You're back," she said, simply.

It was not the greeting he'd expected. He listened as she spoke about her life, its triumphs and disappointments. On the ledge above them sat a beautiful little girl — his sister Lisa's daughter, though he knew she had none.

"All things come to pass in time," his mother explained.

The child had soft, golden hair. She sat high above on the mountain, naked and alone, and did not come down. Warden asked his mother how she was able to maintain suitable living conditions in such a barren place. Her face was serene as she answered. "I use the labours of my ancestors as a foundation whereon I build my city. Nor am I limited to this source, but carry also cedar from Lebanon and gold from Ophir."

"It's very hard," Warden told her, wanting comfort.

"You must be strong," she said.

While his mother spoke he was aware of the colours of her skin, her hair, her dress. Brilliant hues he had never seen before. He felt as though he were basking in her presence. And what of his sister and father? How were they managing? he wanted to know.

"What more do they require of me?" she replied. "Surely not happiness, for that is theirs to have or not have, as they wish. How can I give them anything if they do not know what they are missing? You, being bodiless, can better understand and see immortality in the leaves and the sky and the water. They will just go on getting older. Open your hands, Warden. You will see they were never empty."

A tiny dog yelped at her feet and she turned and did not come back again. When he woke he was crying, tears bathing his pillow. In the dream he felt he had understood everything she said. It no longer made sense when he thought about it now he was awake.

That afternoon Rebekah did not come for her afternoon visit as she did nearly every day.

"I'm alright," Warden told her over the phone. "I'm going to take a walk later."

By the time he returned to the flat, he knew it was time to move on. Right on schedule, without knowing it, his new self had arrived. Leaving him gasping for breath, as though he might drown. He had outgrown England. Nor was Canada his choice. Despite his parents' wishes, he couldn't think of going home. The prodigal son unreturned. If he were ever to return, he knew, it would be a long, jagged line he followed to arrive back where he began.

For now, Italy was calling. He phoned Andreo to say he would be coming.

"Va bene, bello! Leave that world. It is not for you. I cannot wait to see your lovely face."

*   *   *

By the time the plane landed, Warden was not sure he hadn't made a mistake. If he hoped for a miraculous recovery from all that had befallen him, it did not happen. Andreo was shaken by his ragged appearance, as if a look of hope had been stolen from him. He seemed to have vacated his body, leaving an indifferent custodian in place while he resided in some inner land of shadows.

He'd chosen a hotel near the Albergo Sirtori, but Andreo insisted he stay with him. He had no plans to approach his old agency, even just to say hello. He wanted nothing to do with Maura or Calvino and their chimerical world, and was content to leave his presence in the city unknown to them.

Andreo's flat was a beautiful, old-world sanctuary filled with ornate wooden furniture. Gilt-edged paintings, hand-drawn maps, renaissance tapestries covered the walls. The evening of Warden's arrival he'd prepared a meal with his own hands. Spaghetti with fresh basil and a raw meat crudo. They ate on the patio at dusk. Afterwards they walked through the streets together. Warden felt restored somewhat by the sight of the city's tall, grey monuments to other eras.

"I'd forgotten how much I missed this place," he acknowledged.

"Non è verro. It is this place that has missed you," Andreo asserted.

Andreo was able to talk Warden into helping out in his studio in the daytime, though he did not try to convince him to step in front of a camera lens. None of the models passing through seemed to connect his helper's empty stare with the glowing face of the Fabiano Boy.

Evening walks became a part of their routine. The light was luminous at dusk, hinting at unspoken mysteries in the air around them. Soft folds of cloud arrayed themselves with brief splashes of blue. The aquamarine sky hung overhead as if they were walking straight into the clear, clean expanse of ocean. People passing in the streets seemed to smile like silent Buddhas. Glimmering faces of hope strung together in the twilight. And everywhere a blending of voices, the living gospel of a river.

One evening he saw a teenage boy who reminded him of himself waiting at a bus stop. As though he'd come to meet himself there. He looked so young and enviable, Warden thought, feeling himself prematurely old and battered. Like a sieve with holes for the wind to blow through.

They returned to the flat. Andreo indicated for them to sit outside on the patio. Fading light stuck on the edges of the sky, filtering through clouds. As if lit not from behind but from within.

"Once again I have been doing all the talking," Andreo said, settling into his favourite chair. "And now it is your turn."

Warden leaned on the edge of the railing. He hesitated.

"I don't know what there is to say. Sometimes everything seems so unnecessary. Unreal. Like when you stare at something for too long and it loses its perspective. I feel as if I'm not really here and that all this is happening to somebody else. And then... " He shrugged, not knowing where to turn.

"And then?" Softly, gently.

"And then I just feel there's no use. Why should I say or do anything at all?"

"Because you are here. Because you have to go on for now."

"I keep thinking none of this really matters. One day I'll die — we'll all die — and it'll be like waking from a dream."

"But that is no reason to give up. Living means dying to anyone who can truly see it. Time pierces us like a marvellous arrow, toying with us, until it grows tired and puts us aside eventually."

Warden remained motionless for a long time until it seemed he'd gone to sleep or that at last time had come to an end. Everything unchanging forever. Clouds whirling overhead the only movement.

At last he spoke. "While I was in prison I had a lot of time to think about everything that happened and I kept wondering where I would find any meaning in this whole mess. A lesson, or something. I tried to be open to some sort of voice, but nothing came through."

"I think you will find that truth is found in silence, as you once told me that love is colourless. And if justice is truly blind, as they say, then we are lucky we can ever know anything at all."

Warden came and crouched before Andreo as the photographer had once done before him.

"I'm not saying I was unjustly treated. After all, I did walk into that bank to cash those bonds. But it's like hearing about other people's problems on the news, and then one day it's your life they're talking about. It's like you're standing outside looking in and you realize you don't recognize anything."

His face seemed lost in a problem too simple to understand. Like love or warmth or how a shadow manages to resemble in utmost detail the thing from which it is cast no matter how fast it moves, no losing it no matter how much it twists and turns. Nowhere to hide except under the still blazing centre of noon. Andreo pointed up as if to indicate a colony of angels dwelling above.

"We must have fallen a very long way," he said. "If I were God I would take us up one at a time, holding each one in the palm of my hand where we could see one another, just for a second. And then we could know without a shadow of doubt there is something beyond empty space and eternal darkness. And that would make our task of believing a little easier, I think. And then we could just get on with the rest of it."

An ironic smile came over his face. He took Warden's hands in his own and squeezed them.

"But then again, if I were God, I would probably know better. Nothing down here would change and I would be so disappointed."

Warden looked up, spoke again. "While I was in prison, I kept thinking back to when I was a kid and I used to deliver the morning paper. In the winter I had to get up early, while it was still dark, and walk all the way through the snow. The only sound I could hear were the church bells. Before I began I would stand and let the snow fall on my face, waiting for the bells to ring. For one single moment everything else seemed to disappear in the sound. Then, when they stopped ringing, I would deliver my papers and watch the house lights come on one by one."

He paused for a moment, picturing the scene to get it exactly right.

"By the time I was done I was pretty cold. Sometimes I wanted to run to get home faster, but I knew I would get there eventually. So I made myself walk slowly. And by the time I returned, the tracks I made when I left were already filled in by snow. As if I had never been there. I used to think about that all the way back home. Sometimes I found it almost unbearable as I watched hands lifting blinds and unlatching doors, going off to their place in the world, to think all our footsteps will be obliterated by the snow."

He sat back and put his hands on his knees as if to conclude what he had been saying.

"And then what?" Andreo asked, leaning forward.

"And then? And then I leaned into my collar to keep the wind off my neck. And I walked on as I had to," Warden answered with

222

a trace of a smile.

He rested his chin on his hand. After a minute Andreo stood and opened the door, turning on the light in the hallway.

"Come in when you are ready," he said, leaving the door open behind him.

* * *

He had not been there two weeks when he got a phone call from Ivan. He could tell from his voice it was unpleasant news.

"I thought you should know — Rebekah... " The sentence ended in quiet sobs.

Ivan was phoning to tell him Rebekah had been killed in a car crash the day before. Her life ended driving home through the late night streets of the city.

"I think she'd be pleased to know at least that she went out at top speed... " he said, becoming speechless again, sobbing into the receiver. Warden said what he could to console him and thanked him for calling. Hung up the black cradle of the phone.

* * *

One evening, Andreo returned late from the studio, beaming and motioning for Warden to get dressed to go out.

"Where are we going?" he asked.

"Come with me. There's someone I want you to meet."

He would say nothing more. At eight o'clock, they arrived at a small restaurant, not unlike the family trattoria from his early days in the city. They sat and Andreo ordered for them both, ignoring the door as though he were not expecting anyone. After fifteen minutes, Warden looked up to see Valentino in the doorway, looking very much the same except for his head shorn of its curls.

They shook hands hesitantly, almost fearfully, then Valentino grabbed him in an excited hug, lifting him off the ground.

"How can it be so long since I have seen you?" he said. "I miss you so very much."

They sat and talked excitedly, barely able to eat. Once it began, the conversation rolled on as if they had never been apart. How was Paolo? What was training camp like? Had Warden suffered much in prison? They spoke quickly, laughing and reacquainting themselves. Valentino kissed the tips of his fingers, tracing the length of the scar over his face. Following the narrow pathway to where it ended just below his eye.

"I think we are both in the prison, my friend. The first six months, I work myself to death so I don't remember I am so miserable. And still I don't sleep!" Valentino complained. "I miss dancing and having fun and being with you all the time."

He told Warden since his return he had been dating girls, but there had been no one steady since he left.

"It is just to keep myself from being bored," he said, laughing.

And as for the future? His first plan, he said, was to grow back his hair. Then, in the fall he would enrol in a school for architecture.

"Then I will build us both a big house where we can live happily," he said. "And, if we decide to have some wives who like each other the same way we do, even better." He laughed at himself.

"And a room for Andreo where he can come and hide out from the world," Warden added.

Andreo nodded and smiled. "I would like that," he said. "But I warn you now, I am planning to be a very cranky old man, so you should beware."

"We must go to the Riviera on Paolo again," Valentino exclaimed. "That is, if you are free." He winked.

"I'm free," Warden said.

They left in the early afternoon, retracing their route of two summers before. Warden felt the pang of being alive return with the landscape. Racing through the countryside they approached a giant billboard off to one side of the road. It was the infamous Fabiano ad, with Warden as both male and female self, one that had somehow escaped the company's censorship. Or perhaps been left up by some erector of billboards sympathetic to such nameless beauty.

They passed by, leaving it behind them as they tore up the mountainside, climbing the sunset. Vivid colours erupting in the air like over-ripe fruit. Wind picking up. Valentino shouted something over his shoulder Warden couldn't quite make out. It didn't matter. They were almost there. Returning at last to where it all began. Restless. Parched with thirst for the shapings of time.

— *THE END* —